Sanity
Stops
HerE

Marlon A. Ferguson

This Book Is Dedicated
to the
Valorous Few
who have
Challenged and Vanquished
their own
Personal Demons.

CHAPTER I

The imposing old house, perched like a vulture atop a lofty prominence that overlooked the Rundle River, never hurt anyone—not intentionally. Intention implies sentience. The dwelling was no more than stone, timber, glass and a collection of incidental building materials typical of the time of construction. One could hardly hold the aging structure accountable for the men, women and children who died there. Nevertheless, the once elegant marble flooring and sumptuous hand-blocked papered walls had witnessed every degenerate act that could transpire through the course of generations, and each vulgar occurrence indelibly etched its onerous mark upon the dwelling's impassive surfaces.

The estate is char and ash, now, naught but an eerie relic of its insufferable and sinister history. To digest fully the evil that reeked from that primal place, allow me to elaborate on my first impressions of the cursed behemoth and to explain what I have learned of it since.

An ornate rusted gate, chained in iron and oddly posted with a faintly discernable sign that read "Visitation by Appointment Only", fairly warned the curious and misguided on approach. Tall pines with multitudes of remnant branches spiking out from their centers like thorny fingers forged a formidable wall on either side of the deeply eroded drive. The earthen way, through a series of calculated curves, presented a taste of intrigue to the uninitiated that was irresistible and effectively masked the harsh austerity lying in wait beyond.

The substantial rise on which the house rested was nearly stripped of vegetation, except for a skirt of brambles that cringed shyly at the toe of a severe slope. A spattering of pecan trees anchored mid-hill still bore the air of monarchy and spoke of a once productive orchard—their gnarled limbs and rumpled trunks long fouled with decay and drowning under neglect and elemental abuse. The supplicant trees, in their physical contrariness, arched their craggy limbs up-slope towards the house for attention that never came, despite the majesty their presence bestowed upon the land and owner.

Overgrown foundation plantings smothered the manor's colonnaded entrance to one side of the generous portico and thwarted the intended architectural symmetry with a cruel lopsided logic. The sagging, rotted corners of the roofline bore gaping wounds where bats, rodents and other secretive vermin found refuse between the skeletal trusses that crowned the moldy superstructure. Countless layers of bland whitewash applied to the structure's exterior over the years hardened and cracked into scaly schizophrenic patterns. The resultant unsightly chinks in the reptilian armor allowed the weathered grey siding to breathe where exposed.

The most salient elevation offered a commanding, if hazy, view of the bones of a failed crossroads that once held promise as a vital trade center. The energetic and productive entrepreneurs who first populated that austere landscape welcomed the prospect of hardy commerce in the beginning but quickly abandoned their considerable investments of money, toil and blood once the Lovingdale presence corrupted their dreams. Driven to desperation, most migrated north over Hazens Notch to the small town of Milford and resettled there.

Gaps and breaches in the property's walled and fenced perimeter allowed errant cattle access to the meager vegetation sprouting between the stumps of diseased elm trees and shoulders of outcropping rock. Such sporadic growth provided scant nourishment, and a hungry bovine earned little reward for losing its way. Most farmers considered their livestock an indispensable commodity, but no one dared trespass onto the unholy soil to gather strays.

It was said daredevil youths routinely scaled trees on adjacent parcels for unobstructed views of the notorious site and witnessed the ghosts of foraging animals. Their elders quickly dismissed such fanciful tales, but shifted their perspectives after the remains of cloven-hoofed beasts were found strewn along the ribbon of road that connected their properties to the estate.

Rumor had it that demonic forces drove the wretched animals from the hilltops. The few to survive being torn to ribbons by the thorny boma near the property's extremes expired in their madness before reaching their stable sanctuaries. Their bug-eyed carcasses, lagging tongues and flaring nostrils bore testament to their terrific exertions before the indiscriminate hand of damnation weighed in.

Viewed from the grounds proper, the Rundle River glows in the distance like the upturned belly of a lifeless serpent. The emerald sparkle upstream and downstream, where the course dramatically roils around the polished stones dotting the river's bed, offers stark contrast to the chalky metallic sheen peculiar to the half-mile stretch that fronts the Lovingdale property. There the skewed trunks of trees, long-felled to their knees by the blustery demands of time and season, choke the river's vibrancy into sluggish pools.

Anglers still dub this remarkable stretch of water "Dead Run" for its general pall and sterile qualities. Indeed, even birds and amphibians commonly encountered nearby avoid the area altogether, with nary a heron or salamander eager to claim the territory home. Boating enthusiasts adventurous enough to test their mettle in this "den of iniquity" swear the river's deep calm demeanor harbors unseen whirlpools and life grabbing eddies that clutch at their crafts as they speed through. Most folks in Upshire County, even today, steer clear of the river there and abide by the waterway's implicit warning.

The daring fools naively drawn to danger and forbidden folly serve as oblations to feed Evil's dark appetites. While the meek majority hunkered behind barred doors and shuttered windows endure their marginal existence enslaved and emasculated by superstition and fear. It has been so with all cultures and civilizations since stars first fell, and so it was with Lovingdale Manor.

Lovingdale Manor was, and is, an oppressive place, an evil place. It is a place better left to the tragic dead and the skeletal herds haunting its god-forsaken slopes. The ruins near the Rundle River stand as a monument to the irrefutable decay of the hearts and souls of ruthless and ambitious men, and to their miserable failing to recognize and correct their destructive paths.

There will be more concerning this singular manor later—much more. For now, though, let us begin at the beginning.

CHAPTER II

In the Beginning

Life in the waning decades of the eighteenth century was reasonably comfortable for the well-heeled, marginally tolerable for the industrious employed and downright impossible for everyone else. Most families eked out a bread and potato existence working their strip farms or laboring for the noble gentry. The agricultural and industrial revolutions were blossoming, but few benefits trickled down to the lower classes.

Reynolds Lovingdale I was fortunate to be born into the higher echelons of British society and grew up with the arrogance and selfish expectations common to the upper crust's self-proclaimed higher order. His parents, the Duke and Duchess of Hallsworth, of notable old money extraction, were luminaries in European circles and enjoyed great wealth and prestige. But it was the excitement and glamour of the New World that lit the lamp of their first-born.

"I am sorry, but I absolutely must go," the eager lad insisted after much discussion. "The New World is to me a ripe, red apple waiting to be plucked. I simply feel it must be my hand that bends the bough."

"And will you also be first to taste the fruit?" his mother remonstrated. "Have you forgotten the fate that befell Adam? He, too, was beguiled by the unknown."

"Mother..." Reynolds interjected; but before he could finish his father stood up, crooked one arm customarily behind his back and silenced him with the palm of an upturned hand.

"What your mother is trying to say," the Duke dutifully explained, "is that the consequences of your actions may not bend to accommodate your capricious pursuits. Your decision will carry a great weight with it across the seas. You are burning with the passions of youth and blinded by your inexperience. I am afraid that when your eyes finally open, you may discover yourself in a place far different from that which you imagine."

"Father, you know I care deeply for both of you, but surely you understand my desire for adventure and my need to find my own way. Were you not a merchant seaman in the King's navy as a younger man?"

The Duke of Hallsworth peered at his first born over the silver frame of his reading glasses and nodded in confirmation.

The Duchess turned to face the oversized windows of their study, grasped the gold-tasseled edge of the embroidered burgundy drapery and used the bulk of stately fabric to support her sinking frame. When she had gathered her poise sufficiently, she spoke again— her voice tinged with melancholia.

"Go if you must, Reynolds. But I will hold you to a promise of a safe return. Promise, also, that you will not forget the values we have labored so tirelessly to instill in you and that you will let them guide your life daily."

"I promise nothing less, Mother," Reynolds answered affirmatively. "And now, I must beg your leave. I have much to plan and more to do." The young man could not contain his pleasure and excitement at gaining their blessing. He embraced his mother warmly and vigorously shook his father's hand before he departed.

The Duke and Duchess watched from their crown glass window as their son boarded a waiting carriage. The coach rattled across the cobblestone courtyard to the road leading to Kingsbury Harbor and disappeared around the bend. Solemn and smiling weakly, the Duchess turned to her husband. As she approached, his arms opened wide and surrounded her with the reassuring strength of his embrace.

Less than a fortnight later, the Lovingdales reluctantly bid their son farewell at the Port of Kingsbury with a desperate longing in their hearts. They did not wish to taint their son's pilgrimage with overt sentimentality at its beginning. Instead, they hid their dismay and projected a faux air of optimism and stoic detachment.

The year was 1773. The prospect of immigration to English colonial America at the ripe old age of twenty-one set the impatient lad's head spinning even before the schooner Crimson Gale departed Kingsbury Harbor. The pocketed sailcloth billowed before the mast like a gathering of great canvas clouds, puffed with pride and eagerly pointing the way to success and prosperity.

Reynolds waved wildly from the aft deck and watched his parents shrink in the distance. His gestures continued until he could no longer distinguish his own family from the teeming throng of well-wishers hovering about the docks. The ambitious Reynolds had reservations about leaving his parents behind. He may not see them again for many months or years, or ever again. A jolt of panic spurred by his last thought surged up from the pit of his stomach and lodged in the back of his throat. He felt he might choke, but steadied himself with reassurances that 'never' was not an option. He loved them, of course, and his intention was never to sever ties to his heritage and entitlements—blessings far too valuable to forsake. He genuinely anticipated establishing his fortune on virgin soil, and he knew drawing heavily upon his family name and resources would be essential.

The Crimson Gale was a square-rigged, three-masted merchant carrier, a full one hundred ten feet from bowsprit to stern and thirty feet across her beam. Weighing in at over five hundred tons, she was well equipped for trans-Atlantic travel. Her structural members were primarily of pine and oak, her masts of fir. A battery of twelve cannon fitted in her ample belly offered reassurances against pirate attacks so prevalent on the high seas. Twelve miles of rigging and five thousand square feet of canvas sails graced the skies above her teakwood decking.

Unlike most ships of her class, she also sported fore and aft sails stayed to her foremast and mizzen that allowed the craft to carve into the wind. Should the trade winds blow fickle on their journey, the ship should loose little time.

Brass and copper detailing reflected the sun's rays most admirably on clear days and sent the prancing light merrily on its way from wave crest to wave crest. The crow's nest near the top of the craft's one-hundred-foot main mast seemed to scrape the heavens free of clouds, and from the deck appeared a mile distant to the novice's untuned eyes. Aye, she was a fine ship, and she knifed through the water like Neptune's trident.

Reynolds had been at sea a wee shy of two weeks before the uneventful Atlantic crossing began to grate on his nerves and test the limits of his patience. The daily routine aboard a ship sailing a seemingly boundless sea would, in time, erode the enthusiasm of the most ardent seafarer. Conditions were deplorable. Food was scarcer than hen's teeth and of low quality. Redworms and spiders infested food stores, and lice hospitably allowed the seamen to share their berths. Fresh water was anything but fresh, fouled with insects and offal of the most awful kind.

Captain Bainbridge, concerned for the morale of the crew but also valuing their cleanliness and good heath, restricted crew visits to the scuttlebutt to twice daily but allowed watered rum to augment their refreshments. Once weekly, the good captain encouraged revelry and offered more generous rations. Unfortunately, the carousing of the tipsy seamen on those occasions left the deck and sleeping quarters reeking of vomit and dysentery, despite subsequent double scrubbings. The Captain's decision, though applauded by the crew, seemed irresponsible to Reynolds. Yet, the addition of high-proof alcohol to the fresh water stores added a degree of antiseptic benefit without which consumption of said stores might cost lives.

Stories of corsairs, buccaneers, and other fearless seafaring men were the staple of vagabond minstrels across Britain's imperial domain. Reynolds absorbed every detail of the exploits of his daring nautical heroes from the romantic yarns he heard, and he envied their freedom to travel the world and do as they wished. However, he quickly learned the life of the common seaman was anything but free.

Foremost, a body aboard ship was as much a prisoner as one condemned to a prison cell. It was a larger cell, to be sure, but a constricted space nonetheless. The vessel, in turn, danced within the confines of the bounding sea. The mates on board acted in accordance with the captain's directives without question, much as prisoners obey the commands of their oppressors. To do otherwise guaranteed harsh punishment.

Aye, sailors were far from free but, unlike their landlocked cousins, seemingly content to labor under a tyrannical ruler for a meager portion of the spoils. Their scandalous shanties sprinkled with hearty "yo-ho-hos" and "way heys" served to allay the burden of their duties. The musical rhythms forged a spirit of camaraderie among the men and fostered relative happiness.

Yet, the crew was a scurrilous lot not easily given to friendships with passengers and certainly unlikely to befriend the pampered son of an undeserving monarchy. Now, despotism: there was an idea they could understand and embrace wholeheartedly. They were rebels and anarchists, for the most part, sharing an affiliation and love for the open sea.

Most men on board ignored the gangly Lovingdale's attempts at levity and good humor and passed by the sea-green lad as if he were invisible. There was one man on board who was different. He was quiet, observant and hard-working, yet carried an air of learning and wisdom about him that the others did not possess. His name was Laird Cromley.

Captain Bainbridge, who felt an unusual mix of uncertainty and confidence when Cromley approached him for a position, ordered his "operatives" to gather intelligence about the stranger. They reported back promptly, as directed.

"As far as we can tell, no one about has ever 'eard of 'em", began the first agent. His crony angled in. "From all accounts, he arrived in Kingsbury from corners unknown on the day before the ship was to sail. No one can say where he come from, he just appeared, or so we're told." The Captain nodded.

Laird Cromley had the swarthy, weathered look of an able-bodied seaman and his calloused hands spoke of hard work in tough times. Still, hiring the mysterious stranger could portend trouble and asserting absolute control over him once they sailed might prove difficult.

A man of strength, character and experience was paramount to serve as boatswain, a supervisory position with emphasis on rigging, general deck maintenance and task assignments. Seemingly trivial duties at face value, but enormously important when at sea. A brief test insured he was no stranger to knots and the windlass, and his no-nonsense demeanor would set well with the deck crew. Time was short, and to delay sailing was unacceptable.

The Captain took the chance. Tried and true men were few and far between, he reasoned. He christened the newcomer "Chance" when introducing his new addition to the crew assembled for that very purpose—and to serve as a daily reminder, no doubt, that his trust in the man was not lightly given.

"Men, meet Master Cromley, our new boatswain." The Captain began. "Ye shall refer to him as "Chance" when addressing him aboard ship, as shall I." Captain Bainbridge rested a hand upon Laird's right shoulder and gazed upon his able subordinate approvingly. "He is yet unproven, but seems hale, hardy and fit to the task. You will all answer to him, and him to me. That is all."

It was not long before Chance realized the young Lovingdale's plight and took it upon himself to watch out for the fledgling, at least until the greenhorn "found his legs". The lad reminded him of himself not a score ago when he set out to see the world. A ship at sea could be a dangerous place for the unprepared. Chance was willing to talk and listen to his young friend's concerns. The two men quickly established a repartee that developed into an enjoyable and anticipated daily exchange.

At Chance's behest, Reynolds was permitted to share in the boatswain's deck duties. The Captain was undeniably aware of his passenger's pedigree; otherwise, Reynolds would have found himself a galley rat instead of in the covetous position so graciously bestowed. Chance was responsible for the division of labor on deck and, in so keeping, assigned his young protégé to duties befitting his age and experience. As the lad's seamanship evolved, Chance exposed him to tasks requiring greater skill, which Reynolds mastered easily.

All mates had equal share at watch, and Reynolds was no exception. Favoritism aboard ship might spark mutiny and could not be flaunted. Normally, Reynolds served as "second dog", but after a month at sea he earned mid-watch for failing to properly secure a capstan hoist.

One dawn, a topman spied several small pods of baleen whales breaching and cavorting off the starboard bow. The mammals' alabaster bellies flashed like battle flags during the frenzy of their morning ritual. Unusual considering that Minkes, as they were called, were known to be generally solitary by nature, preferring to travel in pairs or in small groups of three or four. They were usually observed nearer shore as well. Perhaps, a healthy shoal of shrimp or fingerlings, secure in their instinctive massing, had been unlucky enough to lure the beasts to breakfast.

This was Providence, indeed!

Although baleens were small by whaling standards, the resources obtained from their numbers would add measurably to already diminishing provisions. Meat and blubber spoiled quickly in the humid expanse and were always in short supply. It was customary, indeed essential, to exploit fully every opportunity to replenish stores.

Captain Bainbridge ordered the jollys let go and several seamen reeled the davit cranks and deployed the jollyboats near the stern. The chase was on! After the hunt, the animals were cleaned and butchered near their weighing stations. Chance tasked Reynolds with retrieving the harvest with hawsers threaded through a cat hole and weighed with an improvised capstan designed for such a purpose. An incorrect twist of his wrist when securing the lanyard to the capstan arm was all it took to send the blankets of cherished blubber back into the sea. As punishment for his carelessness, Captain Bainbridge decreed that Reynolds should pay for time and materials lost by serving as surrogate for any ailing seaman unfit for duty, regardless of danger, for a period of two weeks. The captain castigated Chance, as well, for failing to assign a duty of such importance to one seasoned and well-learned.

After such an embarrassing episode, Reynolds forgave any pretenses of status and courtly privilege he may have formerly entertained. However, his new duties, menial and unglamorous as they were, did much to alleviate the tedium of the endless stream of wind-dogged days and nights. The physical challenges were refreshing, and he realized that his labors clarified his mind. The clarification, in turn, helped him crystallize a strategy for future successes. Reynolds continued to perform his assignments admirably and slowly gained a margin of respect from nearly all the fellow seaman he contacted daily. All but one.

Peter Blythe was the exception. He had it in for the "arrogant snot", as he affectionately called Reynolds from the beginning. Peter was small of body and sported a complexion burned red and raw by exposure to sun and wind, dark even by seafaring standards. A short man was typically more stable on a pitching deck, but being of lesser stature than the rest, Peter adopted an exaggerated gait and puffy pretense. He talked louder and coarser than all the others talked and was quicker with a hook or marlinspike when an enemy's back was turned.

One balmy morning, Reynolds found himself alone with Blythe on a rigging inspection. Normally, Chance would not have assigned the vitriolic pair together, but Peter's usual mate was down with dropsy and failed to muster that day.

"Well, now, if it isn't the royal snotty?" Peter began his caustic rebuke on sight. "What a pleasure it 'tis to be sharin' the company of such a fine example of gentrification as yerself." Peter glanced around the deck to insure their privacy then boldly approached Reynolds to within an inch of his nose. His eyes gleamed with hatred, and jealousy dripped from his skewed jaw like a mad dog's slobber. He drew a dagger from his waistband and held it to his enemy's throat. "Let me be reminding ye that yer blood runs true and red as any man's. I'll be obliged to back me words with action, if you've a mind to test me theory." His grimace was painfully intense.

Reynolds backed away until the bulwarks forestalled further retreat. "I've done nothing to you. Why not leave me alone?"

"Why not, says you? Yer a bugger and a coward, says I, and a mealy-mouthed spawn of a whore. Give me cause, and I'll slit you from gut to gullet."

Reynolds could not control his trembling. He was thankful the thick fabric of his trousers muffled the sound of his knocking knees.

Just then, Chance appeared from around the corner of a stack of crates amidships. "Everything shipshape, here?" He asked, glancing from Reynolds to Peter.

"Aye", Blythe replied, after secreting his knife beneath his cotton weskit.

"Get the rigging on the main and foremast taught and ready," he ordered. "We've a blow behind us, the winds are up and the seas are capping. The fire at dawn this day spells trouble, but we've hours of sailing, yet. Look lively, now." He glanced, again, at his callow protégé and then departed as quietly as he arrived.

"Aye, sir," Peter answered, stepping away, his pretense at conscientiousness failing to fool the astute boatswain. The two incompaticos worked in silence for several minutes, until a cry of despair roused Reynolds from his sullen reverie.

"Waahh!" Peter bellowed, just as a crate of halyard blocks crashed to the deck with a thunderous sound. He strategically positioned his leg beneath the pile of tackle to indicate the accident had pinned it fast. Forgetting their earlier row, Reynolds rushed to the blackguard's aid and lifted the mass from off the man's person. He helped his "injured" mate to the upturned crate to rest, noting by a rudimentary inspection of the man's calf that the professed injuries were not immediately apparent.

"I'll not be a-going topside today," he moaned as pitifully as he could manage. "You best be climbing the shroud by your lonesome to stay the halyards. And don't forget to furl the jib afore ye sling it to."

"All right, I'll go." Reynolds said without thinking. He hopped atop the starboard bulwark and stepped gingerly from the lower deadeye to the upper before pulling himself into the shroud. Slowly, he scaled the netting, ratline by ratline, and paused to rest and look about just beneath the royal mast. The winds forty feet above deck were high and blustery, much fiercer than below. He could hear the sharp snap of the flaxen canvas sails as they resisted the unrelenting force. Constant billowing before the wind had stretched the fabric and loosed their stays, setting the lengths of running hemp vibrating like harp strings all the way down to their deadeyes. The enchanted sailor delighted in the humming effect and whistled a shanty in harmony.

He gazed down upon the vessel's plan. The ship seemed to swing beneath him like a mighty pendulum as it rocked to the ocean's lullaby. Indeed, it was he, not the deck, that enjoyed the greater motion. Had he considered that the extent of the ship's perceived movement beneath him correlated directly to his height above deck, he would not have advanced another inch.

A sudden gust caught him off-guard and twisted him sideways in the shroud. He now faced astern. His mind raced as he clung to the ratlines, trying desperately to re-establish a sound purchase on the pliant cordage. Looking out, he was appalled to see an advancing mass of blue-black clouds filling the eastern horizon. The storm approached must faster now than he first assessed and promised to be the devil and more. Thinking it best to alert his shipmates below him, he averted his gaze from the ominous skies and scoured the foredeck below him for Blythe.

Peter was not where he last was. It was Peter's task to guide him to the main stays running from the royal spar to the topgallant yard, where the flaccid sails screamed for attention. When aloft, it was quite difficult to discern areas most in need, and a sailor might as well be blind as to crawl unguided along a cantilevered yardarm.

"Alooo!" Reynolds shouted, cupping his free hand to one side of his mouth to funnel his call. He heard no response. "Alooo-oo-o!" He shouted again, raising his pitch to make the sound travel as far as possible above the din of the musical strands. He considered retreat, but climbing ropes in gale conditions on an angry sea was no easy matter. He preferred completing his assignment now to attempting a second climb. But where in blazes was Peter?

Unbeknownst to Reynolds, Peter hid on the port side of the main mast where he awaited the decisive moment to act. The time was now. The hardened seafarer sprang from his concealment, knife in hand, and severed the main shroud's master strands. The standing rigging to which Reynolds clung collapsed like a squeezebox and sent him on a dangerous collision course with the main mast. Fortunately, the flailing web, supported by precautionary transverse strands installed before the ship set sail, stopped Reynolds before he collided with the mammoth central pole. Heedless of the young man's peril, the gale blew him about like laundry.

Responding to the alarming screams aloft, the men on the aft deck assembled in a knot directly beneath Reynolds. Experienced hands, strong and sure, quickly secured the swinging netting, allowing the shaken novice to descend unscathed. So weak were his knees upon reaching firmer footing, they buckled beneath his weight. Poor Reynolds collapsed into the arms of two able bodied seamen on either side.

Captain Bainbridge, ever mindful to threats to his vessel of any kind, appeared magically amidst the excited throng of sailors. He eyed Peter Blythe suspiciously, but accepted his protests of innocence pending evidence that suggested otherwise. He dismissed the groveling worm to the galley and ordered Chance to investigate the matter fully and to report his findings as soon as they were completed. "Look sharp, ye landlubbers," the captain barked before returning to his quarters. "Reef the topgallant on the main, boys, and furl the fore and mizzen. Aye, there be a blow about. We'll know soon enough if she be mistral or mistress."

#

That night, as the ship rolled sickeningly on an agitated sea, Reynolds left the stench of his hammock for an overdue breath of rejuvenating air. He climbed the rope ladder that dropped from atop the roundhouse cabins that squatted above the quarter gallery near the stern. He was sleepy-eyed and dog-tired, but his mind sharpened when he saw a shadowy figure hunkered on the upper deck immersed in the throes of some ritualistic and clandestine activity. He could not make the identity of the mysterious practitioner, but the figure's gestures and indecipherable mutterings mesmerized him. Reynolds lowered his body on the rope ladder until only his eyes and forehead protruded above the deck planking.

The figure sat face to the wind within a circle of white powder, which he replenished as needed to keep the circle intact. At the center of the circle, a small flame flickered. Strangely, the prevailing wind did not disperse the silvery smoke swirling about him. The smell of burning wormwood was powerful and prominent. After scribing a circle in the air with a forked stick, the stranger pointed the stick to the four cardinal directions of the compass. He then blew a pinch of the white powder from between his fingers and uttered a chilling summons:

> "Guardian of the Threshold, I call unto Thee.
> Awaken Thy Hidden Light. Hear me, Asmodeus!
> Pass beyond the Realm of Light,
> O, Devil Lords of Wind, Water, Earth, and Fire.
> Hear me, Lord Leviathan!
> Reap the soul of Thy servant, Peter Blythe
> And cleanse this vessel, if it be Thy will.
> Hear me! Send him back beyond the Shadows of Death.
> Let Thy Black Flame within me shine as light.
> Hear me, Asmodeus, Waking Lord of Sabbath!
> Allow Thy servant through the Veil of Wakening
> To stand upon the Hill of Dreams."

As he finished his infernal chant, the stranger extended both arms above his head and arched his back in what appeared to be an exaltation of ecstasy. A flash of lightning followed by an egregious peal of thunder consummated the sorcerer's pleas and illuminated his features. Reynolds was stunned. He sank down below the deck with an expression of surprise and disbelief. The sorcerer was no other than his friend and mentor, Chance Cromley. In the wake of another thunderous clap and with presence of mind regained, Reynolds straightened to his former station that he might confirm his conclusions. To his amazement, there was no one there. Only the portentous glow in the heavens remained. In disbelief, Reynolds returned to his berth, but remained disturbed and awake until exhaustion sealed his eyes just before dawn.

By early morning, force nine conditions battering the ship awakened Reynolds and nearly catapulted him out of his linens. All berths and hammocks were empty, save for his. He had neglected to undress prior to retiring the night before. He readily made his way up the steep ladder to amidships. The storm was raging. Dark clouds swirled menacingly overhead and showered rain in buckets. Wave after ocean wave shattered over the railings. The deck was a pool of brine eight inches deep in which unsecured crates sloshed back and forth like rotting fish.

Amidst the turmoil, Reynolds was amazed to find the entire company of seamen huddled en masse, eyes fixed skyward toward the foremast gallant. Rain drenched his eyes as his gaze fused with that of his fellow men's. Suspended by the neck from the gallant yardarm, swung the lifeless body of Peter Blythe.

Peter's right arm was stiff and frozen outright before him, pointing west. The electron glow of St. Elmo's fire danced over his person, travelled down twin transparent ribbons of water that spiraled from his extremities to the flooded deck and shimmered up the rigging again. Reynolds rubbed his eyes free of the blinding deluge and looked again. His eyes were not mistaken. He fell back against the cabin jam, mouth agape, his eyes fixed on the apparition.

Then, as if numbed by a great truth, each man turned and ghosted past the startled youth with no acknowledgement of his presence. As the sailors passed, Reynolds noted their blank expressionless faces and dead lusterless eyes, like those of the Great White, sunken in a fleshy paleness that rivaled the moon. The one face that should have been present was not. That face was Laird Cromley's.

Reynolds ran to check the boatswain's quarters first. No Chance. He checked the galley next and then the cabin of Captain Bainbridge. No Chance. He knew the Captain's quarters were off limits to every mate aboard, and had his judgement not been fired by the passion of the moment he would never dared to enter.

A general alarm sounded and a search of the ship ensued. No trace of Laird Cromley was ever found. Most hands speculated that their capable boatswain was somehow lost overboard in the churning seas on the night of Peter Blythe's demise. Reynolds would not see Laird Crowley for the duration of the voyage nor ever again.

Reynolds remained unconvinced that his friend and mentor had perished so carelessly at sea. Laird Cromley was much too competent a seaman to ever succumb to a layman's fate. Reynolds knew Chance had passed on to a higher calling…to an untold plane of existence. Perhaps he had found his way through the Veil of Wakening to stand upon the Hill of Dreams?

CHAPTER III

Another month passed before Reynolds caught his first sight of Boston Harbor. He joyously disembarked the stalwart vessel that had been his home that past season and felt the rush and rekindling of the initial fire that drove him when his journey began. The contagious fervor and bustling activity driving the inhabitants smote the ardent immigrant hard. He planted his feet firmly on the cobblestone streets of Boston and gazed about in awe. Here was a land to tame. Here was a world worthy of conquest.

He quickly secured quarters suitable to his station and set about establishing his chosen livelihood. An import/export concern was the logical choice and most likely to enjoy success— due, in no small part, to his family's deep European connections. His venerable family had not cornered the market on trade between England and her colonial interests abroad, but their network was extensive.

As reprehensible as slavery was, it was the moneymaker— growing unpopularity in the northern colonies notwithstanding. A transplant deep in human trafficking from 'jolly olde' England would do well to operate clandestinely and shun controversy and unsolicited attention.

Despite the trade's potential drawbacks and some conscientious misgivings, Reynolds embraced the abhorrent trade as did most of his newly minted associates. There was too much money in importing slave labor to the plantations in the southern colonies and filling the demand for cotton, tobacco, turpentine, tar and seasonal agricultural crops in Europe and beyond to abstain. Surface legitimacy served as the perfect cover. In two years his shipping business thrived, due in no small part to his fervor for the more ignoble aspects of entrepreneurism.

Product shipped out regularly through Boston Harbor bound for England and the Netherlands. On the return voyage, a cargo hold crammed with terrified Africans to be auctioned off in the Dutch West Indies and subsequently delivered to the Chesapeake Bay country brought fifty times the expense of transport.

The War of Independence that exploded around him did little to squelch demand for his services. The same products that fattened the King's coffers were still in demand. Tried and true marketing and distribution guaranteed continued commercial viability. The relevant parties divided the fruits of that commerce differently, that was all.

Reynolds Lovingdale found himself comfortably situated to enjoy the grass on both sides of the fence, and he spent equal time attending to both. However, despite his success and fortune, memories of Chance and the eerie death of Peter Blythe began to haunt him.

A recurrent dream of the death of Peter Blithe aboard the Crimson Gale often awakened Reynolds just as the clock in his bed chamber struck four. This disturbing ritual continued for months leaving him sleep deprived and addle-brained. A hunger for deliverance from the curse drove him to investigate the root cause of the unwelcome disturbance. The deeper he delved, the deeper became his obsession with ancient and forbidden knowledge. The seductive call of the occult was intoxicating and drew him relentlessly down its dark path.

The works of Franz Mesmer in Germany and Luigi Galvani of Italian fame were of particular interest to the novice devotee. He also explored the murky depths of the ultra-secretive 'Illuminati' Order—placing great credit upon its founders for the orchestration of the American Revolution. The history of the Salem witch trials fascinated him and fostered enormous respect for the control that assumed authority wielded over those majorities possessing less robust faculties and resources.

Reynolds devoured every morsel of occult information he could extract from the oppressive puritanical society in which he resided. When in Rome it was good for business to do as Romans do, so he abided by that time-tested adage for the sake of maintaining positive public and professional appearances. But the night was meant for darker things, and it was during the hours from midnight to dawn that he explored the mysteries of satanic conjurations and devil worship to the level of fanaticism.

Neither demons nor gods were predictably agreeable and Reynolds soon learned that, regardless of the deity one worshipped, the mind blurred their singular attractions over time into an indistinguishable mass. Reynolds chose the Dark Lord. He might just as easily have chosen the Lord of Light, but he could not reconcile the numbers.

This was a world of avarice, corruption, famine, greed, jealousy, hatred, prejudice, injustice, poverty, natural catastrophe, genocide, torture, rape and murder on the left hand and kindness, justice and humaneness on the right. The scales seemed heavily tipped in favor of the former. Who was more powerful, more influential and more pervasive...*deus aut daemon*? The answer to Reynolds was obvious.

As the new decade dawned, Reynolds embarked on a radical strategy and instituted a more aggressive plan to achieve control over the elusive Powers of Darkness. Considerable research was necessary before the road to enlightenment straightened and revealed the way. He readied his materiel, transcripts, ancient tomes, offerings and ideas and set his plan in motion.

His virgin foray involved extensive preparation. Flour for the sacred circle was readily available. A sacrificial knife, never used, was at his command as were virgin goats. First, he must bless the ebony-handled knife with fire before slitting the kid's throat and skinning it. The goat's blood must dry and remain on the blade. He would use the same knife to cut the forked boughs of the witch hazel tree. Forked witch hazel boughs were plentiful, but required travel.

He learned that the seeker must discover and select the highest limbs on the tree the day before harvesting. At dawn of the day following selection, just as the sun rises, the branches are to be pruned and cut into seventeen-and-one-half inch lengths. The knife blade must them be melted down and forged into daggered caps for the forked ends. If forged by another, the caps were to be fitted to dummy forked branches of the same size by the non-believer and transferred to the sacred boughs by the seeker in order to avoid cross-contamination.

Consistencies of a personal nature were essential to observe, as well. Step one on the ladder to spiritual purification was to abstain from the company of the opposite sex for a period of one month. Step two was fasting for thirty-six hours with naught but spring water to drink, followed by seven days of eating two meals a day, and then only at the hours of midnight and noon. Prayers must be offered in their entirety to the entities he, or she, wished to summon before and after consuming each meal. Only after addressing the prerequisite details could the conjurations begin.

Reynolds satisfied the prerequisites with religious fervor and anal resolve. He dipped long candles of virgin wax scented with vervain, two white and two black, and bundled them away for later use. He shut himself away from all acquaintances, male and female, for thirty days, fasted the required period and zealously consumed his meals as stipulated in the inscriptions laid down in his Master Grimoire.

He donned his hooded ceremonial robe of black velvet and wore it night and day for twenty-four hours prior to the incantation. At midnight, just after consuming his final meal, Reynolds began the journey that would forever alter his perceptions and damage his psyche beyond repair.

He began by circumscribing a five-foot diameter ring of hand-milled flour surrounding himself upon the dark oak flooring in his study. Within the ring, he scribed an inverted five-pointed star using bloodstone. He removed the vervain candles from their satin coverings and placed the white ones on the tips of the star pointing north and east. These would summon Lucifer. He placed the black ones on the tips of the star pointing south and west. These would summon Leviathan.

After a minute of silent meditation, he spoke in dramatic tones suited to his purpose as he lit the candles from right to left. The powerful odor of vervain wafted into his nostrils with a gentile wave of his hands.

> "O' Daemon, Speaker of Immortal Fire,
> Keeper of the Holy Flame,
> Angel Serpent born of lightning flash and storm,
> Grant my wish for power to assist Thee.
> Blessed be the Knife of Re-birth.
> Guide my hand and sever my soul
> From the bounds of Earthly innocence.
> I pray to Acubis, to Sunubai, and to Azazel,
> Let Thy combined energies and wisdom fill me.
> I, Thy servant, ask no less."

From his seated posture, he repeated his earnest paean twice more, allowing several minutes between chants for the spirits to receive and acknowledge his plea. A dreadful chill overcame him and he started to shiver. His palms sweated despite the chill. His stomach grew sick and sour. He swooned for an eternity until, without warning, the candles extinguished.

He awoke in his own bed. He could not say how long he had been unconscious or how he found his way into his bedchamber. He recalled his intention to perform the ceremony, but could not remember having done so. He felt no different from usual, and a sudden debilitating depression sapped his strength and will. He was convinced of his failure and doubted his talents and worthiness. Perhaps, it had all been in vain.

Disheartened but not dissuaded, Reynolds continued his investigation into the shadowy netherworld of evil. He repeated the ritual weekly with little encouragement. But when warmth arrived on the heels of a dreadful winter colder and snowier than anyone had ever endured, his perceptions of success began to change. It became obvious that the spring equinox was not only a harbinger of reprise in the natural world, but a herald of spiritual renewal as well.

March and April were uneventful, but for several days in mid-May amber imbued the sky and blood stained the moon and stars. Silvery soot materialized in the air and fell like an ashen rain, fouling lakes and rivers. Thick fog and low-lying clouds draped the land in an ominous blanket. Then, on May 19, 1780, the sun disappeared.

At twelve o'clock noon, total darkness encompassed New England. The gloom crept in from west to east—the same direction Reynolds consistently faced when engaged in his demonic conjurations. Chickens returned prematurely to their coops to roost and night birds called to test the blackness. Pocket watches held at arm's length disappeared and were practically unreadable held to noses. Blackbirds dropped from the air by the hundreds and patterned the land for miles around like feathered brimstone.

Citizens filled churches to pray for repentance. Whale oil lamps burned at mid-day were mere translucent orbs along the dingy streets. Residents jealously guarded candles in the uncertainty of their dim lit rooms. Scurvied sailors, barred from the sea due to the sightless conditions, relished the darkness and reveled in the relative anonymity it provided. They spent their idleness tossing vulgar catcalls and halloos indiscriminately to females hurrying past their shadowy lairs in their wayward search for home. The abject darkness remained until dawn of the third day then vanished as mysteriously as it appeared.

Reynolds Lovingdale was ecstatic. The event convinced him his connection with the underworld had unleashed the madness. Not since the dark age of unreason cloaked Salem, Massachusetts in the previous century had such terror gripped the citizenry.

According to Mather, the Devil was "the prince of the air" and commanded his minions to muster the primeval forces of lightning and thunder. Beelzebub, himself, might extinguish the moon and stars if doing so furthered his contemptuous regard for God's creations and the souls of righteous men.

The key to immortality now in his hands could unlock the door to a wealth of knowledge, heretofore, unattainable. He stood a threshold away from the handful of mortals that blazed the way before him. Now that the seductive power was his to control, he vowed to evoke devils from every dark recess of Hell and wrench from them the secrets of life, death and the everlasting. His rotting mind, sick with success, reasoned that bypassing the profusion of lesser lords to communicate with the Supreme Lord and Master required measures he had been remiss to undertake, until now. He knew what he must do. It would be done.

CHAPTER IV

And so, with sociopathic devotion, the practice of child sacrifice began. Innocent dozens perished during his insane quest for omnipotence. Yet, for all his malevolence and dedication, Reynolds Lovingdale I never again passed through the door to the netherworld as he thought he had that fateful day in May, 1780. His labors continued for nearly twenty more years until a son, sired in the womb of one of his debauched captives, was born.

He predictably named the boy Reynolds Lovingdale II. Most of the child's nurturing fell to the baby's teenage mother and a succession of nannies. In all fairness, though, the father did dote upon the newborn on occasion. It was the father's intention from the beginning to instill in his spawn the same ignominious pursuits that dominated the last thirty years of his own life.

Reynolds I, presenting himself as the Marquess of Lovingdale, began design and construction of Lovingdale Manor is the wild reaches of Vermont shortly following the birth of his son. He imported hundreds of slaves and hordes of ivory from the African coast, rare exotic sandalwood and rosewood from Southeast Asia and South America, and Calacatta marble and alabaster from Europe. No indulgence was too vulgar, no expense too excessive. In less than three years, the tremendous effort was complete.

The family moved to their incomparable estate at once. During his son's formative years, the Marquess introduced the young Earl to the natural world in its infinite diversity. Field trips routinely culminated in the tortuous death, dismemberment and dissection of whatever creature failed to elude their inquisitive grasps.

Throughout his teenage years, Reynolds Lovingdale II absorbed and practiced hundreds of secret incantations utilizing props and ceremonial attire donned to convince scouting demons of his sincere dedication to his craft. These incantations, culled from countless manuscripts his father acquired during his studies, were the cornerstones of the foundation from which his monument to Evil would rise.

However, black magic did not monopolize every minute of his life. Indoctrination in the areas of business, commerce and finance engaged him as well. It was paramount that the Lovingdale incomes continue to roll in reliably, if the family's gentrification were to continue. Was the love of money, after all, not the root of all evil? Manna's ready availability was essential for ceremonial funding, and its influence removed the pressing need for necessities and afforded protection in their harsh and discriminating world.

When the Earl of Lovingdale reached a level of sufficient mastery over his studies a cadre of elite Masonic northern capitalists, of which Reynolds I was a member, heartily inducted him into their fellowship. Collectively, they prospered from the backbreaking efforts of over-tasked workers who labored endlessly in the various mining, textile and agricultural interests "The Order" controlled. Their tentacles extended from the major metropolitan centers in the Mid-Atlantic region to the Maine Territories in northern New England.

The Lovingdale connections to southern plantations, where cotton was soon to be king, added immeasurably to the enterprising association's capitalist dominance. The Order commanded hundreds of slaves to pick the cotton. Their railroads shipped the coveted raw material north and cotton gins south. Their financial institutions provided competing plantation owners with long-term high interest credit, and an impressive fleet of steam and sailing ships transported their burgeoning inventories abroad. Times were grand. Yet despite enormous material wealth, mounting opportunities and diligent and industrious application, the spiritual keys to the spectrum of occult knowledge remained elusive.

In 1840, Reynolds I transferred complete and final ownership of his substantial holdings into the competent hands of Reynolds II. Along with his inheritance, he passed instructions that his heirs should "loosely" honor his homeland's tradition of peerage, and adopt appropriate titles to convey their rightful social standing. In 1846, Reynolds Lovingdale II celebrated the birth of his own son, anointing him Viscount Reynolds Lovingdale III. Beaming patriarch and boastful new father toasted the fortuitous occasion with much fanfare and celebration.

The close-knit conspiratorial research betwixt father and son into the practice of sorcery continued until Reynolds I passed away in his sleep during the winter of 1852. The Order saw to all wake and funeral arrangements. Strangely, although hundreds attended the services, the deceased body was denied public viewing. A bronze bust of the departed prominently affixed atop the mahogany lid of a gilded casket with ivory handles served as surrogate during visitation. Inquiries remained unaddressed by The Order as to the unusual nature of the closed service and were summarily dismissed.

#

From the day of his birth at Lovingdale Manor, Reynolds Lovingdale III, or "Rennie", as he came to be called, enjoyed an idyllic childhood. Springing from the loins of progenitors of such high social eminence afforded him access to all the luxuries outstanding wealth provided.

A host of nannies and personal valets meticulously attended to their young lord's needs. As he grew into adulthood, the perpetual indulgences of his formative years left him jaded and difficult. Not content to have his wishes merely fulfilled, he exacted his desires at the appreciable expense of anyone unfortunate enough to be within range.

The scope of his demands grew exponentially in frivolity until his emotional development stagnated and regressed to a near infantile state. He persistently refused to bathe and dress himself for no reason other than the disproportionate pleasure he experienced through bending others to his depraved will. At the slightest provocation, he struck out aggressively with a horsehair whip he religiously carried. Once, he tore an eye from the socket of an apologetic manservant because the attendant neglected to powder his master's foot before applying its brocade silk stocking.

Perhaps, the manifest example of the young sadist's obscene personality was his habit of forcing attendants to catch his excrement in a paper bag. This, they were instructed to secure in their apron pocket while they wiped their master's rear clean to his satisfaction. Only then did he dismiss them to extricate the repulsive burden from their person.

Had it not been for the irreproachable social standing and power of the Lovingdale name, Rennie's head would have adorned the bedpost of any one of his humiliated and tortured underlings. His timely execution would have elevated his assassin to sainthood in the eyes of his peers. As things stood, servers and attendants remained sullen but compliant. They endured the whims of their master for the sake of their families so reliant on the pittance they received for their insufferable labors.

In April 1885, twenty years to the day after General Robert E. Lee surrendered to General Ulysses S. Grant at Appomattox Courthouse, Virginia, the Earl of Lovingdale died, leaving his son and sole heir in control of the family dynasty. Remarkably, the Civil War that ravaged the southern states of the Confederacy and divided the nation for four terrible years left the Lovingdale fortune unscathed. True, the Emancipation Proclamation decimated all slave-related interests, but the various other holdings in the Lovingdale Empire continued to thrive.

For the next seventeen years, Viscount Lovingdale, known as Squire Lovingdale to commoners ignorant of his family's privileged lineage, continued his diabolical practices and indefensible cruelties with fiendish delight. The astute pupil mastered the lessons of Satanism well. A storehouse of supernatural wisdom, gleaned from the ancient texts aggregated over decades by two generations before him, offered priceless insights and experience that would have taken him three lifetimes to otherwise acquire.

Business associates, politicians and newspapermen alike grew to hate him and reviled him at every opportunity in the forum of public debate. Squire Lovingdale took it all in stride, concentrating his warped sensibilities on the indoctrination of his four children. The children's mother, Grace, died during the birth of their fourth child. Consequently, the father assumed dictatorial control over his progeny's education and enlightenment.

The desperation of continued failure in achieving notable results in his practice of the devil arts ignited in him a determination unlike any he had previously known. His grandfather had nearly "captured the light", as he had put it, and hailed the Dark Day of May 19, 1780 as the hallmark of his endeavors and a tremendous milestone of achievement in his chosen craft. Yes, his grandfather certainly set the bar high.

The Squire would have to plot a new course into territory yet unexplored by the Lovingdales. He would have to dig deeper into the belly of demonology, probe its entrails and commit his resources fully towards realizing his ultimate ambition. In early 1901, he liquidated his assets, except for Lovingdale Manor, and retired from public life. Days, weeks and months sequestered in the inner chambers of his mansion melted away. Laboring feverishly with scarcely a break for nourishment, he flooded the stale air with spells, incantations and conjurations steeped in cosmic synergy.

The children rarely saw their father for weeks on end. A succession of caregivers attended to the children's physical needs, but when inquisitiveness as to the Squire's secret activities preoccupied a servant's thoughts that employee mysteriously vanished.

On October 1, 1901, on the eve of a great late season thunderstorm, Squire Lovingdale experienced a flash of genius. The vision might well have been delivered on a bolt of lightning—such was the immediacy and clarity of his epiphany. His head spun deliriously, and time as he knew it ceased to exist.

Everywhere he looked, evidence of his newly discovered truth rang out in confirmation. Ropes and wooden planks collected for no apparent reason took on new significance. The steel edge of cutting weapons gleamed with heightened brightness. The imagery on tapestries and imported floor coverings swirled into reconfigured patterns, all eerily suggestive and profound.

His direction gelled overnight. The following morning, he put his ultimate bestial act into play. When his work was complete the devil would hold title to his soul, but Squire Lovingdale would achieve immortality. He, alone, would hold worlds and universes at bay through all the coming ages and the Lovingdale name would live on in infamy.

Reynolds labored tirelessly until All Hallows Eve, when he dismissed the servants early so their intrusive presence would not impede the flow of his genius. He carefully prepared a powerful opiate-laced nightcap and insisted his children consume equal draughts of the bitter beverage in his presence before leading them upstairs to their respective bedrooms. The potent cocktail had the desired effect in minutes with the youngest daughter, Audrey, falling unconscious before reaching the top of the stairs. Picking her up, he directed the other three to the end of the hallway. When Audrey, Jacob, Ebenezer, and Julius were prone in their beds, their father placed his palm on the forehead of each and mumbled what would have been perceived to be, in normal company, an evening prayer.

During the interminable night, Reynolds sharpened a small scythe blade to razor keenness and polished it until his demented smile sneered back at him from its mirrored surface. Four hemp ropes fashioned into nooses with thirteen twists lay aligned upon the dining table. Four crosses constructed from alder timbers leaned precariously against one another in the dining room archway. The main post of each unit spanned ten feet in the long dimension and met a perpendicular member at a point where the cross would appear to rest upside down when its lower end was buried two feet into the earth.

After insuring all necessary accoutrements were in order, Reynolds set about destroying twenty goats in the estate stables. Before killing the beasts, he enlisted a larger cousin of the breed to serve as 'Judas'; its mission being to lure the oblivious animals to the cross erection site at midnight.

With the aid of his cloven-hoofed assistant, he herded the goats into a circular pen enclosed by a six-foot high, woven-wire fence built specifically for their containment. Reynolds waded in among the unsuspecting rascals, scythe in hand, thrashing wildly in all directions. The panicked bleating of the goats rang into the night, feeding the mad man's lust and increasing his demented fury to bloodthirsty heights. When the mass of ruminants reduced to a handful, Reynolds methodically stalked each one singularly. With his leering face ablaze with an inner light, he chased the terrified beasts over and through the bodies of their fallen brethren. When finally cornered, the animals cowered in submission before their insane assailant.

Reynolds grabbed each of the bleating herbivores by a hind leg and lifted them kicking and squalling from the ground. He dispatched each of them with a single vicious blow to the abdomen, spilling their entrails upon his feet. In less than an hour, the song of death abated. Reynolds stepped outside the gory, burgundy ring and shot a menacing glance to a dim candle flitting in the window on the upper floor of the house. He dropped the scythe where he stood and strode defiantly back to the house. His children were waiting.

He entered the bedroom shared by his first and second born. With a last dispassionate gesture, he slid the down-filled pillow from beneath the head of his eldest son and placed it over the child's face. Though unconscious, the helpless youngster struggled beneath the full weight of his father's body. Only the boy's spastic hands and feet foretold the agony as his life slipped away. In a moment, it was over. Reynolds smiled. One down, three to go. Without delay, he transferred the pillow to the next child's face and then adjourned to the adjacent room where he resumed his madness.

After all four children succumbed, Reynolds carted them outside in succession, aligning their bodies, side by side, from largest to least— their white cotton nightgowns gleaming like prostate ghosts in the ambivalent moonlight. He then erected the crosses at each corner of the enclosure, all strategically pointed to the four cardinal compass points. He sunk the crosses two feet into the pliant earth so that the horizontal member was about three feet above the ground. Upon each cross, he draped a child's lifeless legs over the horizontal beam that served as a natural hook, with the upper part of the post between the young one's knees. He then attached a thin lash of rawhide to one ankle, pulled the leather strip around the post and tied its loose end to the ankle of the child's other leg.

With the corpses thus secured, he was free to execute the next step of his ghoulish enterprise. He arranged five goats around each cross with their rear ends near the cross's upright post. Their gutless carcasses splayed outward to form a five-pointed pentagram. He stripped butt-naked, built a bonfire near the crucifixion site and danced around it with savage glee until he collapsed in exhaustion near the flaming embers. After several minutes, he re-energized and resumed his diabolical experiment.

He produced a large ceremonial dagger and with it slit the throats of his progeny. It was imperative that he catch the first surge of crimson liquid in his mouth. In order to accomplish this vital step, he reclined beneath each dangling child, craned his head until face-to-face, and drew the knife expertly for its entire length across each ivory shaft. After consuming a mouthful of their blood, he allowed the remainder to wash over his head and torso, staining his infernal flesh an abominable red. The sticky mass gelled on his skin, camouflaged his identity and suggested a vile, new species had usurped his bones. A thrilling energy pulsed through his being and somehow trumped the preceding events in pure majesty and power.

Then, as if in answer to his heinous offering, storm clouds gathered in the distance. Thunder pealed with increasing temerity, its frequency and duration magnifying as the storm approached. Dynamic crashes bashed the heavens milliseconds after branching bolts of lightning split the sky.

Reynolds was beside himself in frenzy, reeling like a drunken man and muttering intelligible gibberish to his phantom audience. A gargantuan flash, greater than any he had ever witnessed, reflected eerily from the clouds and revealed the visage of his Lord and Master, Satan. The ethereal portrait glared down with approval from the tortured firmament. Reynolds dropped immediately to his knees, clasped his hands together in a prayerful gesture and pleaded to the Lord of Darkness to fulfill his wish of immortality—to bestow upon him the supreme power he devoted his entire lifetime to pursuing.

In a heartbeat, a single arc of lightning met his upheld hands full force. His body surged electric. An ice blue aura encased his form and curled his skin to blistered translucent flakes that shed from his body like azure snow. The almighty pulse transfixed and transformed his shell into half a man, fusing his lower extremities to the moist loam in a hermetic mass. The residual power of each continued flash cast its wealth upon the haunted scene and prompted the ashen faces of his children to glow again like paper lanterns.

When concerned citizens discovered the horrific display three days later, Squire Lovingdale was a figurine of charred ash still kneeling in prayerful subordination. The children's bodies were extricated and properly interred in the churchyard cemetery—their presumed innocence outweighing the implied guilt by association. The act of atypical compassion was one of the truly righteous events in the town's history. The Squire's "burnt offering" crumbled into dust when disturbed and dispersed in a whisper of wind.

Squire Lovingdale III was dead, as were his four innocent children, but the evil that destroyed them grew fat on their wasted lives. It drifted unopposed over vale and hillock, then haughtily returned with devilish exhilaration to settle down upon the scene of its nightmare of carnage like a pall.

That abandoned altar to depravity rested for the next hundred years, patiently waiting for a spark of malevolence destined to inspire renewed purpose to its dark design. As the twenty-first century dawned, a series of apparently unrelated events freed the Wheel of Evil to again roll forth. Damned be the unfortunates in its way.

CHAPTER V

Clara Connor, or Kim, as she came to be known to family and friends, was just about the prettiest baby the world had ever seen. Her proud father beat this very fact into the heads of everyone who would listen and vehemently vowed that he would whip, without mercy, any man who dared to say it was not so. She was born on December 8, 1984 in the exact house where her mother Ellen was born some twenty-seven years earlier in the small town of Circleville, Ohio, just south of the capitol city of Columbus.

There was no doctor present, just Ellen, of course, her husband Carl, her employer, Bernard Biggs—who insisted on being present if only in an adjoining room—and Cassie, a trusted midwife who helped bring Ellen into the world all those years before. Ellen would have it no other way. Cassie was in her sixties by then but still delivering babies right and left. Ellen felt confident and secure that time had not diminished her good friend's compassionate energy nor dulled her dutiful sense of responsibility. On top of it all, that glorious day just happened to be Ellen's birthday as well. Ellen was ecstatic over sharing a birthday with her daughter, and her labor proceeded as flawlessly and effortlessly as any mother could have wished.

Carl crowed for weeks after the blessed event for having effectuated the one thing that Bernard never could, the birth of a daughter. He chided his wife's employer for his legendary bachelorism whenever the opportunity arose, but he never meant it in a callous or mean-spirited way. Carl and Bernard were from the same town, but Biggs was older than

Carl by ten years. Carl had historically played "second fiddle" to his senior neighbor. It was no secret that Ellen and Biggs had been romantically involved before Carl entered the picture, and Carl could not suppress his satisfaction over finally holding the better cards. Bernard pretended to handle it well, but Carl knew the idea of losing anything put a knot in Bernard's shorts.

Carl Connor was a dreamer. Ellen fell for the romantic fool at first sight. 'One of these days…' he would promise religiously, and Ellen would smile, nod patronizingly and take him by the arm. She truly loved him and would be happy rich or poor and for better or worse. She liked dreaming, too. The two of them 'fit together', as the neighbors were so fond of telling them, and they believed it with all their hearts.

Clara was a bright young girl by any standard and was always ahead of the game. She took her first step at nine months, was potty trained at two years of age and could read simple books by age three. Carl and Ellen chose to forgo kindergarten and, through educational achievement testing, placed their precocious child in first grade by the time she was five.

Clara's physical development was equally rapid and remarkable. She had an astonishing effect on other children, and they flocked to her in droves. Everyone wanted to be Clara's friend, and all her teachers had nothing but high praise for the 'Darling of Circleville'.

Golden tresses softly curled and tinged with strawberry framed her sharp, but delicate, features with an admirable satin radiance. The most extraordinary pair of violet eyes sparkled beneath her locks with dazzling brilliance, and her pleasantly paired and proportioned nose and mouth seemed to hold the mischievous smirk of some delicious secret. Wonderfully transparent skin and long, long lashes completed her list of charms. Clara knew there was something special about her, but she did not flaunt it or take herself too seriously. Whatever the elusive quality was that set the world ablaze, Clara had it in spades.

Ellen bestowed the sobriquet of 'Kim' on her little girl while reading nightly from Rudyard Kipling's great work by the same name. Her mother had started the book while she was pregnant, but the emotional and physical demands of pregnancy drained her energy and she often fell asleep while reading. After Clara was born, she mitigated these lapses by reading the tome aloud while rocking her baby in the nursery Carl had built, and she continued her narration after Clara was old enough to lie still in her own bed and listen.

Clara did not truly understand all in her mother's recitals, but the inflection in her mother's voice and the joy in her delivery brought the narrative to life. The idea of adventures in exotic lands was exciting, and she refused to go to bed without the book and her mother in tow— insisting after she did so that her mother call her "Kim". Ellen happily indulged her daughter's chosen sobriquet. She would read nightly snuggled in a chair near her daughter's bedside until both fell soundly asleep. In all likelihood, they shared the same dream.

Ellen's employer, Bernard Biggs, seemed to come out on top in everything. In high school, he held every student body office obtainable, was editor and chief writer for the school paper and lettered in every sport the school offered. He was voted "most likely to succeed" in his senior year and proved it by starting his own newspaper within two years of graduating. Over the years, it grew into one of the largest dailies in Ohio. Shortly after the Connor wedding, Biggs tried to recruit Carl for some menial position when the newly established firm took legs, but Carl found pride a bitter pill and would have none of it.

Biggs renamed his newspaper, *The Village Clarion*, in Clara's honor after she was born. Ellen had granted him "godfather" status out of deference to his unsolicited gesture, but Biggs took the honorary title to extremes, as he did most things. He was overtly doting and fixated on Clara from the beginning—somewhat disquieting given the child was not his.

But as always, the additional expense of raising a child quickly strained the family budget. To help ends meet, Carl reluctantly agreed to accept a delivery position at Bernard's newspaper. That Biggs renamed his publishing concern in honor of Clara softened Carl's objections and convinced him to come onboard. The extra money certainly helped, but his part-time duties soon expanded and required extended absences from home. Consequently, he saw his family less and less as one year flowed seamlessly into the next, and the next.

On one auspicious occasion, Bernard Biggs arranged for Carl to deliver a semi-trailer filled with recycled newsprint to an associate concern in Atlanta, Georgia. The trip was a long one and the details of the delivery complex. Due to carefully arranged scheduling conflicts, the time required for the trip spanned several days and Carl would have to lay over both ways. There was a hefty bonus waiting at the end of Bernard's faux rainbow, so Carl agreed to go. With Carl out of the way, the true reasons behind the importunate arrangement became provocatively clear.

#

"Ellen, I have a right to see her whenever and for however long I like." Bernard shouted.

"Bernard, please don't do this," Ellen pleaded. "Please...it will ruin my marriage. It will destroy Carl, and Kim. Please..."

"What's mine is mine, Ellen, and what's yours is mine as well. Get used to it. I've taken all the goddamn cockcrowing from Carl I'm gonna take. It's time he understands whose child Clara really is."

"Bernard, please...I'll do anything you say, but not that. I'm begging you." Ellen clutched desperately at his jacket lapels, distraught tears drenching the front of his silk shirt and tie.

"Clara's our daughter, Ellen. The fact you found a husband after our little thing doesn't change it. I've let you pretend for more than eight years, and now you have to face the fiddler. Besides, you enjoyed our little romance as much as I did."

Ellen hissed and attempted to pull away, but Biggs's hands gripped her wrists like manacles. Without hesitation or compunction, he drew her closer to him and clutched her tightly to his chest. With one hand under her rear, he lifted her from the floor and clumsily sought her lips with his own.

"Stop it, Bernie!" Ellen demanded. "You're going to wake Kim." She squirmed to free herself, arching backwards and beating at his chest. In a final fury, she launched a powerful jab to his throat and followed with a two-fisted tug at the man's thinning hair. The resistance caused tears of pain to swell his eyes, and he released her.

"Damn you!" He squalled, rubbing his eyes with the back of his hand.

"Get out, Bernie!" Ellen retorted. "Carl is Kim's father. Do you hear me? Regardless of what you prefer to think, she is ours, not yours!" She turned away from him and supported her weary one-hundred-pound frame on the back of the sofa.

"You can't make it without me, Ellen. You know that."

"I said get out!"

"I'll be back, Ellen. You'll never get rid of me."

#

Two weeks later, Kim's dearest friend invited her to a slumber party hosted by the girl's mother. Ellen's only misgiving about it was that Carl would be gone again and she would be alone. Nevertheless, she dropped her bubbling youngster at the prescribed time and place and went home.

That night at two a.m., Ellen awakened beneath a great bulk. It was Biggs. His rough hands sealed her mouth as he flicked on the small lamp on the nightstand. This time, an attractive woman dressed in pink tights favored by some of the local prostitutes accompanied him. She stood readily by the bed holding a video camera and slender tripod.

Ellen's eyes darted back and forth between the two intruders in hopes of ascertaining their motives. She screamed and kicked her legs, but Biggs pushed her head into her pillow with such force she felt she would smother in her own linens. His right hand gripped her throat, and she was terrified he would kill her if she continued to resist. She understood that Bernard Biggs was capable of anything and willing to do it without qualm.

"Ellen, are you gonna be a good girl?" he asked in hushed tones. "Where's Clara?" He slowly removed his hand from her mouth.

"She's not here."

"Don't lie to me, Ellen. You know I can't stand liars."

"I'm not lying. Look for yourself. She's spending a couple of days with a friend."

Bernard relaxed a bit. "Ellen, this is Tanya. Isn't she pretty? Tanya, take a look around the place for me while I help Ellen settle down. Check the rest of the rooms and make sure the back door is locked. Then hurry back, ok, doll?"

Tanya set the photographic equipment on the bed and promptly left. She returned shortly and confirmed Ellen's claims. "She's telling the truth, Bernie. There's no one else here."

"Well now, that's real nice. It looks like we'll have plenty of time to get to know one another. What do you think about that, Ellie, my dear?

Wanna get to know Tanya a little better?"

"Bernie, please," Ellen pleaded. "Please get out before you do something you can't undo. I won't say anything to anyone, I swear. Just leave now. Bernie, you..."

His powerful hands stifled her pleading again. His manner grew maniacal. The bitterness in his eyes reflected his cruel intentions.

Ellen battled with her mind, and the fear of what may occur swept over her like a tidal wave. She had to get out of there fast. With a quick maneuver, she slipped from beneath her assailant's grasp and fell to the floor. Despite having nothing on but a sheer satin slip, she bolted for the door, knocking the complicit harlot across the room in the process. Before she secured her freedom, a wrenching tug at the back of her head stalled her progress and sent her reeling back into the room.

"This won't do, Ellen," Biggs scolded. "You're not being a good...gal...at...all." He slapped her to emphasize each of his last four words. The accent on the final blow knocked Ellen senseless. She was out cold. The bastard picked her up and laid her on the bed. Without further ado, he and Tanya began readying the camera equipment in preparation for their big debut as filmmakers. His sick plan was getting sicker.

When Ellen awoke, she found one hand tied to the headboard post and one foot likewise to the footboard. This allowed her some freedom of movement while preventing her from rising from the bed. It also afforded Biggs and Tanya a necessary element of control that facilitated repositioning Ellen to their advantage when a particularly base capriciousness entered the equation.

Biggs operated the camera while Tanya entertained their humiliated and helpless captive with pornographic delight and expertise. When Biggs determined that he had collected enough footage, he released Ellen from her bonds.

Biggs threatened exposing her "libertine excesses" with a hooker through his formidable, tri-state newspaper network. Not only would the community she was born and reared in and the church she attended ostracize her, she would certainly lose her precious daughter to the blind discretion of the state. Biggs assured Ellen he would have little difficulty wrangling custody of Kim, and he would prevent her from seeing her daughter ever again unless she willingly complied with his demands without reservation.

Ellen was distraught, exhausted and devastated. Even though no lesbian acts were consummated, she had no choice but to agree. She could never tell Carl about this. No matter how much he loved her, and she him, he would never understand or accept such an inconceivable situation. Carl would explode in anger and destroy Biggs without question. She would still lose everything. The scandal would rip her life to shreds and damage them all irreparably. She had to find a way to free herself and her daughter from the coils of her venomous former lover. Resolving the how and when of her dilemma would have to wait until her thoughts cleared and the numbness abated.

Ellen's dazed and confused mind sought refuse in the sanctity of sleep. She drifted off unopposed into a better world. When she awoke around eight that evening, her violators had departed. There was no sign that villainy had occurred in her home, and she desperately hoped everything had been an ugly nightmare. However, the bruises on her torso and abrasions on her wrists and ankles belied self-deception. She hobbled to the bathroom and ran a cleansing bath. She paused before the vanity mirror and burst into uncontrollable sobs. Her reflection ordered her to the cold tile floor in a fit of despair.

CHAPTER VI

Bernard Biggs was a man of considerable wealth with connections and holdings in several states. Associates knew him as a pragmatic, ruthless individual endowed with enviable business acumen and adroit at furthering his own selfish interests. He travelled extensively and marked his expanding territory with the telltale odor of his princely, Cohiba Cuban cigars.

Biggs knew from experience that a hands-on approach to management of his real estate acquisitions offered the greatest measure of return. He distrusted brokers as a rule and used them solely out of necessity to expedite and legitimize his activities.

He had recently purchased an admittedly forsaken property overlooking the Rundle River in upstate Vermont. He had purchased the estate sight unseen. The price he paid was a steal, and he was still patting himself on the back for his latest bulls-eye. This purchase merited a routine visit so, as the weather was seasonably warm and inviting, he opted to drive himself to the closing in his new Mercedes Benz S-class automobile. It was high time he enjoyed the fruits of his labor, and he looked forward to cruising enveloped in hand-tooled Nappa leather and burled walnut veneer.

A mortgage bank had launched foreclosure proceedings against the estate over delinquent taxes and a small investment corporation had acquired it, abruptly choosing to subsequently unload their investment for pennies on the dollar. The land alone was worth twice, even three times, what they were asking and the offer was too good for Biggs to resist.

The house and grounds had been under the Lovingdale banner for nearly two centuries, but suffered from mismanagement and neglect after the last known descendants resident at the house met horrible deaths in the year 1901 at the hands of their father, Viscount Reynolds Lovingdale III, Esq. Since that notorious time, few occupants roamed the mansion's baroque halls. Each empty season drained another vial of its lifeblood and left it more withered and anemic than the year before.

Biggs was astonished at the estimated cost of revitalizing the grounds and structures. The prohibitive expense convinced him to pursue the option of allowing the land to appreciate naturally over the course of years, until such time borrowing against the equity covered renovations. He would sit on it for now. At present, he had monies to shelter. He recently sold a downtown Cleveland office building and had a tiny window of opportunity to re-invest before incurring substantial penalties on capital gains.

Since leaving early that morning, he had followed the freeway and the incessant noise and stress of being sandwiched between semi-trailers had him in a state of rage. The time was approaching six-thirty in the evening. Allentown, Pennsylvania lay a good fifty miles behind him. He achieved excellent time thus far and saw no reason why he should not adopt a more leisurely pace for the remaining miles ahead. New England autumns were beautiful by any standard and, although he was not one prone to stop to smell the roses, he anticipated enjoying the fall splendor.

The bucolic stretch between the towns of East Stroudsburg and Port Jervis was a welcome departure and freed his mind to focus on something other than death by semi. The sun had set and enough light remained to proceed without warranting the cars headlights—although dusk was on its heels.

Biggs was cruising along, ruminating over business concerns, when the figure of a young man stepped quickly from behind a road sign and stuck out his thumb in hobo fashion. Biggs slowed the big black sedan but did not stop. He scrutinized the figure in passing merely to satisfy a curiosity. As the hitchhiker met his approval, he braked the vehicle to a full stop and reversed it to where the man stood. He could now tell that the fellow, no more than seventeen or eighteen years of age, had a desperate look about him. The boy was physically burdened by no more than the clothes on his back. Biggs attributed the hitchhiker's disheveled appearance to the nature of his circumstance. "What the hell," he thought to himself. He could use a little company.

Biggs swung wide the door to the "shotgun" seat, but the young man ignored the gesture and opted to enter the car through the rear passenger door. His red hair was closely cropped and his manner slovenly. A thin grove of light whiskers sprouted from his chin and a face scrubbing was long overdue. He slouched in the back seat as if he were lounging at a sophomoric frat party and extended no respect normally due a stranger's impromptu hospitality.

Biggs set aside his disapproval for the moment. "Where you headed, son?" He asked in an uncharacteristically friendly, though transparent, tone.

The boy stared blankly at the older man and replied coldly, "I'm not your son."

Biggs, caught off-guard by the coarse and unappreciative remark, considered extricating the offensive youth from his vehicle to continue his miserable sojourn alone along the empty highway, but something in the young man's face talked him out of it and he let it pass. "I understand that," he conceded. "Do you have a name?"

"Yes," the boy replied, offering nothing else.

Biggs sighed, his patience wearing thin. "Mine's Bernie. Do you mind telling me where you are headed?"

The taciturn stranger shifted further back in the seat and dissolved into the shadows. "Right now, I'm going with you," he replied enigmatically.

Biggs smiled with mild chagrin, and edged the sedan off the shoulder and back on the highway. The next thirty miles were notable for brief remarks and protracted stretches of silence. He could feel the boy's eyes burning into the back of his head as he drove along. He sometimes met the young man's intense gaze when he checked his posture in the rear view mirror. On one occasion when their eyes locked, the boy spoke audibly but sans emotion. "Roger," he said. "My name is Roger."

As darkness fell, the travelers approached a diner set back several yards from an intersecting road. Both men forswore nourishment for several hours. Biggs suggested they stop for a bite, to which his bizarre companion readily agreed. There were few vehicles in the gravel parking lot, just two large trucks parked side by side. They assumed the trucks were the only vehicles there until a police cruiser revealed itself on one semi's far side as they drove past the diner's front entrance.

Roger glanced suspiciously at the "blue light special", but Biggs apparently did not notice. He also did not notice his passenger slide across the back seat and exit through the driver side door—the side farthest from the patrol car.

Inside, a handful of patrons chomped steadily at their vittles and paid little heed to the newly arrived strangers. Everyone except the patrol officer seated at the counter, who turned slowly on his stool and eyed them both as they entered. They subconsciously selected a booth in the rear of the establishment. Biggs sat on the seat facing the officer who projected more than a passing interest in his unkempt acquaintance and himself. The officer's deliberate scrutiny was unnerving. Biggs was about to confront the man when the cop abruptly rose and left the diner.

"Strange," Biggs noted. "What was he looking at?"

Roger remained cool, collected and noticeably silent. He excused himself to the restroom and entered the dingy space and locked the door behind him. He was disappointed to learn the bathroom was windowless and vented solely by an obnoxious exhaust fan. After a believable amount of time elapsed, he left the toilet and discovered the police officer standing next to Biggs. The officer's back was turned, but Roger could tell he was interrogating his driver about some matter of immediate concern. Roger sensed danger and headed directly towards the exit. He paused at the counter near the officer's seat and slipped a steak knife into the sleeve of his denim jacket. Once outside, he melted into the darkness where he waited and watched the front entrance. He clutched the steak knife in his fist and ran the thumb of his other hand over the serrated edge.

Close on Roger's heels, the cop emerged from the diner into the cold night air but found his suspect nowhere in sight. He strode directly to his patrol car, opened the door and withdrew his radio. A moment before he contacted the station, someone grabbed him from behind. Determined hands wielding a deadly keen-edged weapon sawed aggressively across his throat from ear to ear. The attack severed the poor man's esophagus and jugular. The policeman stood stone still gripped with shock. Great globs of blood percolated up into his mouth and spewed forth from his "Kool-Aid smile" to paint his shoes and the white gravel beneath them a loathsome red.

Roger reached around and removed the radio from the dying man's grasp and supported his convulsing victim with his left arm. He threw the handset back inside the vehicle and forced the officer behind the wheel. In doing so, he inadvertently engaged the blue emergency lights. Roger's first instinct was to shut the signal down immediately, but his whimsical side found the idea great fun and he resisted. He noticed a warrant notification on the front seat with none other than himself as the center of interest. He was positive the cop had made him as soon as they entered the diner, but now it made no difference. He crumpled the flier into a wad and stuffed it into the pocket of his jean jacket. After wiping the radio free of prints, he cast his improvised implement of death into the bordering vegetation. Roger returned to the Mercedes and nonchalantly positioned himself against the front passenger door as if nothing had transpired.

Biggs grew tired of waiting for his fellow traveler to exit the lavatory and left the diner. His face registered surprise when he discovered Roger leaning against the side of his Mercedes. Biggs was visibly perplexed at his passenger's unorthodox behavior and intrigued by the policeman's probing questions. "Did you see that cop, Roger?"

Roger remained dead calm for a moment before responding. "What did he say to you?" he answered in a detached tone.

"He was asking about you...all sorts of questions...how I knew you, what we were doing together, where we were going. He seemed genuinely concerned and was about to elaborate when his radar went up and he left quickly. Did he speak with you?"

"Yeah, we spoke," Roger lied. "It was a case of mistaken identity. He's in his squad car now calling in a report."

"Strange," Biggs concluded. He started the sedan rolling again and glanced over at the patrol car in passing. The officer was sitting upright in the front seat, blue lights flashing. Biggs resolutely tightened his lips in disconcerted amazement and returned to the main road. The incident apparently haunted them both and prompted an eerie silence for some time. Biggs sought to brighten the mood with a dirty joke or two, but the humor seemed lost on the introverted lad. The conversation was decidedly one-sided with Biggs doing all the talking.

Eventually, the topic turned to sex, as topics between males often do. "Do you have a girl friend?" he asked Roger casually and seemingly out-of-the-blue.

"No," Roger replied, looking straight ahead.

Biggs continued asserting his vulgar, lascivious side. "What, a good looking stud like you? I'll bet you're hung like a race horse!" He glanced at Roger for any revealing reaction that might offer him encouragement to continue his sophomoric soliloquy. He thought he caught the shadow of a smile cross Roger's lips.

Roger disengaged from the prurient babblings of the much older man. He rested his head upon the window glass and watched the silhouetted treetops commence their frantic race against the lost and lonesome sky. His driver's mutterings faded into a drone. The stark light from a full moon broke through the scattered clouds and showered down upon them, illuminating Roger's face. His disembodied reflection in the window was now quite visible—as clear and clean as the face of a fellow pilgrim across the aisle on a bus or train. Roger and his alter ego smiled in unison at each other. He watched in awe as his reflection morphed into the wild, red-eyed, fanged deviant of his other self.

Around midnight, Biggs decided further driving would accomplish little and a good night's sleep just might insure he arrived at his destination tomorrow without incident. He stopped at the next motor lodge and paid for separate rooms. Both men retired to their respective beds with little fanfare and great relief.

Biggs was lying in bed by one a.m. flipping through the television channels, when a report on CNN caught his undivided attention: "Early this evening, a New York police officer was discovered outside the Wayside Diner near the Pennsylvania/ New York state line with his throat cut. At first report, there were no witnesses to the crime, but the owner of the diner remembered seeing two men—one possibly in his late forties or early fifties, the other in his late teens or early twenties—who left the establishment without ordering. The proprietor also observed the officer talking to the older man while in the restaurant. A truck driver found the police officer sitting in his patrol car with the emergency lights flashing. Local and state police are currently seeking the two men as 'persons-of-interest' in the case and have notified the FBI. Anyone with information concerning this crime is advised to contact the authorities at..."

Biggs flipped off the television with the remote control and sat upright in the bed, scarcely believing what he had just seen and heard. He recollected the events of the evening and compared them to the broadcast images he had just observed. He weighed each seemingly insignificant occurrence against another until a cohesive picture emerged. "It could all be coincidence," he reasoned, "but if it isn't?" A calculating smile augmented his bewildered features with relief and realization. "Roger, my boy," he commented softly, "you might just prove useful after all."

Around eight a.m. the next morning, Biggs knocked on Roger's door, but no one answered. He tried the knob, but the door was locked. Thinking the young man had abandoned their relationship overnight he shrugged, stretched his lips tight in a grimace of resignation and proceeded to the office desk to check out. The clerk was engaged in a news broadcast concerning the capital murder of the patrolman. Biggs feigned disinterest, and the clerk absentmindedly processed his checkout request while barely averting her eyes from the television screen. He left without thanking her and walked straight to his Mercedes.

As Biggs slid behind the wheel, Roger materialized from a crouched position on the opposite side of the Benz, his face pressed distortedly against the passenger-side window glass and his fingers splayed to each side of his head.

The brusqueness of the maneuver and Roger's crude and corrupt appearance alarmed Biggs. "Jesus, Roger!" He remarked with disgust after settling down. He unlocked the passenger door with a click. "Get in."

"Did I scare you?" Roger chided sarcastically.

"I don't scare easily, Roger. You had best remember that."

"I'll remember," Roger answered immediately, the playful glimmer in his eyes dulling to the sheen of pool table slate.

Biggs grunted, gunned the big V-8, and set the Michelin radial tires to squalling. "Let's go to Vermont," he said.

Roger was up for anything. He told Biggs as much. He had nowhere to go, little to look forward to and nothing to do. Nothing, that is, but to pay an overdue visit to his folks. He had some unfinished business to attend to and a present to bestow upon his beloved parents. However, that could wait. He was in no hurry to see them. All in good time. He would visit Vermont first and learn what Bernie Biggs had up his sleeve.

After an hour or more of driving, they stopped for gas and a bathroom break. While Biggs was topping off the tank, he saw Roger pull something from his jacket pocket and dispose of it in the trash bin as he walked to the john. When the boy disappeared behind the door of the restroom, Biggs quickly retrieved the material and returned to the car where he smoothed the crinkled paper on his leg and confirmed his suspicions. It was the wanted flier with Roger's picture on it. The person in the photograph sported a Mohawk haircut. Roger wore his hair closely cropped. Other than that, they were dead ringers.

According to the flier, the felon had escaped from the state hospital in Fairview a week earlier and had nearly killed an attendant while doing so. "He could have shaved his head after escaping," Biggs surmised. "It's him, I know it is." Biggs never mentioned his suspicions when Roger returned, and he remained silent and smug in his newfound knowledge for the duration of the trip to Lovingdale Manor.

The noirish, rambling estate had Roger at hello. Its mysterious history, tortured landscape and overall foreboding appearance held an unhealthy appeal for the young man. He wandered the length and breadth of the property while Biggs and his broker discussed details from inside the broker's car. They preferred concluding their affairs in a more accommodating environment and were considerably peeved at Roger's late return.

Biggs denied Roger's request to remain at the mansion and thought the premise ludicrous and unwise. What would the boy eat? How could anyone possibly live in a place so obviously hostile and void of human comforts? However, he did inform Roger of a matter that concerned him greatly and if Roger helped him resolve his "difficulty", perhaps, they could arrange something—the particulars of which they would discuss on their return trip.

Roger agreed and was hopeful and lighthearted for the remains of the day.

On the way back, Biggs outlined his situation to his young protégé, explaining only as much as he felt Roger needed to hear. He told him about Carl, though not by name, and of how the man had stolen his wife and daughter from him. He told him about a trip that Carl would soon be making, of how and when the time would be right for Roger to utilize his special skills.

Biggs waited until they approached the location where the police officer was murdered before showing Roger the wanted flier he had retrieved from the trash bin. He tossed the wrinkled paper in Roger's lap just as the sign for the Wayside Diner came into view. Biggs considered it best to employ every advantage to his favor and figured Roger might be a little on edge when he recalled the diner and what happened there.

"Hey, remember that spot?" Biggs asked matter-of-factly.

Roger glanced down at the flier between his legs then over at the man who had put it there. "So you know. Big fucking deal."

"You killed that cop, didn't you, Roger?" Biggs accused.

Roger remained silent and looked straight ahead. He was formulating a strategy in his mind in case certain things required doing.

"Look, I don't care how many people you've killed, understand? Only now, you have involved me in your little escapade. Now, it is up to me to make certain you don't sink and take me down with you."

Roger turned towards the older man and cut through him with the blankest of stares.

Biggs continued. "In exchange for my silence, I want you to help me solve my little problem. That way, we both have something on each other, get it?"

Roger turned his head and stared straight ahead again. "I get it," Roger admitted. "I also get to live in the old house in Vermont as long as I like, or it's no deal." Roger paused to note any exception, and then continued. "I have some business of my own to see to first. Give me a phone number or an address, and I'll look you up as soon as I'm finished."

"That will work," Biggs answered happily. His tone changed quickly to one of deadly earnest. "Only don't screw with me, Roger. You don't know who you're dealing with."

Roger turned again to face Biggs. His blazing eyes displayed remarkable intensity and power. They wiggled wildly in their sockets with energy incongruent with every other non-emotive feature of his pallid face. "Neither do you," he warned with a whisper.

They parted company where the highway leading to Roger's family home intersected the interstate. Biggs headed west toward Circleville while Roger vanished into the woods. The authorities would be combing the highways and byways of the state in search of him. Better to travel cross-country. He knew the rolling land like the insides of his own pockets, and they would not find him there. He should reach his parent's house in a day or two, if all went well. Then, he would conclude his business with his father and mother and bid them a final farewell.

CHAPTER VII

Beryl Perry had laundered clothes all day and stood in the yard removing sheets and shams hung earlier upon the wire clothesline to dry. The linens had grown crisp and crinkly in the brisk autumn chill, and they made sharp sighs of relief as Beryl pulled them free. She expertly folded them into manageable squares before she placed them in the tan wicker basket at her feet. When she plucked the last clothespins free and swept the final sheet from off the line, a bedraggled Roger was facing her.

A retarded smile smeared his features and slumped shoulders accentuated his slovenly manner. Roger began laughing his ass off. The longer he looked at his mother's dumbstruck face and speechless expression, the harder he laughed. "Hi, Mom, it's nice to see you, too." He choked back the laughter to a more manageable level and straightened his posture in a mocked, semi-serious gesture. "Did you miss me, Mother dear?"

After the initial shock wore off, Beryl relaxed her clenched fingers, folded the bed sheet uneasily and placed it on top of the others. "Roger, what are you doing here?" she asked, straining to reel in her fleeing composure. "The police have been looking for you. They said you escaped…and that you hurt someone doing it."

"Naah, I never hurt nobody. You know how cops are, always exaggerating. They let me out, Ma, honest. They say I am cured. You can't trust cops. They'll tell you anything."

His mother picked up the clothesbasket and side-stepped toward the back door in an attempt at putting as much distance between her and her son as possible without arousing his suspicions.

Roger caught on right away and hopped menacingly between his mother and the house, causing her to drop and upset her laundry basket. "Where ya off to, Ma?" he asked, grabbing her by her arm.

"Roger, you're hurting me!" She cried. "Let go of me!" She backed away as her son followed, matching her movements stride for stride.

"I wouldn't hurt you, Ma. Not like you did me. Why did you let them take me away and lock me up in that place? Didn't you want me?" His grip tightened and his voice deepened and turned more aggressive. He was speaking through a wall of teeth and tilting his head side to side as if he were trying to unravel the incomprehensible. "Where's Pop, Ma? Flat on his drunk, sorry ass again?"

His mother grasped his vice-like fingers and tried to pry them from her bruising wrist. "Roger, please," she begged. "Let go!"

A trail of dust in the distance alerted Roger to an approaching vehicle. In a moment, he identified the maroon Renault Dauphin his father drove. 'It was a classic,' his father had boasted. No one drove a Renault around here except his father. It had to be him.

"There's Father dear, now," he sneered. "Let us go and greet him, shall we? What do you say?" Twisting his mother's arm behind her back was all the encouragement needed to convince her to comply. He marched her quickly to the back porch and re-entered the house of his childhood. Any fond memories he may have had loitered outside the door.

Once inside, he bound his mother's legs together at the ankles with his belt. He ripped a dishtowel into several strips lengthwise and tied her hands behind her back. He muzzled her with another strip of fabric. Just as his old man opened the front door, Roger kissed her on her covered mouth, stuffed her into the hallway closet and repaired to the living room.

His father sauntered down the hall while glancing at the headlines of the newspaper he had picked up in town. When he lifted his head, he saw his son standing idly by the living room window. Roger's father realized the potential danger facing him. His eyes darted to the fireplace for a weapon of any kind should defense be necessary. "Roger, what are you doing here?" he asked with presumed authority.

Roger laughed heartily again, his body arching backwards and shaking. "That's the same thing Mom said. You two sure are peas in a pod!" He wiped a pretend tear from his iron eyes with the back of his soiled hand.

His father glowered. "Where's your mother, Roger? If you've hurt her, I'll kill you where you stand. Beryl," he shouted. "Beryl, are you here?"

A dull, thudding sound bounced from within the walls. A louder bang forced the closet door wide, and Beryl rolled out onto the floor. Her tempered whining strained through the greasy fabric tied around her face still conveyed her terror and excitability.

"My god, Roger, you little bastard!" He moved swiftly to free his frantic wife. When he bent down to assist her, a powerful blow from a fireplace poker sent him sprawling on top of her.

"You made me, Daddy, aren't you proud?" Roger exclaimed lightheartedly as he peered down upon his father's prostate form. "I'm *your* little bastard, only I ain't so little anymore."

When Vernon Perry regained consciousness, he found himself trussed upright to a support column that flanked an over-stuffed orange divan that, together, distinguished the living area from the entrance hall. His son had bound his neck and knees tightly to the post that he might not slump while unconscious. A small tangerine had found its way into his mouth and remained imprisoned there with duct tape. His eyes were large as boulder marbles and focused on his deranged son. He could see his wife's bare feet and naked legs on the floor beyond a recliner, but he could hear no sound from her.

Roger was careful not to tie the shredded bed sheets too tightly about his father's throat. There would be little fun in his father dying prematurely. His final staging before his presentation was to push a reclining loveseat from the middle of the room to in front of the far window. He jabbered incoherently while he labored but stopped briefly to insure his father was alert and watching. His labors finished, Roger smiled happily and rubbed his palms together with obvious glee. His actions insured his mother and father were now in full view of each other.

"Can you see ok, Daddy, dear? I made sure you had the best seat in the house. Or should I say best post?" Roger chuckled at his cleverness. "I wouldn't want you to miss anything."

His father squirmed as much as his bindings allowed, which amounted to very little. His son was thorough, if nothing else.

Beryl began struggling again. She bent her legs at the knees and fought to right herself, but the constraints about her ankles proved too hobbling. She craned her head backwards and traced the blue and yellow, braided nylon rope that bound her hands to where it rounded the jam of the archway that separated the living and dining areas. She held the contorted, supine position for several seconds before she collapsed.

With the preliminaries complete, Roger set upon the more demented aspect of his design. He positioned himself squarely between both parents and proceeded to disrobe. His slender, muscular flesh glowed like a frog's belly in stark-white contrast to the august earthen hues that predominated the space. He shed his jacket and his shirt, balled the latter and angrily tossed it at his father's head. He removed his pants next while teasingly astride his mother; so helpless to escape her fate or dissuade her son from his obvious intentions.

Roger's performance adhered faithfully to the plan he had hatched while he sweated two long years at the Pennsylvania State Hospital. Now that the blessed hour was at hand he wanted to relish each beat and retard every measure before consummating his masterpiece. But, spontaneously chose, instead, to sift his manic opus through the filter of improvisation.

Roger excused himself to the kitchen and fetched a bowl of fruit from the counter. He returned in a moment to place the bowl of fruit on the floor near his mother's head. He picked a banana from the bunch, peeled it playfully before his mother's eyes and lay next to her. He longed for the taste of the cherry flavored lipstick she preferred. He removed the tattered gag from her mouth and exposed her trembling lips to his own.

As soon as he removed the gag, Beryl let out a wild ear-splitting scream. "Vernon! Oh God, no! Vern..."

Immediately, Roger stuffed the peeled banana into his mother's mouth, nearly choking her. To underscore his ardor, he placed his own mouth over the protruding end of the banana and swallowed half its length until their lips met. Beryl twisted her head savagely to one side. Roger paused befuddled. He felt far from satiated, but, in an uncharacteristic display of compassion, he slackened his mother's restraints and covered her quivering form with a warm crocheted legwarmer he found draped across the back of the orange divan. He bent down, kissed her ear and turned his attentions to his father.

He took the rope used to secure his mother, fashioned a slipknot at one end and placed the noose over his father's head. He then cut the strips that secured his father to the post but kept his father's hands bound and legs tethered closely together. So immersed was Roger in the part he played, he neglected to dress before dragging his confounded progenitor by the rope leash through the kitchen and out the back door. The temperature outside was chilly, but Roger was impervious to the cold. He jerked at the rope when his father stumbled, bawling at him as if addressing a stubborn mule. "Woah there, buck! Come on, now!"

When they reached the smokehouse Roger was so intimately acquainted with, he smacked his father over the head with a length of black gas pipe. The blow knocked the man senseless. He then threw the loose end of the rope over an exposed rafter and hoisted his father heavenward like a slab of meat until his feet were inches from the pine flooring.

He began rambling to himself again while rummaging through bins of miscellaneous items hoping something would strike his fancy. He picked up a strand of barbed wire, inspected it and tossed it aside. He did likewise with a spool of ten-gauge soldering wire and a worn extension cord with the plug end missing before settling on a defective tractor fan belt about one inch wide. He doubled it, grabbed the looped ends in each hand, pushed the ends toward each other and shaped the doubled strips into an irregular oval. Holding the belt in front of his face, he peered through the oval at his suspended prize and snapped the opening shut several times with a loud aggressive noise. He moved to within inches of his father's face, repeated the motion and tried to snare his father's nose between the sections of belt. He giggled like a school girl each time he met with success.

He quickly tired of his new trick but found the helpless attitude of his victim insanely stimulating. Roger's interest turned more brazen and vicious. He flailed his captive with the tractor belt, much like his father had flailed him over the endless years of his childhood. The force of his raining blows spun his father's dangling body like a fish on a twisted line.

Suddenly, the barking report of a pistol shattered Roger's morbid concentration and caused him to pause mid-lash and listen. Not hearing any subsequent sound, he dropped his corporeal weapon to the floor and sprinted back to the house. There on the kitchen floor lay his mother. A brilliant maroon thread escaped from a single bullet hole in her temple and sketched the remaining seconds of her existence onto the yellowed linoleum.

Roger stood spellbound as he watched the crimson pool of liquid spill forth and thicken. He knelt down beside his dying mother and pressed his lips to hers in a prolonged goodbye kiss. The sweet, briny taste of her blood excited him. A fullness of vigor and renewal thrilled him as her ebbing life stream mingled with his own. The sickness that overpowered his senses drove him to lap at the gore like a desert dog.

After his mother's blood offering, Roger imagined himself a mightier man—no, an immortal. The salty nourishment transformed him into an invincible force the world would envy and fear. His face blushed with evil. His eyesight grew more acute, his hearing keener, his strength exponentially. He felt he had lived a thousand lives yet died not once. His meandering thoughts coalesced into a crystal purpose as a wraith of delusion descended upon him.

Henceforth, he would judge all as all had judged him—with impunity and a detached, compassionless will. He vowed to thrive on the blood and death of lesser creatures The depths of their suffering would transport him to the heights of hegemony. The way had greened before him. The crown was his.

His delusions of grandeur dulled a little as the outline of his outstretched bloody fingers revealed themselves to his conscious mind. He remembered his father hanging in the smokehouse, and the chilling sight of his mother's corpse at his feet prompted him to gather his clothes and dress. He leveraged his father's Harrington & Richards 22-caliber, seven-shot 'Buntline' revolver from his mother's inanimate grasp, borrowed a bottle of Four Roses 'tonic' from the cabinet where his father usually kept it and made haste to his father's side.

Vernon Perry was awake now and struggling to free himself. Blood from his head wound had clotted about his eyes, and he could barely see. He had loosed a hand and managed to remove the tape and citrus from his mouth. He was attempting to undo the knot at his other wrist with his teeth while slackening the suspending rope by pulling his weight upward with the strength of one arm.

"Here, now!" Roger exclaimed upon entering the shed and discovering his father's efforts. "That won't do." Roger chuckled to himself as he sat the liquor bottle and pistol on a nearby bench. "You look like you've got a turd cross-ways."

His father kicked ferociously as his son neared but ceased his exertions after Roger seized him by one leg and spun him repeatedly around by the tether.

"There we go," Roger cooed as his father calmed. "That's better."

Roger secured his father's dangling arm and removed the thin, black belt from his father's trousers. He pulled the man's pants to his ankles and arranged them inside out and lumped about his feet. He then retrieved the whiskey and gun from where they rested and enjoyed an extended draught of the amber beverage. He passed the mouth of the open bottle beneath his father's nose. "Want some?" he teased. "Yes...no....yes? Ok, but be careful what you wish for, you just might get it. Get it?" He laughed maniacally.

With no more compunction than one would show drowning a fly, Roger emptied the liquor over his father's head and saturated his white dress shirt. He inverted the bottle and dumped the remainder of the firewater, bottle and all, into the cusp of his father's britches. With one white-tipped sulfur match borrowed from the kitchen, he set his effigy to the past ablaze.

His father's screams were no more effective at commuting his sentence than Roger's pleading had been years before when his father doled out punishment for infractions, real and imagined. The dumb walls and deafened timbers of the old smokehouse absorbed his father's cries, as they had his own, and held them from all ears.

He watched his father burn. The stinking mass of scorching flesh spun violently in the rising heat. He focused on his father's petrified face but saw the visage of the trembling dog, Bruno, he nearly shot as a child. Roger slowly lifted the revolver to his eye and levelled the elongated barrel at the blazing creature's head. "Bang," he barked. "Bang, bang!" This time, he pulled the trigger for real and without hesitation, emptying the remaining six chambers of deadly ordinance into his father's head.

The flames scurried up the ropes like rats, licked at the ancient rafters and set them alight. Roger backed out the door and tossed the empty revolver back inside. He watched the roof collapse in a terrible conflagration. Several large fiery embers detached themselves from the pyre in an unexpected explosion. Roger picked them up by ends unconsumed and tossed them through the windows of his childhood home.

One burning missile ignited the yellow-checked kitchen curtains on contact. The seasoned wood of the sill flared hungrily as if it awaited the chance, and soon the entire hillside glowed with the beauty of it all.

Twilight descended with the comfort of darkness close behind. A full moon peeped over the eastern ridgeline and addressed Roger's eye. He stood a long while admiring its symmetry and magnificent glow. He again felt invigorated, strengthened and reborn enveloped in the restorative light. He grew hungry, bold and adventurous.

The light of the moon stirred up long dormant emotions from deep within his soul; feelings long hidden and remote grew recognizable and real. A curious satisfaction flooded his rising blood like a narcotic. He recognized the face of his alter ego on the moon's surface and hailed it as an old friend. A lascivious smirk twisted his mouth as his tongue lashed his exposed teeth and he re-savored the essence of his mother's blood.

As the peepers in the nearby bogs began their evening chorus, Roger sank to all fours and looked dispassionately upon the scorched relics of his former life. The thrill of the hunt surged through all the fibers of his being. The world would never contain him, nor would it fail to bend to the demands of his iron will. He sniffed the crisping air and bounded away into the forest. He felt complete at last, and life was good.

CHAPTER VIII

No one in his right mind would have wandered the highways freely with every lawman in three states on the prowl, but Roger was anything but right-minded. He had little trouble making his way to the home of his new associate in Circleville, Ohio. Truckers were the most accommodating of ride givers and 'in it for the long haul', so to speak. They drove at night, too. One even radioed ahead to a truck stop diner to line Roger up with a rig going to Columbus. He was in Circleville in less than twenty-four hours.

Biggs was leaving his office around six o'clock one evening when he spotted Roger leaning on a lamppost across the street. Biggs wheeled his big Mercedes S-Class in a U-turn and passed slowly by him. He leaned over towards the passenger window and called to the young man. "Go around the corner so no one will see you. I'll pick you up at the end of the alley."

Roger nodded arrogantly and strolled, hands pocketed, to the alley where he made an abrupt right. He walked on while Biggs turned right at the light, then right again. When Biggs felt confident that no one was watching, he stopped the car. Roger hopped eagerly into the front seat with a smirk staining his face.

"What are you doing here?" Biggs demanded.

"You said to look you up when my business was finished. Well, I finished it."

'I didn't mean for you to stake out the front of *my* business," Biggs grimaced angrily. "Do you want everyone in town to see you?"

"What do I care who sees me?" Roger spat back.

"You'd damn well better care, moron. We're not playing here."

Roger peered blankly at Biggs. "Don't call me moron, moron."

"Look Roger, We've got some business to do, some very illegal business. We can't be advertising that we know each other, ok?"

"Ok," Roger agreed, knowing Biggs was right, but still not caring.

Biggs scoured the streets for potential witnesses. He took a card from the console and handed it to Roger. Meet me at this address tonight and we'll settle the particulars."

Roger nodded and asked Biggs to let him out in the next alley. After Biggs was out of sight, Roger wrangled the town dry of information on his new partner in crime. He pretended to be the nephew of the newspaperman and conned directions to the home of Bernard Biggs from a woman at the drugstore. One could never know too much about one's enemies or conniving business partners. Besides, he might find something useful at the old man's place.

Roger kept his appointment with Biggs at the newspaper warehouse, and there amidst giant rolls of newsprint and great machines Biggs outlined his nefarious plan. His instructions included killing the nameless driver of a delivery truck. He had Roger memorize the US DOT fleet number lettered on the front fender and told him when the deed was to occur. Roger did not ask why he was to kill the man. It did not matter why. The reward would be handsome, and he liked the idea of having a jingle in his jeans for a change.

He stole a handful of cash from the register at the drugstore, but it would not go far. His employer scheduled the assignment two days hence. Biggs even offered to let Roger stay in his horse stable until then. Roger smiled. Things could not be better. Biggs also provided a blue, paisley neckerchief and suggested Roger fashion it into a covering for his head. His red Mohawk haircut was more than a shadow now and would be easily noticed and identifiable. Their mission called for discretion of the highest order.

On the decisive day, Biggs provided Roger access to the motor pool and left Roger last minute instructions. The truck would depart early. He advised Roger to wait until several hours had passed and the cover of darkness before making his move. He reassured his murderous agent that generous compensation would be forthcoming and wished him luck.

Roger hid his wiry frame beneath the berth in the sleeper compartment and waited. At four in the morning, Carl Connor appeared and the wheels were literally in motion.

Carl's itinerary took him to Cleveland first, but bad luck cursed the trip from the start. A flat tire derailed the rig after no more than a hundred miles. After attendants replaced the tire, Carl unknowingly topped the tanks with diesel fuel tainted with water that had unknowingly infiltrated the station's aging reservoirs following an over-night deluge. A half day was lost while technicians drained the tanks and flushed the engine free of contaminants. Thankfully, the happenstance caused no permanent damage and rig and driver were on their way again by late afternoon. Had Carl been possessed of a superstitious nature, he would have labelled the chain of events omens and cancelled the trip.

After concluding his Cleveland business, Carl decided to make up the time lost by driving non-stop. The night was half gone before the monotony of the traffic markings speeding towards him lulled him into the hypnotic state known universally to truckers as "white line fever". He rolled his window full open and fidgeted with the radio dial, convinced the fresh air and spirited music would alleviate the humdrum of the road.

He had driven the big rig nearly six hundred miles since leaving Cleveland and was nearing the Georgia border when a rustling in the berth behind him distracted his attentions from the nearly deserted highway. There was a roadside rest just ahead and Carl eased the rig off the highway and into the meager unimproved lot that offered travelers a place to stretch their legs and little more.

After rolling to a complete stop, he previewed the rearview mirror just as the uncanny face of an uninvited guest burst from behind the drapery that divided the cab from the truck's extended sleeper. His first reaction was total disbelief, and he turned in his seat to confront the stowaway. Before he could maneuver fully, a steel 'handler's hook', similar to the one he used to load the ungainly squares of newsprint onto the truck, sprung like a rattlesnake from behind the barrier and withdrew just as quickly. The tool's spiked terminus penetrated the back of Carl's neck and emerged from his mouth, fixing him to the headrest like a minnow bait impaled on an angler's fishhook.

A gargle of blood filled Carl's throat and spurted from his mouth with each beat of his heart. Roger braced his feet against the back of the driver's seat and leaned back. The force at the hidden end of the implement matched Carl's struggling efforts kip for kip and pinned him to the seat cushion. Carl thrashed wildly and grasped and clawed at the crude weapon until the loss of blood dimmed his bulbous incredulous eyes.

When all movement ceased and Carl was convincingly dead, the shadowy form of his covert assassin slipped from his secret place inside the cab. Roger calmly reached around the dead man's contorted torso to scan the radio until a country station met his approval and then disappeared into the night. He left the running lights on. The semi's engine was still idling and the passenger door still agape when an astonished member of the Tennessee Highway Patrol found Carl's turgid body in the dim light of morning.

News of the horrific murder in Tennessee spread back to Ohio and immediately permeated the region thanks in no little part to the *Village Clarion*, that iconic bastion of integrity and truth. The investigation led authorities to Biggs' office, of course, but the wily editor's prepared statements and explanations gave them no reason to suspect him and no justification for further questioning at that time.

When detectives notified Ellen of her husband's reprehensible murder, she feinted in shock and disbelief. She had no doubt Bernard Biggs was involved, but she could confide in no one lest the incriminating material he kept as security came to light. Surviving this latest calamity nearly cost the poor woman her sanity, and she seriously entertained notions of ceasing her own existence. Had it not been for her precious Kim, she certainly would have done so.

Ellen could not jeopardize her daughter's welfare by leaving her unprotected in a world with vipers like Bernard Biggs within striking distance. Sadly, her options were limited and she had no strategy that would secure their future or even maintain the status quo. She could not abandon her dear one at the most important and devastating moment in her young life.

Local and state investigators interrogated Biggs with grueling efficiency on several occasions following the murder, but the well-regarded newspaperman and community benefactor had his facts in a row and never wavered in the telling and re-telling of the event as he saw it. The authorities, completely satisfied with his explanation, were beginning to fan out in different directions and expand their sphere of inquiry. They consulted the FBI and discussed the probability that the perpetrator, or perpetrators, had crossed state lines prior to the commission of the heinous act. Full-scale involvement at the federal level was warranted and mandatory. Murder was, after all, a federal crime.

A week passed, then two, with no word from Roger. Biggs could not explain Roger's unwillingness or inability to re-establish contact, but he was thankful just the same. He prayed the young fool had met his own demise, but knew better than to take too much for granted.

Eventually, the uproar settled down to a murmur that allowed Biggs room to breathe. As each passing day further distanced him, in his own mind, from all culpability, Biggs began to assert himself in his usual bombastic manner. He publically proclaimed a ten-thousand-dollar reward for information leading to the arrest and conviction of the party, or parties, responsible. He conveyed daily condolences to Carl Connor's distraught widow and daughter in the form of floral arrangements and accompanying dictated notes always signed: '…with love and support, Uncle Bernie'. He also announced cleverly timed phone calls when numerous witnesses were on hand to hear them. He relished playing to the hilt the role of grieving godfather, and no one suspected him of anything but genuine concern and devotion.

In her heart of hearts Ellen knew Biggs was responsible for her husband's horrific murder but, lacking proof, she had no ammunition to back her suspicions. The fact that she previously appeared with her employer at social gatherings and charity occasions confirmed his intimations as a close and favored friend. Their debased relationship was too explosive to see daylight. No one must ever know. The secret she buried in her heart would have to die with her and molder in her grave along with her sullied flesh.

The news of her father's untimely and horrific death forced Kim into a world of unimaginable denial and disbelief. For weeks, she refused to emerge from her room. She gazed for hours from her bedroom window that overlooked the meadow across the road. The tranquil visions of the mares and foals that grazed there quieted her frazzled nerves. Her aversion to nourishment resulted in weight loss and listlessness, and her mood progressed from melancholic shock to deep depression.

Ellen's family doctor aphoristically explained that "time would heal all wounds" and prescribed close monitoring and patience. He could do little more than offer reassurances and spout platitudes. He recommended counseling after an appropriate term of bereavement and left Ellen with the names of several renowned practitioners to call when such time presented itself.

Biggs resumed his orderly routine at work and in the business community without a twinge of conscience. His champions admired him greatly for his stoic acceptance of his employee's plight and his unfaltering Christian readiness to help her through her time of trial. When he spoke of Clara in the public forum, he maintained the illusion of a familial connection in the minds of the ever-inquisitive press. But, on the third month anniversary of Carl's murder, another unforeseen turn of events tested the veracity of his web of lies.

Biggs promised to take Kim riding one Saturday with hopes that the outing would infuse her spirit with youthful vitality and restore the bloom of adolescence to her pallid cheeks. They rode for several hours before stopping near a quiet little stream that meandered near the extent of the Biggs estate. Lunch was minimal but satisfying, and by the time they returned to the stables late that afternoon the young girl's attitude was much improved.

After the weekend equestrians unsaddled the mares, Kim got busy brushing the golden mane of her Palomino pony. She bade Bernard fetch oats and water for their noble steeds. She cooed soft reassurances as she curried the stiff bristles through the mare's coarse coat and plucked burrs from its feathery tail. When she focused her attentions on the pony's tangled mane, she was shaken to find the face of a stranger staring at her across the animal's withers.

"Hello," the stranger called out with a smile.

After the initial surge of surprise, Kim's heart regained its normal rhythm. She remained cautiously alert before lowering her guard, but then only to eye level. The stranger's pleasant voice and innocuous manner softened her natural defenses. "Who are you?" She asked.

"I'm a friend of your "uncle," the boy explained, holding his hands chest high and animating his index and middle fingers into expressive quotation gestures. Roger had followed Bernard's public outpourings of grief from a distance and was well aware of his partner's ingratiating falsity and of his desire to infiltrate and dominate the Connor household. His sarcasm and contempt were growing.

"Do you mean Bernie? He's really not my uncle. How do you know him?"

Roger looked down at his feet with an 'aw shucks' attitude, spreading strands of hay to one side with the toe of his boot as if searching for an elusive object. "Oh, I guess you could say we're business partners," he answered, not lifting his eyes from his busy boot.

Kim resumed her grooming chores and chatted openly with the young man about their mutual real world concerns. She did not trust the stranger explicitly, but she saw no reason to mistrust him either. He looked to be about ten years older than she was, but she could not be sure. She began to enjoy his friendly and engaging company, and they were jabbering away like magpies when Biggs returned.

Biggs froze in his footsteps when he re-entered the barn. He stooped down slowly and sat the feedbags of oats and pail of water on the earth and never averted his gaze from Roger for an instant. "Clara, step away from your pony," he ordered steel-eyed and serious.

"What?" She answered innocently. "Why?"

"Never mind why. Just do as you're told."

"Bernie, we were just talk..."

"Do it!" He roared, cutting her off mid-sentence.

Kim was alarmed and confused, but she knew better that to disobey when Bernard's ire was up. She backed away nervously until her shoulder blades crushed against the rough stall railing. She reinforced her stance by grasping the wooden slat behind her firmly with both hands. She glanced quizzically from man to man and could feel the thrill of confrontation building in her breast.

Roger slinked cat-like around the horse's head, stepping gingerly in Clara's direction. A curious smile of intent teased his lips.

"Roger, stay away from her," Biggs warned.

Roger continued his slow advance. "Or what...?" He challenged menacingly.

"I'm warning you. I told you to stay away from her."

The air of danger frightened Kim and warned her away from the mysterious young man and closer to Biggs. 'Better a devil you know, than a devil you don't know,' she recalled her mother's counsel. Her gaze fixed on Roger.

Roger stilled his movements when he sensed the change in the pretty girl's attitude and body language. "Ok," he laughed, throwing up his hands. "I'm away now." His smile faded to a smirk as he stared at the man for whom he had killed. He wondered what had occurred to make his formerly amiable compatriot so hostile.

Biggs grabbed Kim by the arm and pulled her behind him. "Go to the house, child," he ordered.

"But I haven't finished brushing Saint yet, and he needs food and water."

Biggs was impatient and hard. "Go, now!" He bellowed. "We'll finish caring for Saint and Sunny later." He retrieved a pitchfork near the outside corner of the first stall and held it soldierly to his front in a defensive posture.

Kim bowed her head and left the area. She had not walked far before Biggs bellowed again. "Kim!" When Kim re-entered the picture, it was apparent to her that Bernard Biggs sensed great peril from the person standing to his front. "Kim, phone the sheriff and inform him that I've cornered a trespasser in the barn. Tell him I don't know how long I can hold the man and that he looks dangerous".

"But, Bernie, he said you were business partners."

"He lied to you, girl. I have no business with the likes of him. Go on and do what I told you. Go on, now."

Kim left immediately, more scared and confused than ever. Why was she always in the midst of some appalling drama? Why was her life an incessant calamity? Was she destined to remain friendless and alone forever? These questions and others burned inside her as she ran to the sprawling house. She struggled to suppress her inner turmoil, but it stayed with her during her conversation with the sheriff.

Biggs and Roger faced off for several minutes with Biggs denying events and Roger threatening full disclosure. Biggs explained his actions as merely a rational response to the discovery of a home invader in the commission of a crime. "They'll believe me, Roger. Make no mistake about that."

Roger knew Biggs was right, and he hated him more for it. The betrayal cut him to the quick. With little to lose and no time for argument, Roger grabbed a handful of the palomino's forelock and swung its head in the direction of his adversary. With a powerful smack to the animal's rump and a shrill "git out of here...git!" he sent the pony bolting for the door, knocking Biggs aside. Roger bolted too and spritely disappeared over the treeless rise behind the two-story barn. Biggs chased the boy to the top of the hill. Although he was close on Roger's heels, Biggs could see neither hide nor hair of the slippery fellow from the hillock's superior elevation.

The sheriff arrived within minutes and radioed his office and the highway patrol after noting Biggs' complaint. He ordered every available man to the area and every road blocked within a ten-mile radius. "We'll get him," he remarked assuredly. "Can you tell me how you know this man?" he asked.

"I don't know him," Biggs lied, "never seen him before."

"The girl says you called him by name. Roger something, wasn't it?"

"The girl is mistaken. I have never seen the man before. She must have learned his name while I was absent. I went to get feed and water for the horses, and I found them together when I returned. If I called him by name, it was because I heard her say it first."

"Yes, well, I suppose that would explain it. We are going to need some additional information from you, Mr. Biggs. Deputy Saunders, here, will take down your statement. Any additional details you may recall could prove helpful. We will have to talk to the girl again, too."

"Of course," Biggs answered, relieved that his explanation apparently had satisfied the sheriff, at least for now. He accompanied the deputy to his patrol car while Sheriff Vanderlin went inside the house to question Kim.

Roger managed to elude his pursuers for the better part of two days. But the sheriff's savvy posse finally spotted and apprehended him crossing a small creek underneath a state highway bridge.

The sheriff charged Roger with trespassing, felony menacing, and eluding capture and booked him into the county criminal justice system to await arraignment. A subsequent fingerprint check revealed the rascal used an IV pole to assault an orderly in an escape from a mental facility in Pennsylvania. The authorities there also wanted to question the suspect in connection with arson and the murder of his parents. Evidently, the sheriff and his posse had corralled quite a rebellious handful. They dropped the local charges and agreed to extradite the felon back to Pennsylvania to answer to the more egregious offenses.

With Roger out of the way, Biggs regained supreme control over his criminal empire. With Carl out of the way, Ellen was irrefutably his and his alone and Kim was his by default. He could have wished for nothing more and, indeed, would have settled for nothing less.

The icing on the cake came some weeks later, when Sheriff Vanderlin paid Biggs an unexpected visit at his office to inform him that Roger Perry pled guilty to all charges. An unsympathetic judge sentenced him to two life terms, without parole, in the Pennsylvania State Prison at Frackville.

Biggs could scarcely contain himself at hearing this latest and most welcome development. He thanked Vanderlin for delivering the good news personally and offered a drink in celebration, which the officer dutifully refused. After the sheriff left, Biggs retired home where he began to outline his strategy for reaping the maximum benefit from his not unsubstantial accomplishments.

CHAPTER IX

Over the ensuing months, Kim slowly regained a half-measure of her once vibrant spirit. Kim's doctor intimated that exposure to those persons most familiar might revitalize the girl's frail constitution and speed recovery. Bernard patiently waited in the wings until he felt the time was right. To Ellen's surprise, Kim did brighten measurably when Bernard visited. Ellen embraced the change, albeit, with warranted reservation and concern.

Biggs continued to blackmail Ellen into submission and visited whenever the spirit moved him. In exchange for unquestioned compliance, he provided much-needed funds for her mortgage and living expenses. He also secured excellent professional medical and dental care for both her and Kim. The impossibility of living under desperate subjugation to her boss and his atrocious demands kept Ellen on the verge of suicide.

Nevertheless, she was thankful to anyone or anything that rescued her little girl from oblivion. She managed to adopt a benign expression and demeanor towards Biggs in Kim's presence, never correcting him when he insisted Kim call him "Uncle Bernie" despite her certainty the inevitable would transpire. Perhaps, it already had.

That inevitability hung in the air over the Connor household for eighteen months after Carl's death before becoming a reality. Kim, now ten years of age, was more communicative and endearing than she had been for some time. Although still shy with strangers, she seemed at ease and content in the company of those closest to her.

One September day, Bernard dropped by and suggested Ellen go to the city for the afternoon while he and Kim spent some quality time together. Ellen was not comfortable with the arrangement and said so. Her vehement objection brought an expression of naïveté and innocence to her daughter's face. Kim saw Bernard Biggs in a different light and had, so far, no exposure to the darker side of his nature.

Biggs took Ellen aside and firmly led her by the arm into the kitchen. "I know you are not going to be any trouble, are you?" He exclaimed hatefully. "I said you would never be free of me, and I meant it. Remember your night with Tanya? I watch our little movie from time to time. I get so hot seeing you stretched out on your bed with Tanya between your legs." He grabbed her breast with a callous hand while pulling her head back by her hair. "Remember?" he taunted. He ran his tongue along the side of her neck from clavicle to chin. Ellen broke free just as Kim entered the kitchen.

"What's going on, mom?" She asked innocently. "Are you going to town, or not?"

Ellen turned from Kim to compose herself and then faced her again with an exasperating sigh. "Yes, dear, I'm going. I won't be long." She held her daughter's face in her trembling hands. "Be good, darling. I'll be back shortly."

"Take your time, dear." Biggs interjected. "We won't expect you back before dinner. Maybe you can stop on your way back and pick up some chicken?"

"Yeah," Kim chimed in exuberantly, "the extra crispy kind!"

"Alright, Kim," her mother agreed, smiling as bravely as she could. She shot a warning glance to Bernard before leaving the kitchen.

They watched Ellen's car pull from the driveway and drift slowly down the gravel road to the main highway. The sound of the engine had scarcely melted away before Biggs suggested they go for a walk in the meadow and watch the horses. It was a beautiful, crisp autumn day, and the walk would do them both a world of good.

#

The day Ellen left her daughter in the hands of her tormentor was the longest day of her life. She fully understood the ramifications of doing so, but the fear of losing custody of her little girl to the auspices of the state, or worse still to her conniving immoral employer, overruled her objections. Rumors of a dalliance, coerced or not, with a known lesbian prostitute would destroy what remained of her family. She could never allow that to happen.

The evidence supporting her unique dilemma presented far greater peril than rumor or innuendo. It did not matter that Bernard Biggs and the slut, Tanya, held her against her will and forced her to participate. There was a tape. It would be a classic case of he said / she said; only *he* had all the ammunition. Ellen had not filed charges for fear that the small-minded authorities populating social services might harbor a different view and now, of course, it was too late. If only she knew where the video recording was she could possibly turn the tables. This fact remained; she was hopelessly bound to obey the bastard's commands as long as the tape existed.

So, she buried her heartache away and busied herself with distracting, self-indulgent activities for most of the day. Her jet-black hair was short and newly cut. Nevertheless, she had it washed, blow-dried and styled. She even sprang for a rare pedicure for good measure.

She wandered through the boutiques on Chestnut Street with their banal message: *'Lovely to look at, delightful to hold, but if you break it, consider it sold'* boldly displayed with bourgeois regularity. In a grander mood, she might have scratched the cheap veneer on a vase or hid the lid to a creamery. Instead, she browsed like an herbivore in a field of dead grass and did neither. Gaiety was a stranger today.

She squirmed through a matinee showing of *Gone with the Wind* at the Skybo theatre on Whitaker Avenue until the agony of sitting still while her daughter faced possible harm drove her to leave the premises far in advance of General Sherman. Atlanta would have to burn another day.

#

Kim, on the other hand, had an entirely different day. After they watched the carefree foals cavorting in the neighboring fields, Bernie suggested Kim prepare them both lunch. She returned to the kitchen and readied the apple juice and turkey sandwiches, careful to spread the mayonnaise evenly upon the Kaiser roll and allot each sandwich a single ample leaf of romaine lettuce and full slice of Big Boy tomato. Bernie sidled from the room and slinked upstairs.

With the meal prepared, Kim piled the menu high on a serving tray and whisked to the living room only to find it as empty as her growling stomach. "Uncle Bernie? Soup's on." Hearing no response, she walked into the hall, tray held chest high. "Uncle Bernie?"

A noise from upstairs beckoned her and she responded naively, thumping her feet playfully upon the stairs as she ascended. At the top of the stairs, she called out again.

"In here, dear," a muffled voice directed her to the bedroom at the end of the hallway.

Mystified and curious, the young girl slowly walked the length of the hall to the far bedroom and halted in her tracks. This was the one room in the Connor household Kim's parents had forbidden her to enter. She slowly approached the door, peeked through the narrow opening and entered. Kim immediately became aware of the room's depressing character. Obviously, no one had slept in the room for years. Dust-heavy sheets covering the sparse furnishings accentuated the minimalist décor. Tangles of cobwebs hugged the corners, their wispy tentacles dangled like flypaper and stirred at the slightest disturbance.

Kim's parents designed the room to accommodate guests, but few visitors who slept over would do so twice. Excuses ranged from 'disturbing noises' to 'smothering sensations' to 'abject terror'. The bizarre explanations perplexed the Connors, and those who graced the residence with their presence overnight became rarer than hen's teeth. Naturally, the room sank into neglect.

"Uncle Bernie?" she repeated uneasily.

"Come in, dear. I thought we would eat somewhere different today. You know. Air out the old room."

Biggs had set up a small folding table and chairs near the only window that overlooked the pasture they had just visited.

"I don't like this room. Kim replied. "Daddy always said not to play here."

"You can see the horses from here. Come here and take a look."

Kim placed the tray of sandwiches on the folding table and moved silently to the window.

"I wish my daddy were here." She whispered and turned away with a discernable sob.

"I can be your daddy, now, if you want." Biggs offered.

Kim grew silent and stared at the floor.

"Ok, then. Let's see what you brought us." Biggs continued. "My, these sandwiches look wonderful!"

Ellen Connor returned home around suppertime as directed. Mother and daughter embraced on sight for a considerable time. Ellen sensed that "something" may have occurred, but, perhaps, her misgivings were just paranoia. Her daughter insisted they had simply played games and watched the horses. Her mother let it pass. If anything untoward occurred on that day, it remained undefined.

Biggs occasionally finagled time alone with Kim over the years, thereafter, and during those times Ellen was typically absent. Kim saw this as an approval of sorts. Her mom was devastatingly forlorn and wounded following the murder of her husband and only true friend. Kim believed their time apart seemed to do her mother some good. Naturally, she wanted her mother to be happy. If those hours apart helped her mother in any way, Kim could hardly object.

CHAPTER X

When Kim, or Clara (the name she now preferred), turned sixteen, the nightmares began. The terrible dreams were always the same. She dreamed she awoke suddenly and bolted up right in her bed, drenched in a vapid sweat. Incredible fear and anxiousness consumed her. A black ominous shadow formed in the open doorway to her room. Slowly, the amorphous shape melted to the ground in a pool of indiscernible matter and flowed almost imperceptibly towards her like oozing blood. She gasped for air and fought to leave her bed, but unseen hands restrained her and held her fast within the sodden sheets.

The shadow approached menacingly close where it reconstituted its vertical shape and hovered above her. Her eyes froze open in terror and her mouth, wide with anguish, remained desperately mute though she tried to scream. The evil cloud settled down upon her and smothered her with an oppressive stench and immeasurable weight. She gasped for air until death felt imminent, even welcome. Suddenly, the creature vanished.

After the monster was gone and her strength and mobility restored, she darted from the room to the top of the stairs. A glance over her shoulder to the black end of the upstairs hall revealed a haggard grey-haired woman seated at an organ festooned with dead flowers. The old woman was frighteningly witchy. A mysterious wind disturbed the witch's coarse strands of hair alternately revealing and concealing a dreadful countenance, red-eyed and seemingly fleshed from grey-green clay. The hag cackled insanely as she played some discordant melody in a minor key.

A tremendous force dragged her backwards as she attempted to flee down the stairs. The harder she resisted, the greater the invisible tether reciprocated. Then, as sharply as a snapping elastic band, the force released her. The unexpected freedom propelled her forward allowing her to break away and descend to the lower level. The staircase vanished on her heels into a void as the witch's powerful reverberating vocals reached a crescendo before dissipating into an unearthly echo.

Once Clara awakened for real, cold clammy sweat skinned her nightgown to her shivering flesh like a death shroud. Her shallow and rapid respirations would cause her fingers to splay in a paroxysm of hyperventilation.

Clara dreaded sleep for fear of the recurrent nightmare. She grew to hate Bernard Biggs and held him somehow responsible for her nocturnal torment. She refused to call him 'Uncle Bernie' anymore, opting instead for "Bernard" or the polite 'yes, sir' or 'no, sir' in response to his personal inquiries as to her health or well-being.

Still, inexplicable longings she could not completely dispel brought her to the realization that Bernard Biggs maintained an unhealthy hold over her. She managed to repress this inner turmoil of guilt and emotion, but the effort created a dichotomy in the impressionable teen's personality and she could not totally reconcile her desires.

Platonic though it was, opportunities for Biggs to indulge his weakness became less and less frequent. Clara astutely recognized her benefactor's personal failings and exploited them to full advantage. She enjoyed power over Biggs and discovered she could coerce him to her will on occasions when he was vulnerable and off guard. Clara demanded and received substantial remuneration for the pleasure of her company, her reluctance notwithstanding.

Throughout high school, Clara matured into a levelheaded, though jaded, beauty. An adherence to the prescribed one hundred brush strokes nightly finessed her luxuriant mane to the shimmer of the finest silk. But it was her startlingly dramatic violet eyes that exaggerated her exotic aspect and granted her a most desirable and fascinating appearance. Rumors of promiscuity flourished at her school, but, like all rumors, vanished under scrutiny. If one were to believe every young male who boasted of a liaison with the charming beauty, the entire countryside and half the county had enjoyed her company at one time or another. Before graduating from high school, Clara contacted various seats of higher learning, but found few colleges offering degrees in her desired major—historical culinary arts and traditions.

The years had rolled comfortably and profitably by for Bernard Biggs since he orchestrated the brutal removal of Carl Connor. Varied investments returned handsome dividends and blessed his existence with continued financial prosperity. It was just like the man to measure his successes in terms of personal benefit. Never did his conscience (as minute a thing as it was) argue that a great deal of suffering befell those closest to him or that his relative prosperity was matched inversely by a loss to everyone else.

It came to Biggs' attention that a player of considerable stature in the culinary world recently set up shop in the great state of Vermont not twenty miles from the old estate he had purchased a few years before. Biggs was ecstatic with the news. Opportunity certainly knocks for those attuned to hear. Coercing Clara to attend should not be difficult. He would pay for everything, of course, and as the 'cash cow', he could demand the recipient of his generosity grant the respect and consideration due one's primary benefactor. It was only fair.

With Clara so conveniently disposed, he re-entertained thoughts of revamping the ailing Lovingdale Manor and using it as a high-end rendezvous, an effort quite in keeping with his fashioned self-image of country squire and nouveau gentry. It would also serve as his base of operations for any business negotiated in the northeastern United States and the eastern Canadian provinces. New Yorkers loved Vermont, and his numerous clients would relish a weekend "lost in a castle" amidst the splendor of the New England countryside. It was a capital plan all around, and he lost no time convincing Clara of the benefits of selecting Culinary Arts International as her alma mater.

By now, Ellen had resigned herself to her fate but still held high hopes for Clara. Her only daughter's success and happiness were paramount. She did everything humanly possible to guide Clara down the road of opportunity—a road Ellen, through no fault of her own, had been so unfairly barred from travelling.

On the day of Clara's departure, Bernard drove Ellen and her daughter to the airport. After wishing Clara well with a hug and an insufferable kiss, he showed remarkable and unprecedented decency in excusing himself early to allow mother and daughter a chance to share their remaining minutes together in private.

Ellen watched the 747 holding her daughter taxi away from the gate and maneuver down the runway. She lost sight of the jet after a short while but remained near the boarding gate scanning the skies until two silver wings heading in an easterly direction appeared on the low horizon. She convinced herself it was Clara's flight and watched the airplane rise until gigantic cumulus clouds swallowed it whole. Clara likewise observed the tarmac closely as the jet lifted off. She swore she could see her mother's face and wild waving gestures through the large plate-glass terminal windows near her departure gate.

Clara enjoyed her undergraduate life immensely. She corresponded by weekly long letter to her mother informing her of all the excitement and activities she was immersed in. She endured regular phone calls from Bernard out of feelings of obligation. After all, she was in no position to provide her own means of support. Tuition alone at the exclusive college was far beyond her means. Besides, it was easier now that she was away from him. She could exchange a few obligatory pleasantries over the phone when required.

Unfortunately, the nightmares continued unabated at unpredictable intervals, but Clara held on to the promise of a brighter future and tried to accept her situation in stride. She was relieved to be free of her sponsor's influence and she delighted in the unfamiliar exhilaration and rarified atmosphere of academia. At long last, she could breathe easily again.

Clara settled in promptly and discovered her love of cooking was a true calling. With so many travelled individuals of diverse backgrounds and common interests surrounding her, it was easy to immerse herself in her studies.

Weekly culinary contests and the demands of her curriculum kept her absorbed on an immediate level. She spent her evenings alone, studying fantastic recipes to try for the dreamy surprise concoctions to showcase in her class competitions on Fridays. Wednesday afternoons were free, and students were strongly encouraged to delegate that time exploring local farmer's markets for the magic ingredients central to the success of their creations.

She had no interest whatsoever in boys, although admittedly, they all seemed interested in her. However, one fellow intrigued her like no other. His name was Nadir Rah Medeev, a Persian prince and sole heir to the throne of Iran. His experiments with caviar and middle-eastern spices were wonders to behold.

The Shah-to-be learned cooking from his great-grandmother and vowed his first official act as Shah would be to decree her 'Ash-e anar', a thick pomegranate soup served over white rice, or 'pollo', a national dish. Sadly, a family emergency called Nadir home shortly before their relationship gathered any steam. It seemed they had barely said hello. She vowed, thereafter, to focus on cooking and put her academic responsibilities above all else.

Her mother visited after two months had passed, and they spent a wonderful weekend together sampling soups, salads and desserts at the school's annual "Foods from Around the Globe" extravaganza. There were fungi, or 'truffles' from Spain, snails, or 'escargot' from France, fish eggs, or 'caviar' from Russia and ethnic domestic dishes from every region of the United States and Canada.

Connoisseurs never called anything what it actually was, it seemed. They were wont to pair every food with an equally savory appellation designed to excite the palate and satisfy the senses. Afterwards, while indulging in a mutual 'guilty pleasure' of peanut butter and bananas on toast, they laughed hardily at the pretense of it all.

Ellen had great pride and love for Clara and showered her with constant praise and affection while they were together. The weekend inevitably closed, and mother and daughter cried shamelessly and hugged each other to pieces before parting at the train station. They would not see each other again until the school adjourned for the Christmas holidays.

#

Christmas was never a merry occasion in the Biggs household, but this year would be an exception. Biggs had already received the newspaperman of the year award for his shrewd managerial skills. His exemplary expansion efforts resulted in the acquisition of no less than six metropolitan markets, making him the most powerful and significant media figure in the Mid-Atlantic region. Revenues were up a whopping twenty-seven percent over the preceding year, and several major U.S.

papers contacted his corporate headquarters with offers of potential mergers and/or partnerships. As important as these matters were, nothing stimulated him quite as magically as knowing Clara was coming home for the holidays.

Ellen was ecstatic, too, albeit for different reasons, and busied herself vigorously with plans and preparations for her family reunion. Letters and phone calls were poor substitutes for having her daughter a hug away, and she anticipated Christmas with all the patience and containment of a thirteen-year-old awaiting her first junior prom.

She insisted on decorating a massive ten-foot conifer with bells, bulbs, lights and tinsel; even going the distance and threading buckets of popcorn into lengthy strands of nostalgic delight. Clara would love the old-timey touch. Of course, there were frenzied shopping days searching for the perfect gift. She settled on an imported Italian cooking set complete with sleek utensils and matching oven mitts, and smaller presents too numerous to list.

Clara arrived on schedule more beautiful and radiant than ever. Her time away had worked wonders on her mental state, and she exuded buckets of confidence and charm. Her spirits were high and she gushed endlessly to her mother about all the fascinating people she had encountered and the host of heavenly dishes she had sampled. Bernard left her alone during her visit and, for that, she was thankful and relieved. Proximity to him was the only reservation she had against travelling home for the season, but the man was surprisingly cordial and civilized. At the airport, Clara even rewarded him with a genuine good-bye kiss on both cheeks for his meritorious and uncharacteristic chivalry.

Ellen's mood sank to near depression levels after her daughter returned to school, and Clara's weekly letters and phone calls were all she had to elevate her spirits. She relied on them heavily. When the correspondence stopped abruptly, Ellen's sixth-sense spiked to high alert. Biggs did not share equally in her concern for the lapse in communication and attempted to sooth Ellen's suspicions and settle her unraveling nerves with plausible explanations. It took an incident of immediate consequence to convince the hardened cynic that a mother's instinct is rarely misguided.

CHAPTER XI

Five weeks confined in an eight-foot by six-foot space would test the sanity of any human. To Roger Perry, the cage was just another example of humankind's inability to accept or correct its inherent malignity. Prisons were human zoos. The incarcerated therein no more than a select breed of Homo sapiens; those specimens incompatible with adopted norms and outside civilized society's illusory safety net.

Roger displayed one idiosyncrasy among many common to the caged animal. He paced. He paced the extents of his cage, and it was a cage, for days following his initial incarceration. When granted outside privileges in the exercise yard he paced around the perimeter of the security fence. When he attended the mandated sessions in the office of the prison psychiatrist he plastered his body against the grey-green walls and crawled like a bug at the baseboard, refusing to sit or prone his fidgety form upon the doctor's couch.

Roger, by nature, could never abide limits or boundaries. Although no one in authority abused him at Frackville, he resented the fact that someone, anyone, could challenge his liberty so cavalierly. So, he watched religiously for a lapse of attention or an impartial shutting of his cell door, but the guards were customarily thorough and conscientious and the opportunity to capitalize on an error never materialized. The guards, used to dealing with resentment and hostility, kept him within arm's reach when escorting him to and from his cell. But Roger's fellow prisoners, a worthless and amoral lot, gave him wide berth. They, no doubt, recognized the burning fire of pure evil when they beheld it.

Dr. Werner, the consulting criminal psychologist that examined Roger following his involuntary commitment, found Roger to be reticent to open up but a fractured picture of the circumstances surrounding the troubled man's psychosis eventually merged.

Through a lengthy series of interviews with Roger, his closest relatives and neighbors who knew the family well, Dr. Werner garnered an incredibly in-depth account of Roger's formative years. Roger eventually co-operated fully, even going as far as to contribute a detailed memoir in his own hand. Dr. Werner posted the illuminating text verbatim in Roger's permanent record and submitted the following synopsis in his own words:

#

Roger Perry was a freak of nature. He was born on April Fool's Day and raised in a backward, rural section of northeastern Pennsylvania. His parents, Vernon and Beryl Perry, provided a modest home and adequate care. Their first recollection of their infant son was that he compulsively poked their eyes when they held him, but they would laugh and endure the pain in trusting bemusement.

Before Roger could walk, the young boy developed a fascination for a pair of canaries his mother owned named 'Sugar' and 'Spice'. Their cage rested on a table by the living room window. Roger would pull himself up on his wobbly legs and study the feathered creatures for hours on end. One morning, Roger's mother awoke early to find her nude year-old son sitting by the birdcage.

The cage had toppled to the floor and the wire door was ajar. The canaries were missing. Roger's parents considerately left the window partially open that night so their feathered friends might experience the cool summer air. They surmised the critters must have escaped through fault of their own though the window screens were intact and undamaged. They were at a complete loss to explain the abundance of feathers scattered about the room.

It was not until Roger broke from their grasp at age three and attacked an infant in a carriage at the local supermarket that they became genuinely concerned. He had struck the baby girl repeatedly and clawed at her face. Roger had not seriously injured the child in the fray, but the poor baby's mother was aghast and furious. Great measures were necessary, including monetary compensation, to forestall civil action.

Roger fell behind the curve of normal pre-adolescent development. His doctor insisted that the boy's case was by no means singular and, given proper nourishment and attention, Roger would soon be back on track. By the time Roger reached five years of age, his growth rate did, in fact, improve and his parents were relieved and reassured.

Unfortunately, his was a stature still smaller than that of children his age. In order to free their son from potential bullying, Roger's parents refused to integrate him into the society of his chronological peers, opting instead to place him in the company of children of like size. This decision cast Roger in the role of bully in kindergarten, and he secured his position by terrifying those around him into submission. The situation at school came to a head when several mothers and fathers discovered that someone had bitten their children on the neck with such force as to draw blood. All fingers pointed to Roger Perry.

For the next several years, Roger's antisocial—some said psychopathic—behavior steadily worsened. Due to his history of incessantly taunting fellow classmates and his past and then escalating aggressions, the educational authorities branded Roger with 'pervasive developmental disorder' and ruled him 'unsuitable for group interaction'. They summarily removed him from the public school system. It was determined that home tutoring by an assortment of solicited social workers would benefit all parties to the greatest degree. The community's resources and patience were quickly depleted. By the time Roger was nine, the educational powers-that-be divested themselves of responsibility and abandoned the troubled boy to his own devices and the will of the State.

Roger's parents were beside themselves. Convinced of their marginal fostering intuition, they followed faithfully the advice of psychologists and social experts. They began an intensive home-schooling program that held Roger's attention for a total of three weeks. After that, their misguided, single-minded son abandoned his studies for daily excursions over the rolling hills and farmlands of his native state.

Roger's attentions were fixated on the outdoors and the animals that existed there. He often disappeared into the woods at first light, roaming twenty miles or more and returning at dusk to eat and sleep. Many times, he slipped out at night to wander the countryside under the moonlight pretending to be one of the monstrous characters of his dreams. He howled at the moon, ran on all fours and tried to eat and drink without using his hands.

On one of his frequent rambles, Roger collected no fewer than five stray dogs of varying breeds as his travelling companions. His journey home along U.S. Highway 13 invited the attention of the state police who warned the wayfarer of the dangers his pack posed to himself and motorists. After calling the A.S.P.C.A. to corral the canines, the officers returned the prodigal alpha male to the family fold.

Despite Roger's annoying proclivities, he befriended many of the local boys and spent much of his time cavorting in creeks, rivers, hills and hollows. On winter days, they would sled through the trees at breakneck speed, dodging pines and hardwoods, becoming airborne with every hummock in their way and jumping the creek at the bottom of the slippery slope. They flew down icy, earthen roads on their balloon-tired bicycles, locked their brakes and dropped like stuntmen sending their two-wheeled rockets spiraling ahead of them. They skated on iced ponds and frozen tangent lengths of stream channel.

On summer nights, a hilltop campsite a mile from Roger's home, locally dubbed the 'Poplar Grove', served as stage for games of 'Catch Me'— whereby, one boy, the anointed prey, slithered deeper into the woods and misdirected his predatory pursuers with mocking calls and whistles. Then, following customary suppers of biscuits and jerky, the timeless ghost tale, 'One Step', survived another retelling before the warriors wrapped their lithe frames in blankets and stretched, head to toe, around the dying embers of the crackling campfire.

On other occasions, the chaps constructed minnow traps from funneled screen wire and mason jars and baited them with crusts of white sandwich bread. When trapping proved too slow, they hunted the miniature shiners with BB guns—learning from experience that firing just below the darting transparent forms allowed for the parallax effect of the water and increased the kill quotient tenfold. The insatiable hunters killed dragonflies and butterflies, too, by the hundreds.

When streams were low and clear, the Spartans hunted crawdads and brought them home by the bucketsful. They paired the mightiest of the pincered warriors against each other in staged contests of primal fury. The winner won his freedom. The loser, often missing a pincer or leg to the battle, had its remaining pincer torn from its body and its defenseless carapace tossed callously to the chickens. When streams roiled at flood stage after a soaking rain, the boys swam and played fearlessly in the dangerous currents and constructed temporary dams to divert the powerful channel flows.

With practice, Roger learned to recognize the stench of snake habitat. He would sniff them out, smash them to bits with rocks and drag their lifeless forms behind him like thick ropes. Roger always skinned and dissected his trophies. The other young men were a bit more squeamish but still watched in awe and amazement as Roger displayed his unparalleled skills.

Various species of wasps lived beneath the multi-layered paper covering Roger's bedroom ceiling, and the poor child endured a nightly fear of the horrid little things. Many times an errant wasp would find its way beneath his covers at night, and Roger would receive a painful wallop when he rolled upon it. He tried to eradicate the stinging threats from his room by smashing every one he encountered, but there were just too many of them.

The strategy he adopted finally made a game of his predicament. Roger excelled at devising ingenious traps to ensnare the hostile creatures. Once he placed on his bed a large doll stolen from a local girl and smeared it with jelly and peanut butter. Roger knew that wasps loved peanut butter and jelly just as he did. After a half-hour or so, the wasps would emerge and descend on the mannequin one by one.

The concoction was sticky and adhered to the insects' legs and wings like cement. Roger would gather them on a spoon and, without endangering the lives of the insects, press the stingers from their abdomens with the edge of a table knife. It was a great trick. Now, Roger had the power, and it tickled him to think of how stupid the fearless creatures actually were. They could crawl on him and his bed now to their hearts content and he would never fear them again.

This realization had a profound effect on Roger and changed his conception of himself from wary victim to benevolent predator. He convinced himself that all creatures were powerless against his intellect. Their continued existence would be in his hands. He alone would choose who lived and who died.

Roger's parents ignorantly dismissed their son's fixations and fantasies as the cruel indiscretions of youth—that is, until they discovered the bodies of a dozen newborn chicks. Someone had squeezed them so forcefully that their entrails spilled from their rectums and their tiny eyes exploded from their sockets. Someone, with undeniable ritualistic depravity, impaled the chick's flattened downy forms on ten penny nails and displayed them like trophies upon the molded walls of a creepy canning cellar that lurked like a troll beneath the weathered smokehouse situated a scant thirty feet from the family's shambling back porch.

That someone was Roger. He admitted it freely when confronted. It was then the magnitude of their son's disturbed mind became evident and the frightening awareness of what he may or had already become truly settled in.

Roger loved comic books and never began or ended the day without re-reading one or two. He had an enviable collection of horror stories concerning the Frankenstein monster, tales of werewolves, mummies, zombies, Dracula and his minions of the undead, select issues of *Twilight Zone, Tales from the Crypt*, and *Monster Monthly* magazines. Universal trading cards depicting the greatest fiends of motion pictures filled his bureau drawers, and posters and fiberglass models of his deviant heroes adorned the walls and shelves of his room. Roger relished reading and devoured everything he could find on witches, demons, hauntings and ghosts and goblins.

On Rogers' thirteenth birthday, he and a bevy of his more daring acquaintances descended on Blakelock Cemetery for an evening of devilish revelry. Roger's extensive interest in matters supernatural led, unsurprisingly, to questions of death and resurrection. A séance was planned, complete with Ouija board and candles. The seekers stumbled about for several minutes guided only by their inclinations until the diminutive light from the candles they carried rested upon a sunken gravesite adorned with a circle of mushrooms Roger knew to be called a witches' ring.

"This is the place!" Roger cried. His cohorts dropped excitedly to their knees and arrayed their candles near the Ouija board's perimeter. With fingertips placed on the critical planchette, Roger began a low, guttural chant designed to evoke those spirits most eager to expose themselves. After several minutes of disappointing calm, a breeze stirred the air and Roger's breath grew noticeably shallow and rapid. The planchette raced from letter to letter, delineating gibberish too rapidly for the novices to comprehend, then sprang from the board and crashed against the face of the overgrown headstone. Everyone sat in astonishment and silence for what seemed an eternity before Roger crawled cautiously toward the planchette. As he retrieved the item, the light from the candle in his other hand cast its eerie illumination across the scarred and forgotten stone. Roger fell back upon his rump when the significance of what he saw crystalized in his mind. The surname 'Perry' stood out in bold relief just as a rumble of thunder pealed ominously in the distance.

Roger's co-revelers scattered to their respective lairs. Roger, alone, remained within the 'witches ring' as the sudden storm ensued.

Several days later, those at the graveyard ceremony learned from Roger's mother that her son had taken seriously ill and had run a high fever. Roger was rushed to St. John's Hospital where doctors labored to diagnose his unknown condition. Everyone thought Roger would return home that week.

No one saw Roger Perry again for nearly a year. News of his return from his curious hiatus spread quickly. When Roger re-surfaced, his speech was slurred and his face had taken on the look of idiocy and evil. His former mates, eager to reacquaint themselves at first, devolved into strangers. Family acquaintances made themselves scarce and the Perry home grew more wretched and barren as the seasons dragged on. But by the following year, Roger's condition improved rapidly. He never fully regained one hundred percent mobility. His mind seemed a little slower than before, but the recovery was remarkable.

Soon after this momentous turn, Roger experienced another tumultuous and defining episode in his young life.

Roger's nearest neighbors lived a quarter of a mile away in a small ranch-style house with a huge, brindle, mixed-breed dog named Bruno. The menacing animal sometimes strayed from its master and would find its way to Roger's home. On one such visit, Bruno ambled up behind Roger and lay on the cool concrete of the porch at Roger's back. Surprised at the misanthropic animal's unusual display of friendship and affection, Roger turned to pet the beast. The first stroke of the animal's fur revealed an infestation of blood-gorged ticks just beneath the dog's collar. The ticks had embedded their mouthparts tenaciously into their host's flesh. Roger respectfully sought to remove the first parasite with a tug. Bruno yelped and lunged at the surprised boy's throat, snapping and snarling ferociously.

Roger fell backwards off the porch, landing belly up with Bruno slobbering over him with a rabid snarl. A frantic kick to the animal's groin displaced the beast from its station. Roger fled on all fours for twenty feet or more towards his house until he managed an upright posture again. He was fearful of looking back lest the incensed animal be addressing his heels. When he arrived home, the steaming youth stormed directly to the pigeon-hole desk in his father's bedroom and removed a Harrington & Richards 22-caliber, seven-shot Buntline revolver and a box of shells.

Roger immediately returned to the scene of the assault. After spotting the beast that attacked him, he emptied the revolver in the animal's direction. Sensing danger, Bruno dodged the buzzing lead whizzing around its head and hauled home where it cowered underneath its master's Pontiac GTO. Roger strode the distance to his neighbor's farm with unwavering, ruthless intent. He reloaded the gun with seven more rounds as he marched along. When he discovered Bruno shivering beneath the vehicle, Roger lay down on his right side with his pistol arm beneath him. He was ready to fire and determined to kill. The panicked animal shivered with eyes bulged and its tongue lagging from its drooling mouth. Roger pointed the gun at the beast's head and yelled, "Bang." The dog flinched. Roger could kill it here and now, or he could let it live. Today was Bruno's lucky day.

Vernon Perry, Roger's father, was not a happy man. He drank heavily and blamed his eccentric son for the loss of intimacy in his marriage. He beat Roger at the slightest provocation, using whatever weapon was at hand.

The smokehouse, so called for the long-abandoned practice of smoking hams, found renewed life as an impromptu punishment chamber where Roger endured belt lashings and beatings at the hands of his father. The punishments meted out were of intensity and duration often disproportionate to the egregiousness of Roger's transgressions. Electrical cords, wire hangers, belts, lengths of lumber and broken broom handles knew Roger's flesh and signed their work with distinctively cruel and unusual marks.

One summer day Roger accompanied his parents to town and rode in the bed of his father's Ford pickup truck for the return trip. When the truck wheeled into the driveway that ran by the front of their home, Roger thought it would be great fun to spring from the moving vehicle and roll the way he had seen characters on television do countless times. The jump progressed as planned, but the roll became a series of head-over-heel summersaults culminating with Roger narrowly cheating death beneath the truck's spinning wheels. A scared Roger, confused as to why his choreography went awry, sprang to his feet and ran directly into the house.

His father entered moments later and found his son staring apprehensively into the bathroom mirror. He slowly advanced upon the unsuspecting boy and planted the toe of his work boot squarely in the young man's posterior. Roger squalled as a bolt of pain shot up his tailbone. His father turned and left the room without uttering a single word.

When Roger turned fifteen, his cousin Lori and her friend Molly visited from out of state. Lori was the daughter of his mother's sister. She was a pretty girl, like most are, and Roger was enamored with her charm and genuine graciousness from the start. When everyone retired for the night, the girls occupied Roger's room and Roger moved to the smaller adjacent bedroom at the end of the upstairs hallway.

Around midnight, Roger awoke to giggles emanating from the young girls' room. He crept quietly to the closet that had a counterpart in the opposite bedroom. Wooden slats separated the adjoining closets. A nightlight lit the space beyond. Roger pressed his eye to a void near a knothole and spied upon the merry maids.

The girls were sitting upright on the bed facing each other. The young nymphs cavorted playfully on the bed for nearly fifteen minutes, oblivious to the prying eyes of their "next-door neighbor". What began as an innocent light-hearted romp segued into wanton stares as the girls slid beneath the covers.

Roger continued to spy on his unsuspecting guests for several minutes until the wriggling subsided and the tousled-headed girls emerged from beneath their shroud. His breath was nearly imperceptible, but his heart beat so loudly he was certain the girls had heard. He scurried to his bed and pulled the woolen blankets over his head in feigned sleep.

At daybreak, Roger awoke to find Lori and Molly in the bed beside him. The unexpected company confused him, and he did not know how to react. He made an effort to rise, but the young women pulled him back beneath the covers. Roger was confused, but embarrassingly stimulated and excited. The girls took turns playfully trying to kiss him on the mouth. Roger's obvious inexperience and boorish ineptness inevitably sent the mischievous nymphs scurrying back to their room. Roger slept uneasily from that night forward.

He dreamed often of his cousin and her Sapphic friend for weeks after they returned home and prayed they would visit again. He watched girls from afar and yearned to decipher the mysteries surrounding them, but he still felt more comfortable in the company of animals than with people.

On his sixteenth birthday, Roger's mother spent the morning painting the kitchen a cheerful yellow. Roger took a position beneath the ladder on which his mother perched and busied himself with some imaginary task. As she extended her slender form to reach the area nearest the ceiling, Roger caught a glimpse of her braless breasts bouncing beneath her oversized denim shirt. He glanced as often as he dared, not knowing if his mother would object to his peeping or not.

After the painting was complete, Beryl showered and changed into her best dress. She dutifully baked Roger a cake and made a rare attempt at normalcy by staging a party for her son. Vernon Perry had gone to town for a customary bottle of Four Roses. When the cake and ice cream were ready, Roger and his mother repaired to the front porch swing. Roger was delighted with this rare expression of love and concern and eyed his mother intently as she placed the celebratory desserts on the small table in front of them.

As she seated herself, Roger stealthily positioned his hand beneath her posterior and wiggled his fingers suggestively. His shocked mother screamed and slapped at him and struggled to rise, Roger clawed at her dress. The garment split at the shoulder and exposed the cotton bra she now wore. Beryl broke free of her son's clutches and ran screaming into the house. She slammed and bolted the door behind her. Roger watched the flowing cream trickle down the back of the steel porch swing and gel on the smooth, slate-grey concrete. Immersed in the moment, he lapped the pooling substance like a cat at a saucer of milk.

When his father returned and learned of his boy's disgraceful conduct, he apprehended his son and dragged him by his hair to the smokehouse. Roger suffered the most severe beating of his life. His father flailed him with everything he could find. When the weapons shattered and were unfit for corporal use, he pummeled his son with his fists until he reduced the battered boy to a stain on the wooden floor.

The bruises and scars remained for weeks. Roger withdrew into darkness deeper than he had ever known. Morose, silent and uncooperative, he spoke to no one for weeks. He ate little, if at all, and slept in his clothes. The State had no option but to order Roger to the Fairview State Hospital for the Criminally Insane for observation. The admitting psychiatrist diagnosed him with bipolar personality disorder coupled with homicidal/suicidal tendencies and recommended commitment in the facility until the State deemed the young man fit to return to society.

Roger did not comprehend why strangers took him from his parents and the home he had lived in all his life. He resented their interference and vowed the society that had persecuted him would pay, and pay dearly. Consequently, he concluded that his fate would reside in his hands alone. After nine months of incarceration and psychiatric therapy, Roger viciously attacked an orderly and escaped.

The rest of Roger Perry's sordid escapades were a matter of recent record. Dr. Werner concluded that any hope for rehabilitation and re-introduction of his patient into mainstream society was shattered by the twists of fate and acts of unbridled rage directed at the young man from a world that created and then abandoned him. Such total rejection set the youth on a singular path of self-destructive and psychopathic mutation that was virtually irreversible. Ironically, Roger's unchecked angst spawned a war of retribution upon the heartless system that refused his integration into its illusion of comfort and conformity. Dr. Werner feared, with good cause, those persons Roger held responsible would ultimately pay the price of indulging their self-righteous indignation at the expense of the maligned and misunderstood youth.

CHAPTER XII

Dr. Werner suffixed his report with a diagnosis of paranoid schizophrenia, acute delusional disorder and clinical depression. He concluded that the projection of hostilities toward Bernard Biggs, the last person Roger had contact with before the police apprehended him, was merely a manifestation of textbook fixation and transference entirely in line with his diagnosis of persecution complex and paranoid neurosis. He prescribed 100 mg of chlorpromazine, four times daily, with orders to increase the dosage until optimized patient control was realized. Daily counseling would begin immediately after achieving subjugation. His final recommendation was to place the tormented fellow on suicide watch indefinitely.

The anti-psychotic regimen continued for ten months before Dr. Werner felt comfortable weaning Roger from the chemical agents. Roger's system absorbed the powerful drugs like a sponge until the medication had no discernable effect. His appearance and demeanor suggested progress and the good doctor, quick to take credit for the improvement, arrogantly ignored even the possibility of a false positive.

Yet, despite Dr. Werner's sunny prognosis, Roger remained delusional and fixated on Bernard Biggs. Roger had apprised the authorities of Biggs' involvement in the conspiracy to murder Carl Connor, but the district attorney effectively argued that the defendant's insistences were the ravings of a psychotic intent on saving himself at the expense of another. Anyone could have availed themselves of details concerning Mr. Connor's heinous murder by simply following pervasive television and newspaper coverage.

Over the ensuing months, Roger saw Biggs in his dreams. He saw him in the harsh dispassionate faces of the guards. He saw him in the cells lining D Block and in the exercise yard. Biggs served him his meals and brought him magazines. Biggs ironed his orange jumpsuit in the prison laundry and took his temperature in the prison infirmary when he was ill.

There were so many of them. He could not kill them all. The rational side of Roger's mind finally convinced the irrational side that if he destroyed the Biggs that sent him here, the clones would disappear as well. Kill the head and the body dies. Soon, he would watch Biggs die a death as sick and twisted as the coils of razor wire that encircled his private hell. For now, he had to remain sharp. He had to have a plan.

Roger realized he needed to focus his mental powers on escape if he was to achieve his ambition of destroying Biggs. Things would have to change and change dramatically. He could no longer afford to wait for an opportunity to escape; he would have to create one. From now on he would be the model prisoner and behave as expected. He must master his impatience. Time was on his side and sweet freedom was just a dream away.

His decision to modify his behavior began to bear fruit after the third year. He fought the urge to pace nervously about and modeled his actions on observations of his fellow prisoners. He cultivated few friendships, except for the nominal number required to solicit a nod from the house shrink as proof of his moderating sociopathic personality.

His redrawn persona soon begat extended privileges. The progressively minded warden, eager to chronical evidence to validate a vision often derided by his peers, soon allowed Roger to mingle freely with the general population. In short order, Roger earned a coveted spot in the galley where he judiciously scrubbed pots and pans. His responsibilities expanded quickly to include inventory management. If supplies ran low, he quantified the discrepancies and notified the commissary procurement officer. Eventually, he helped supervise deliveries and returns.

Roger perfected his front with flawless dedication, but it was nearly impossible to elude monitoring. Cameras and guards were everywhere. Prison trustees assigned to the more desirable tasks were not to be trusted, so Roger relied on the support of his newly minted friendships to aid and abet him.

One such friend was Kevin Merritt—a three-time loser with a string of brutal assaults to his credit. Merritt favored the elderly and delighted in their inability to defend themselves. Roger and Kevin were cellmates for a time. It was during late-night games of "chicken" that Roger earned Kevin's respect and loyalty. The inmates would sit facing each other with their forearms side by side and across their knees. Lit cigarettes, puffed to a fierce glow, would then be placed on their forearms. The first one to withdraw lost the bet. Kevin had scars aplenty, but Roger always won. Usually, without a flinch.

Kevin worked with the maintenance detail and had access to many essential tools. A suction-activated glass-handling cup was one of the specialty items required. Roger insinuated himself easily into Kevin's routine and secured a pledge of cooperation. There would be little opportunity for welding or other forms of fabrication, so a minimalist approach was best.

On the eve of the seventh anniversary of his incarceration, Roger went to work. He convinced a night supervisor to allow him to cover the graveyard shift under pretense of advancing his understanding of round-the-clock operations. The super agreed that Roger could replace another inmate who requested an opposite arrangement. A 'coincidence' surreptitiously compelled by Kevin and facilitated with a bribe of two cans of Bugler tobacco and the threat of a shiv to the eye.

Roger bled his midnight cohorts of information regarding warehouse deliveries and learned that a truck arrived twice weekly at three a.m. with a supply of cooking oil for the prison kitchen. It departed forty-five minutes later with fifty-gallon drums filled with discarded oil destined for an afterlife as biofuel. Roger shrewdly volunteered to move several full drums to the loading platform and used the opportunity to judge their weight. If his guesstimate was correct, and he could endure the stench and immersion in the sickening liquid, he would be free in a matter of hours. If not, and he was discovered, he would be no worse off. For the first week, Roger verified the accuracy of the gathered intelligence. When he determined the information was credible, he scheduled the getaway for the following Tuesday.

The big day arrived. Accomplices had removed one end of an oil drum and replaced it with another fitted with the suction device. They also filled the selected drum with oil to a level just over one-half the drum's capacity and insured it was ready and waiting. Used cooking oil is lighter than water but not by much. If his combined weight did not approximate the absent oil, Roger would risk certain discovery by alert handlers.

That night, Roger volunteered again to transport the drums to the loading dock, and the shift super granted permission without question. His special drum was marked with a dusting of flour on its lid. He lifted the top quickly to insure the lid was equipped with the suction cup secured to its underside. Roger methodically transported the drum to the dock and set it aside with the explanation that the super wanted to try a different loading schedule in order to compare relative efficiencies.

After several more routine runs, he managed to slip from his station under guise of a bathroom break. He edged along the back wall and slinked in and out of intermittent shadows until he reached the edge of the loading dock. His escape pod with the dusting of flour on its lid was right where he had left it.

Normally, one handler would be loading while the other returned for another barrel. This created a limited window for chicanery and insured that workers spent minimal time socializing. Tonight, though (thanks to clever abettors), a drum was mishandled and the contents spewed over the galley floor. The guards ordered both handlers at once to assist in the cleanup.

Roger smiled as the wheels of fortune turned his way. His plan of action reeked of success. He stripped naked and waited until both handlers and the two guards were engaged before he made his move. How stealthily he stepped into the viscous bath. How remarkable his idea to secure the lid from within with the suction device. He gloated as the petals of his design unfolded flawlessly. The oil withheld from the drum was the precise quantity required to prevent the displaced substance from overflowing the rim.

He was neck high in the solution with scarcely room for his head. He had wisely replaced the solid fill cap with a screened variety that allowed the noxious fumes to escape, but breathing was still a chore. The minutes seemed eternal. Soon, the clattering approach of the handlers and their wheeled hand trucks resounded from within the vaulted facility, prompting Roger to quiet his thoughts and nervously await the movement of his capsule.

After a brief jostling, his drum began its journey up the ramp of the loading platform and into the waiting truck. Roger cleverly placed his palm over the fill opening to prevent a telltale splash of oil spilling out. A few moments more and someone would notice his absence. He crouched in agonizing anticipation, taught and explosive as a coiled spring. He waited breathlessly for the slide of the closing rear door. When at last he heard the unmistakable sound, reassurance and accomplishment drew his lips into a mischievous v-shaped smile.

Roger was intent to remain submerged in spent cooling oil no longer than necessary and freed himself from the confining space as soon as the truck stopped and continued for a third time. Only then would he be outside the prison walls and beyond the second razor-wired security perimeter. The greasy film clung to his person like surrogate skin. His breathing was labored and shallow. The oily coating suffocated his body. He scraped at his flesh with the web of his thumb and forefinger to reduce the oil's multi-millimeter thickness.

He had to disrobe before entering the drum for obvious reasons, and that was a problem now; the only factor for which he could not mitigate. Luckily, a cloth lab coat similar to the kind butcher's wore lay across some boxes near the truck's sliding back door. He used the coat to dry the remaining oil from his body and then put the garment on. His mind raced for ideas. The challenge of improvisation lay ahead, and he had to be ready for anything.

Despite the early hour, the building buzzed with activity when the delivery truck arrived at its destination. The truck's rear door slid open with a heavy clang. Roger remained hidden behind the wall of drums, watching the workers unload the first line of material from the trailer. He timed his emergence to coincide with their movements.

When the last in a line of workers engaged his cargo and turned his back, Roger moved quickly to the door, dropped from the trailer bed and grabbed a large carton from the side of the loading platform. He lifted it high to obscure most of his face with his eyes peering above the carton's top edge just enough to facilitate navigation. He followed the handlers as if he were one of their own. His naked legs and feet betrayed his status, yet, amazingly, all remained oblivious to his unauthorized presence.

At his first opportunity, Roger discarded his burden. A series of twists and turns through unfamiliar corridors led him to a locker room of sorts. Inside, various and sundry wardrobes hung on wooden pegs. Lockers lined the opposite wall. The workers secured their valuables in small metal cabinets with padlocks, but their civilian clothes were there for the taking. He had no time to indulge personal taste, but he did allow a minute or two browsing for a suitable shirt and trousers in his size. After donning his mismatched apparel, he jumped into a waiting pair of boots and speedily departed.

No one spotted the fugitive as he exited the locker room and slipped through the stairwell door. Nobody witnessed his descent down the stairs or observed his defection from the warehouse. Once outside, Roger Perry strolled away with a spirited gate and an impish glance over his right shoulder. His plan had worked like a charm.

CHAPTER XIII

A week later, Roger found himself back in Circleville, Ohio. He proceeded straight away to the home of Bernard Biggs, where he waited beyond the arbor vitae hedgerow for the cover of darkness. Around eight p.m., the man who betrayed him walked the brick-paved path leading from the front door of his house to his black Mercedes Benz and drove away. Roger would finish his business with his nemesis at some future time. He could not accomplish what he had in mind within the man's local circle of influence. No, he would have to remove the man to a neutral location; the how and when yet unknown.

Roger moved closer to the impressive residence with a cool twinge of excitement. The light from a three-quarter moon sparkled like a diamond on a thin line of drool seeping from the upturned corners of his cruel mouth. Not to be outdone, an illuminated second-story window bid for and won his eye. He felt the urge to kill bubble up from the pit of his stomach. A primal, bloodthirsty hunger gnawed at his insides—a familiar precursor to the anticipated metamorphosis he knew was about to transpire. Fueled by the moon's energy, his body lurched forward, his back bowed and his shoulders broadened. Tendons and ligaments bulged on lengthened arms and legs. His fingers twisted into talons.

By the front entrance, large Doric columns reared up on each side of the glass-smooth marble porch. English ivy encircled each column and ascended as high as the ornate frieze spanning between them would allow.

Roger grasped the vines aggressively in his hands and climbed upward. Before he rose five feet, a German Shepherd burst from the far edge of the shrubbery, barked fiercely and snapped at his heels. Roger dropped to the ground immediately and faced the animal with reciprocal fury. Stunned momentarily by the unexpected action of the intruder, the guard dog ceased barking then re-engaged with a full-body lunge at Roger's throat.

Roger met with the animal halfway. The correlative force when they tangled repelled their bodies several feet. Their re-engagement could not have been launched with graver threat or commitment. The Shepherd's training centered on control and neutralization of a perceived threat and not lethal offensive strategies. Roger had received no training. He drew only from his innate taste for blood and his willingness to destroy—a trait deeply ingrained in his character and as undeniable as the rising moon that nourished his inner beast.

Roger fell beneath the brute's one hundred ten pounds of muscle, his right arm vised within the dog's tremendously powerful jaws. Roger bared his own teeth and sunk them deeply into the canine's neck. The dog yelped in pain and relaxed its jaw muscles, but immediately resumed its programmed attack.

Roger's eyes held the crisp moon's stare over the animal's bristled back. Atoms of light infused through his dilated pupils granted him a dramatic surge in strength. His pulsing heart drove him to his feet even though the attack dog dangled by its teeth from his bloody arm. With a decisive movement, Roger slammed the beast to the ground and pounced upon it. The dog's spine snapped like a pretzel stick, leaving it limp and lifeless.

Roger raised the Shepherd until its hind paws barely brushed the dew-stained pavers. Biting ferociously into the canine's throat, he repeatedly tore quantities of flesh and fur from the carcass and spat each mouthful into a pile at his feet. He knew the threat was silenced, but he could not stop himself from ravaging the remains. He clawed into the wounds he had just inflicted and ripped the animal's head from its body.

Roger turned his gaze skyward again and uttered a grotesque and shivering howl of defiance. With the agility of a lizard, he scaled the vine-covered column to its terminus, traversed the front of the building and forced his way inside through the lighted window.

He entered the chestnut paneled room a different being. He was calm now and recalled the reason he had come. Roger was astonished at his luck. This room was the one he had hoped to find and he found it without looking. He stood in the private office of Bernard Biggs. A true believer would have thanked God for small miracles, but Roger's contention was there was no deity but himself to thank.

A few minutes browsing uncovered a letter in a top desk drawer. The postmark read Vermont—a curious coincidence considering Vermont was the place he intended going after concluding his business with Biggs. Attached to the letter with a paper clip was a picture of a pretty young woman. Roger glanced around the room and noticed various pictures of the same pretty young woman in a frame on the desk and on the wall opposite the chair.

He moved closer to the wall picture. Something familiar in the girl's face grabbed him. Raised eyebrows signaled his recognition of the face. He had talked to the same girl in the stable many years ago. How could anyone forget those amazing violet eyes?

He withdrew the letter from the envelope and began reading. He smiled as the possibilities presented themselves to his devious mind. The contents of the letter mentioned a school the girl was attending, but nothing more of immediate interest. It was signed, 'Clara'. The sender scribbled the return address in the upper left hand corner of the envelope in an impatient hand, but the writing was legible enough to read.

"Hmmm...You are obviously still very dear to my old friend," he whispered, sliding the letter and picture into the back pocket of his trousers. Further rummaging uncovered a locked drawer. Always intrigued by the forbidden, Roger could not resist. A trophy Japanese nihontō from World War II hung prominently on an adjacent wall. Roger tore it away from its mooring and relished a cursory swing or two to test its balance. Satisfied with the article's fit and finish, he employed the instrument to pry the drawer open. The clay-tempered steel sword made short work of the mahogany desk.

Inside the drawer lay a digital tape cassette and a tan leather-bound journal replete with detailed descriptions and dates concerning intimate musings of a special relationship. Roger read aloud several passages and was barely able to contain his delight. He slapped his knee playfully when he realized the import of what he had discovered. The journal shed light on an entirely new course of action, but he would need time to consider his alternatives. He would watch the tape later after he secured an appropriate playback device. There was no telling what goodies resided therein. Leaving a message for his former partner seemed apropos and sufficient for now.

Fumbling through the middle desk drawer produced a letter opener of exotic Asian design. He considered taking it, but instead, pulled Clara's photograph from the wall and shattered it on the corner of the desk. He freed the picture from its gilded frame and used a jagged shard of glass to scratch the violet eyes away. On the edge of the picture, he scrawled these words: '*I'll be in touch*'. After admiring his handiwork, he used the letter knife to impale the image to the wall behind Biggs's desk. "That should do it," he proclaimed decisively.

Thoughts of Vermont and the security he felt in the old house comforted him. He could not remain here or anywhere near here much longer. "Yes, Vermont would be best," he muttered. He spoke as if in consultation with another. "They will never consider looking for you that far north. Why would they? Why don't you send Biggs your own letter when you get there, along with a memento? He'll understand." With a final look around, Roger slipped through the broken window and wrapped himself in the comforting cloak of obscurity.

#

Bernard Biggs returned around two a.m. The demented minimalist message he found in his study sent chills up his spine. His personal journal and tape were missing! He had felt particularly lascivious recently and had indulged in an evening of visual and literary debauchery just two nights before. Intrepid Alarm Services was in the middle of installing a new video surveillance system designed to monitor the entire house and grounds and had disabled the existing systems that morning. The locked desk drawer on the second floor of his secured house that lay beyond a ten-foot steel fence with controlled entrance gate seemed adequate protection for a few days. What could happen in the interim? Apparently a lot, he admitted. He kicked himself for not placing the items in his private safe.

Biggs found his dog, Thor, the next morning. He immediately suspected Roger Perry of the savage mutilation and destruction of his prized Schutzhund and of the scribbled message and defaced photograph of his darling, Clara. He could not risk involving the police, who might easily establish a connection between himself and the escaped killer. Blood was plentifully distributed about his office—indiscriminately, he thought, as if the intruder hadn't given it a second thought. Forensic crime specialists could type the blood easily. No, he would have to handle the cleaning chores personally. He buried Thor near the hedges in the back corner of the property and made surreptitious inquiries into Roger Perry's prison status.

Roger's ingenious escape made national news, and a countrywide manhunt was now in effect. If Biggs had taken the time to read the headlines in his own rags or stay abreast of current events, he might have been forewarned. As in most things with Biggs, it was 'out-of-sight, out-of-mind', and he lived accordingly—at times, regretfully. No one apprised Biggs of Roger's daring escape. Nothing had implicated Biggs in any way, and the authorities had no cause to believe him to be in any immediate danger. There was no reason for anyone to suspect Roger had left Pennsylvania either, so police were concentrating their considerable search efforts in that state alone.

His sources confirmed that Roger Perry had escaped from prison and his pursuers, yet again, and was on the prowl. Biggs was worried. The ubiquitous fellow might turn up anywhere at any moment. Roger had eluded re-capture despite the interstate all-points bulletins issued by federal and state authorities and still made his way across two states and into his private office. There was no telling where the lunatic might be or where he might strike next.

One thing Biggs knew: Roger had a score to settle. If he harbored thoughts of revenge for seven years and still had enough rage inside him to rip a guard dog to pieces, he was capable of things even Biggs could not imagine. Roger was obviously now fixated on Clara. If he knew where she was and could find her, she was in undeniably grave danger.

Biggs could not remember if the return address was printed on the missing letter's envelope or not, but the postmark alone could betray her. He tried several times to reach Clara over the next two days, but either she was in class or otherwise indisposed. Messages on her cell phone remained unanswered.

Clara never returned calls promptly from Biggs anyway. He was surprised she had sent the letter. Most information about her health and wellbeing came channeled through her mother, with Biggs receiving the information secondhand. He intended to address this unacceptable situation soon via a trip to Vermont, but local business matters kept interfering with his plans.

#

After the international food soiree that fall and the interruption of the subsequent holidays, a mysterious fire ripped through the CAI campus putting the school's weekly cooking contests on hiatus. Clara decided to get a jump on the first competition and began her shopping early. She would be ready and raring to go when normality rolled back around.

It was a cold day. Her only transportation was a bicycle—a purple Schwinn with a generous wire basket mounted in front of the handlebars. She donned her favorite red wool jacket with the white leather sleeves, hopped astride her bike and began peddling the four miles to the nearest market. She preferred riding on the unpaved service road that paralleled the highway. Vehicular traffic was practically nil on frontage roads, but the considerable dust raised when the errant car or truck travelled it could be overbearing.

No one is ever prepared when destiny calls. Clara heard the vehicle approaching from behind. The redlined engine was whining at high rpm and its ragged muffler announced its coming far in advance. She glanced over her shoulder at the rooster tail of dust and clocked the projectile's excessive speed. She wisely chose to angle a safe distance from the edge of the gravel to the outer fringe of the road's right-of-way.

As the vehicle approached, she could see it was a truck. The color and make of the gritty machine was indiscernible. It seemed to be of older vintage with makeshift side rails that rattled and flopped about their inadequate fasteners like suffocating fish. The driver braked hard as he passed and skidded tens of yards to a stop in an impenetrable ochre cloud.

Clara strained her eyes, but their rays failed to pierce the swirling blanket of dust. All was literally confusion. Unconvinced the truck had crashed, she stepped cautiously forward pushing her bicycle alongside. Gradually, a figure emerged, shadowy and mysterious at first then unsettlingly revealed.

The man before her seemed vaguely familiar, possibly in his early to mid-twenties with wild mistrustful eyes and sporting a crude Mohawk haircut. With no word and without hesitation, the stranger flung the bicycle from Clara with a crash. He spun her around aggressively and covered her mouth with a cold and calloused hand.

Clara kicked and screamed for all she was worth, but could not forestall the attack. She fought valiantly, but no level of resistance could dissuade the man from dragging her by her heels to the truck and spiriting her away.

CHAPTER XIV

"Oh, where, oh, where has my little lamb gone? Oh, where, oh, where can she be? Oh, where, oh, where..." The faint lilting melody, like the dreamy stirrings from oversleeping, roused Clara back to consciousness. Violet sparks flashed beneath tangled strands of golden hair as her eyes fluttered open.

The room was cold enough to condense breath, but much warmer than outside. The thick walls of the structure that imprisoned her helped insulate her from the bitter New England winter. Light bursting through a battered window reminded her that there was still a beautiful world outside waiting for her return.

The screeching sound of nails drawn from hardwood planks near the door prompted her to rise. Someone was forcing entry. Her gaze fixed on the door. She held her breath as it creaked open. She sought to rise and discovered, to her dismay, that heavy black straps a sixteenth inch thick bound her fast to the rocking chair in which she sat.

"Oh, where, oh, where can she be?" the melody continued. "Oh, where, oh... there she is!" her captor exclaimed lightheartedly in mocked surprise as he entered. "Hello there, lovely. I thought you would never waken. I bet you're hungry, too. I brought you some peaches... a peach for a peach." Roger placed his offering on Clara's lap. On the flat bamboo tray sat an open can of peach halves in heavy syrup. He freed one of her hands from its Velcro restraint and kneeled down in front of her to watch her eat.

Clara watched the young man in front of her with a mixture of disgust, fear, hatred and curiosity. His face was unexpectedly pleasant, but the coldness in his eyes and shock of bristling red hair shaved into a radical Mohawk elicited a defensive response from deep inside her. Here was a human to avoid. Here was a problem that demanded deconstruction and control. To act on impulse could prove disastrous, yet, doing nothing could prove fatal. Once again, circumstance mired her in a quandary. Her incredulous stare tasked Roger's patience.

Roger grasped the wooden spoon from the tray, cradled an ounce of liquid therein and presented it to her like an inexperienced father feeding a toddler. He winced as she turned her head and shut her lips tightly. He moved the spoon playfully before her face, and Clara turned away again. Roger had little time for game playing and snatched the girl by the nose. His action forced her to face him.

Realizing that she was at a distinct disadvantage, she parted her lips invitingly and sucked in the juice. It was warm and sweet, and she relished the delicate flavor.

"That's better," Roger praised, releasing her nose, "now for the good stuff." He scooped a massive peach halve onto the spoon and offered it to her with a big smile.

Clara stared intently at Roger's face. Her intriguing violet eyes sparkled with clarity and depth and held the young man transfixed. She opened her mouth wide to engulf the fruit whole and pretended to chew. At the decisive moment, she spat the amorphous mass back into Roger's face. The force of the unexpected sent him reeling backwards. His mind flashed on the dog, Bruno, and the terrific lunge the animal had made for his throat when he was a young boy. His startled look signaled a rare vulnerability.

Leveraging the opportunity, Clara tore madly at the restraining strap in an effort to free her immobilized arm. It was futile. Roger had bound her well for just such an eventuality. The realization forged new fears in the girl and tears of despair crept from the corners of her eyes.

Roger found his feet and sprang erect to tower over his captive in a sadistic and aggressive manner. The integrity of the straps allayed his concerns. He relaxed his clinched fists and pushed Clara down into her seat. After refastening her free arm and insuring that her legs were adequately secured to the chair, he turned to the small window.

From here, a clear view of the driveway and the point where it intersected with the main road provided ample warning of the arrival of visitors. He expected to welcome his old friend, Bernard Biggs, any day, and the thought etched a smile where his tense grimace had been. He turned back to Clara; his lanky form silhouetted into a shadow.

Clara dropped her chin to her chest. She spoke without lifting her head. "Who are you," she moaned in despair. "What do you want with me?" Her whimpering voice would have melted the heart of any normal human being.

Roger was unmoved. He stepped closer and straddled one of the young woman's tethered legs. "You don't remember me, do you? I'm crushed Clara. I could never forget you. I recall meeting you in the stable like it was yesterday. We talked about your pony. You seemed to like me, and I liked you. Then Biggs appeared and drove me away, remember, Clara? He made you call the sheriff. I don't blame you. I blame him. That's why you're here. I want him, and he wants you. See how it is?" Roger unsnapped the fastener on his jeans with a swift motion of his hand and rubbed his knee gently against Clara's inner thigh.

Clara slowly raised her head, dreading the inevitable. She did not feel excited, scared, nervous or angry. She only felt numbness, as if the blood flow in her entire body had evaporated and her flesh had fallen asleep. Her features condensed into the cold plastic mask of a retail mannequin—her lips timorous and compressed against the anticipated assault.

Roger touched her forehead softly and moved his fluttering fingers slowly down her face like the brush of angel wings. He stopped at the tip of her nose and lifted his hand with the precursory springing motion of a practiced high-diver and landed on her plump lower lip. He traced the lines of her exquisite mouth with his middle finger and playfully inserted the tip between her lips.

Clara jerked her head to one side in revulsion at his crude suggestion. She closed her eyes and wished that she were blind.

Roger ceased his attentiveness and swung his leg free of her. He moved behind her and bunched her long voluminous hair together to expose her delicate neck and shoulders. He bent over her and sniffed near her ear for the fragrance of the forbidden—cajoling her with each probing inhalation to release the pheromones he craved.

Clara's pulsing jugular vein betrayed her pounding heart. Roger watched it swell and subside with each measured beat and imagined the salty maroon liquid surging just beneath her ivory skin. With the exaggerated grimace of a yawning beast, he glued his cavernous mouth to the throbbing vein and held it there like a lioness awaiting the suffocation and expiration of its inferior prey. He shut his eyes and dreamed the life force within her body to awaken and enter his own. He relished each palpitation, anticipated the next and felt his own heartbeat synchronize with the sinus rhythm of the young nymph's heart.

"You're insane!" Clara protested through clenched teeth. The fear that her movements might incite injury choked her and melted the iron façade she strived so hard to maintain.

"That's what they said at the hospital," Roger laughed. "But I'm out here, and they're all still there. I say that makes them insane, wouldn't you?"

Clara did not answer. She discerned the man's reflection in the large mirror occupying the corner. Roger's image appeared dwarfed in the magnificent glass and her own was a picture of sorrow and frailty. When Roger's intense gaze met her own, Clara averted her eyes, fearing the convergent glances in the mirror would intensify the experience to an unbearable level.

Roger's first reaction was of rejection, but he brushed the unpleasantness aside with a scoff and tossed Clara's hair over her head as if he was bored with her sanguine pretense. "I'll leave you now so you and the mirror can get better acquainted," he stated flatly. With no elaboration on his remark, he left the room and noisily refastened the planks to the outside door jamb with a series of sharp, hammered blows.

Clara assumed her captor's comment alluded to her vanity and gave his curtness little thought. By her recollection, she had been a prisoner for no more than two days. Her third night of captivity was fast approaching and she felt starved. It took every ounce of her will to spit out the peach halve, but she had to exploit every opportunity presented to escape. Her last attempt convinced her that she would have to employ a different strategy to secure her freedom. Hunger and thirst was as much her enemy as her heathen kidnapper. She would have to vanquish both soon for she would need considerable strength to square off against this man again.

Around eight o'clock that evening, Roger returned with biscuits and apple cider. Clara gobbled the offerings like a hungry wolf. Roger smiled, pleasantly amused by his young trophy's ravenous appetite and altered demeanor. She even thanked him for his consideration.

"Don't thank me," Roger snarled. "You're no good to me dead."

Clara let the comment pass. The food was an enormous boon to her spirit and person. She asked for nothing else, though she wanted more. She needed to get a handle on this man's nature and purpose, but he was an enigma if ever there was one.

Recollections of his earlier statements and the muddled memories surrounding their first encounter in the stable years ago ordered themselves into a cognitive sequence. "I remember you now," she said, her demure delivery bathed in the intimacy of innocence. "Why do you hate Bernard so?"

Roger shot a castigating leer at Clara from beneath furrowed brows and snapped, "You mean your "uncle", don't you?" He employed air quotes again to emphasize his point. "He and I had a deal," he explained. "I kept my end of the bargain, and he didn't. It's as simple as that."

"If it's so simple, why kidnap me? I can talk to him for you and straighten this whole thing out. He listens to me." She continued after a pause. "I'll make him listen."

Roger felt a flash of anger warm his face. "Do you know what happened to me after I left the stable that day? They sent me to a prison for the criminally insane. Biggs could have helped me. We were partners, and after he used me he acted as if we never met. Do you think I can forget that? I spent seven years in a loony bin, and he gets another medal from the Chamber of Commerce for being citizen of the year. No, he's gonna pay for what he did."

"What's your name," Clara asked, moved by the young man's sincerity.

Roger considered not telling her for an instant, but then relented. "Roger," he muttered.

"Roger, I know Bernard can be mean and uncaring at times, and I can see that he has hurt you, but whatever he's done is not worth going back to prison for, is it?"

"I'm not going back to prison."

"Roger, they're going to find you and send you back. You can't keep something like this a secret. Bernard doesn't even know I'm here. How is he going to find me?"

Roger smiled. "He'll find you. He won't stop looking for his little playmate until he does."

Clara looked stunned. How could this person possess any knowledge of any intimate details of her past?

"I read the journal he wrote," Roger explained, sensing her amazement. "You didn't know he kept a journal, did you? Probably so he could relive all those delicious moments you shared."

"Roger..."

"Shut up!" Roger barked, jumping to his feet. "You've said enough." The boy Clara thought she was reaching morphed into a thing of stone. A callous shell usurped his flesh and the glint of humanity once apparent in his eyes deadened into mounting rage.

Roger tightened the straps that bound Clara's frame to the wicker rocker. He spun her around with a contemptible disregard and lack of empathy until she faced the ancient mirror. He was completely lost in himself now and seemed to forget Clara's presence. He tiptoed to the mirror and pressed his ear against the glass and listened for the echoes his warped mind alone could hear. His arms stretched unnaturally as he cradled the mirror's enormous frame. In a dazed delirium, he whispered incoherently to whatever it was he saw.

Clara stared spellbound, twice calling Roger by name. There was no response. After a minute or two, the spell was broken and he turned away. A tear captured the dying candlelight and held it fast as it drizzled down his sullen cheek. Then, as if he recalled a forgotten appointment, he stepped briskly to the door and left.

Outside, the night matured and bade the stars welcome. The tiny, white candle that had stoically held the darkness at bay in Clara's room relinquished its station to the more formidable power. The flame flickered out and left the mystified girl alone again in darkness.

Over the next couple of days Clara's strength returned, thanks in great part to the sustenance Roger provided. It was the least the son-of-a-bitch could do. Lunch was always bread, a vegetable and a fruit. The variety delivered at regular intervals alleviated Clara's distress, but only by a little. Punctuality seemed the only redeeming quality the man possessed.

Clara was thankful for the well-prepared daily meal she received. Sometimes it was breakfast, sometimes dinner. She often grew impatient for the food to arrive. Ironically, the meals evoked painful reminders of her love of cooking and the former life awaiting her return.

She disciplined herself by mentally offering criticisms of the preparations before eating, as if she were a master chef in a five-star restaurant overseeing the efforts of her industrious understudies. The exercise rooted her identity and helped her retain an aspect of her true self in the face of the dire circumstances that colored her reality.

Her atypical host mysteriously and creepily concluded each visitation by seizing Clara by the throat in his jaws and silently holding his position for several minutes before departing. This peculiar ritual disturbed her more than any in Roger's deplorable arsenal of idiosyncrasies. Still, aside from crudely removing a sample of her hair, he had yet to harm her physically.

It was the end of Clara's first week in captivity that Roger inexplicably changed their routine. He now insisted Clara accompany him at various times of the day while he attended his duties. Typically, when he arrived, he blindfolded her with a scarlet scarf and then led her like a dog on a leash to an unfamiliar area—her ankles hobbled with rope, her hands tied behind her back. The hobbles, long enough to allow a normal step, would not tolerate an expanded stride. Should she attempt to flee, she would quickly find herself face down.

Roger was an industrious fellow and kept himself busy on projects of various kinds. He focused diligently on preparations for an event about which Clara could only speculate. The man hardly ever spoke, and when he did he barked an order to which he expected swift compliance. If Clara hesitated to obey, Roger insisted forcefully that she do so. He was serious and deranged, and Clara learned quickly not to test his resolve.

On one occasion, after lunch, Roger placed the obligatory blind over Clara's eyes, hobbled and tied her as before and led her down the stairs by the rope leash encircling her neck. He allowed her to wear her jacket, signifying this adventure would culminate outdoors.

Clara, though blindfolded, tried to impress upon her memory the extents of Roger's charade. She noted each entry and exit from the building and the ascent and descent of every stair or steep slope. From the onset and diminution of chilling winds on her face, she surmised they emerged outside several times. Roger could have misdirected her in and out of the same building for the sake of disorientation, though why he would go to such lengths was another oddity. If disorientation was the mad man's intention, the strategy worked. When Roger removed the blind and her eyes adjusted to the bright light of day, she could not orient herself to her surroundings.

He staked her out as one would a sacrificial lamb in an area surrounded on three sides by looming wax myrtle shrubbery nearly eight feet in height. The niche she occupied was about ten feet square and created by the deliberate planting of similar hedges at perpendicular angles to the main line. The overgrown vegetation constrained her sight line and afforded her a frontal view only. She remained still as marble in the token space and would have been mistaken for garden statuary to unknowing passers-by.

Roger labored tirelessly a good thirty yards away but was clearly visible within Clara's limited field of vision. Apparently, he was constructing a platform of some sort between two large oak trees. He pilfered the lumber required for his project from the littered structural timbers of a corner of Lovingdale house that had suffered from neglect and the ravages of weather. Torrential downpours and calamitous gales ripped great riffs in the building's exterior and scattered shakes and siding for nearly fifty yards in all directions.

A length of rope girthed the knotty trunks of each oak and an extended lanyard ran from each tree to its respective side of the platform. A single wooden step provided access to the "stage" front to back. 'Curious, indeed,' Clara thought. 'What on Earth is he up to?' She had no doubt of the depth of Roger's convictions and was equally convinced the fiend labored for no uncertain purpose.

CHAPTER XV

When Clara's letters ceased coming, Ellen was beside herself with worry. It was not like her daughter to stop communicating so suddenly. She implored her boss to investigate. Biggs knew immediately how serious the situation could be but offered assurances that Clara was, in all probability, enamored of a pastry chef and enjoying a long overdue and well-deserved romantic interlude.

Ellen was dissatisfied with Bernard's chauvinistic explanation and relayed her anxieties to the Circleville police. The authorities informed her that they could not issue a missing persons report unless there was sufficient cause to conclude that the party was indeed missing. Ellen would not take no for an answer and returned the next day and the next. Her heartfelt and prolonged pleading finally softened the acting lieutenant's bureaucratic stance and he agreed to contact the school in Vermont.

Ellen returned home to wait. Twenty-four hours later, news arrived that the International Culinary Institute in Vermont suffered a mysterious fire in late January. The school suspended all classes for at least thirty days to assess damages and make repairs. The lieutenant's assurances that her daughter's missing status was untenable and her lapse in letter writing understandable under the circumstances only whetted Ellen's conviction that something was wrong. Clara would never have failed to mention an incident of such paramount importance. She would have called immediately and informed her mother about it. Biggs was less convinced but, to quell Ellen's agitation, he acquiesced with a promise to engage an investigator immediately.

He called upon the services of a contract free-lancer he used on occasion when special circumstances warranted delicate handling. The man was cheap, by Biggs' standards, reliable, thoroughly corrupt and more than qualified to ask questions—and he could keep his mouth shut providing the price was right.

His name was Paul Case or "Harry" to everyone who knew him. Biggs laughed aloud when meeting Harry for the first time. The man stated stone-faced when introducing himself that, 'All my friends call me Harry, but you can too.' Biggs liked Harry straight away.

Biggs did a little investigation of his own or, rather, hired it done. He thought it wise to prevue a man's background before enlisting his services for the first time. His associates uncovered the sordid skeletons in Harry's closet in short order. Biggs believed one could never hold enough swords over the heads of potential bedfellows. He soon knew all he needed to know.

According to Biggs' intelligence sources, Mr. Case had a history as a private dick some years back. The end came when Harry agreed to burglarize the office of a female client's husband to look for evidence that might jeopardize her impending legal proceedings. The bungled episode was a farce from the beginning and quickly imploded. It did not help that Harry was intimate with the woman, or that the woman's husband was found lying sprawled out on the floor of his library with a preposterous silver ashtray where his head had been. The situation was complicated and messy, as affairs of this type generally are. Harry faced an extended stretch in San Quentin, if convicted.

The state initially threatened to charge Harry as an accomplice to murder. Luckily for Harry, the District Attorney considered another boneheaded P.I. to be small potatoes. The prosecutor offered Harry the choice between defending his shabby reputation in court and leaving California. The understanding being that the state would levy its full prosecutorial power against him should he ever return. When confronted with charges of burglary, obstruction of justice and felonious assault, Harry wisely chose a less stimulating career path. He surrendered his P.I. license and caught the next available eastbound train. He spent the next two years exploring career options and struggling to rebuild his ravaged reputation.

#

The sharp clang of the telephone awoke Harry from his customary self-approbation. He had just lathered his face with the last dregs from a can of Barbasol. With a sigh of exasperation, he hastily toweled the quickly evaporating soap from one side of his stubbled face. He grabbed the bottle of Sam Adams he had been nursing and answered the phone. It was Bernard Biggs.

Harry spat sarcastically into the receiver after swallowing a mighty mouthful of the lukewarm brew. "Oh, hello, Biggs, I was just not thinking of you." It was his fifth beer since breakfast, but who was counting...certainly not Harry.

Biggs snorted at the other end. "Harry, I got a job for you."

"Yeah, what is it this time? Do you want me to break some old lady's legs for allowing her subscription to expire?"

"You're a funny guy," Biggs spat back. "How 'bout I send over an old lady to break *your* legs for being such a smart ass, huh? How 'bout that?"

"Ok, Biggs, we could dance all day, but, to tell you the truth, my feet are killing me. Do you mind if we sit this one out?"

"Be at my office at nine a.m. tomorrow morning and I'll fill you in."

"I'll be there."

Harry was not one for dropping everything for one client and answering to anyone's beckon call, but he currently had nothing to drop but his razor. He hung up the phone and took another bitter swig from the long-necked bottle. The tepid brew went down with a hard burn, not that it mattered.

"Here we go again," he sighed, "time to pay the bills."

The next day, Harry stood in his cozy apartment challenging the bathroom mirror, ruminating over his average face and examining the lines and creases that were not visible a month before. The bottom of his white sleeveless undershirt, shrunken and threadbare from too frequent washes, rode up his generous belly and rested at navel height. His formerly muscular arms showed their softer side from lack of stimulation and rigor in his daily routine.

He neglected to shave after Biggs called the day before and now

111

had to lather with Lava soap. He moved closer to his reflection as if trying to view himself from the opposite side of the glass. He did not like what he saw, but then he never had. He was conscious of his declining appearance and reluctant to entertain thoughts that he might not be the man he used to be or even the realist he thought he was.

His appearance was average but not altogether unattractive. True, his hair was thinning and receding, but plenty of guys he knew had a lot less. He fought the desperate tendency to comb-over, choosing instead to brush his precious remaining locks defiantly straight back, flying fearlessly in the face of aging. He convinced himself that the resultant visual enlargement of his frontal lobe cast him in an intellectual light, but in his heart of hearts he knew that was bullshit.

His nose was too big for his face, his chin too recessive and his ears overtly large and perpendicularly obtrusive—a trait blatantly obvious now due to a jarhead haircut. In short, he was in dire need of a makeover, top to bottom—a solution he could not afford and would stubbornly refuse out of manly pride even if he could.

Harry imagined his dismal reflection to be a flaw in the glass or the fractal effects of steam. He ran his hand in little concentric circles across the fogged pane and watched the haze vanish and reappear with each stroke. As he moved closer to the mirror, a strange sensation of déjà vu overcame him. In a moment of mental relapse, he transported deep into his past to a time he was neither proud of nor ashamed to recollect.

#

I was born Paul Harold Case, and everything about my early life was quite ordinary. The tiny berg in southern Illinois I grew up in was typical small town America with all the corn fields, grain silos, railroad tracks and swimming holes any red blooded American child could ever want. It had little to its credit except that it was small and people were generally genuinely friendly with an eagerness to help their neighbors in need.

There was plenty to preoccupy an adolescent, but as I grew I found very little that appealed to a mid-late teen mentality. Not that it mattered. I gave my station in life little consideration, devoting no time or effort towards personal betterment. I spent the bulk of my Friday and Saturday nights during that period in my life tearing up and down backcountry roads and deserted highways in one souped-up rod or another, autographing the pavement with black tire marks and bragging about them Monday morning.

One day it all changed. During my junior year in high school, a close friend died and two lovely sisters were disfigured when their Dodge Charger left the road at high speed and slammed into an unforgiving pine tree. The accident scarred the evergreen's trunk fifteen feet above the ground and the sisters for the rest of their lives. My little town survived the tragedy, as it had and would all others, but something inside of me died that night. I was only marginally acquainted with the two girls, but the tragedy was, for me, a life-altering existential event.

From that point forward, I spent innumerable hours wandering the deer paths paralleling the scraggly banks of the Wabash River. I took a sudden deep interest in all living things and marveled how the common act of survival could manifest itself in such a multitude of strategies and adaptations. I studied them all, from the lowliest tadpole swilling about happily in its lime-green gelatinous mass to the noble white-tailed deer and red-tailed hawk. Flora and fauna abounded in the Wabash flood plain and forest bands, even as disproportionate agricultural acreage cut mercilessly into their ever-shrinking domains.

It was on one of my early morning jaunts in April that my world changed again. While I was walking along the mist-shrouded banks of the river, I happened upon a great blue heron standing still as a fence post patiently waiting for a chub or bluegill to saunter past its reedy legs. My abrupt appearance on the scene startled the creature from its repose and caused it to vault into the air. As it cleared the tops of the fresh budding trees, a diamond formation of silver jet planes painted the blue heavens with crisp lines of vapor. I watched them soar past in tight synchronization and spontaneously decided my future lay with the United States Air Force. I made a beeline for the local recruiting office on Dexter Avenue.

A few months earlier in the year, I had talked briefly with a recruiter who visited our senior class at Vilmer High School. I was due to graduate in May, but the military powers that ruled the universe could not resist the opportunity to woo as many young able bodies as they could before the halls of higher learning set them free. At the time, I had no interest in military service and considered either chroming car bumpers or operating a corn columbine as my only career options.

Psychological placement testing given to all graduating seniors, courtesy of the Aptitude and Resource Development Council of the state of Illinois, determined my personality and learning capacity to be suitable for the waste disposal profession. Confident in the integrity of their findings, the state offered me a position in the Delta Regional Landfill in Pulaski County.

My mother suggested nursing, my father barbering. I considered all three but concluded, as did my derisive peers, that the latter two constituted women's work and would be beneath my manly dignity. Had I the foresight to realize that being the only male in both fields of the fairer sex had distinct advantages, I would have been first in line.

At any rate, the lure of the skies proved stronger—that, and the verbal guarantee from my recruiter that I would ship out for Toulee, Greenland after basic training to become a Weather Radar Specialist. I informed my parents of my decision that night at the dinner table.

"You did no such thing," Mom stated, convinced the abrupt declaration was nothing more than another of her droll son's arid musings.

"I did. I'm heading for Lackland Air Force Base near San Antonio, Texas a week from Tuesday."

Assured of my sincerity, Mom cast a glance in Dad's direction, hopelessly anticipating his involvement in the discussion. Dad continued sopping up the juice from his plate of pinto beans with a pone of cornbread as if nothing were askew.

"Did you hear what our son said?" my mother asked.

"I heard it."

"Well, don't you have anything to say?"

"What can I say? What's done is done." His eyes darted at me briefly then returned to his cornbread.

"Arthur, there's a war going on, in case you haven't heard. What if they send our son to Viet Nam?"

"For Pete's sake, Grace, It's not the gaddum infantry. He'll be alright. Besides, if it don't kill him, it'll make him stronger."

My mother stared at the man she had been married to for far too long and then pushed away from the table. "That's reassuring. We all know Arthur Case is never wrong," she replied as she left the room.

Dad was convinced he was always right. But as Mom never failed to remind him, 'even a stopped clock is right twice a day'. He often half-jested when reproached for his righteous attitude by stating: "I thought I made a mistake once, but I was mistaken."

Dad winked at me and went on eating. "Pass the pepper, son."

I passed the pepper and then went upstairs to proactively pack.

#

Basic training was a snap for me. I was already in great shape, thanks, in part, to my youthful enthusiasm for the great outdoors. The routine of rising at four a.m., calisthenics until six, breakfast at seven, training and drilling until five p.m., dinner at six and lights out at ten soon began to have an invigorating and stabilizing quality about it.

I found the obstacle course almost a joke, unlike most of my flight mates who seemed unable to carry, lift or pull their own weight. I passed with flying colors (no pun intended) and the great day for deployment to our new posts finally arrived. At the end of six weeks, I was in the best shape of my young life.

The day before I was to ship out to my permanent assignment, I stood quietly, but nervously, at the foot of my impeccably made bed while our TI declared each airman's future aloud. When our TI reached my name, he smirked with his typical sociopathic indifference. "Airman Case—you will report to Chanute Technical Training Center in Illinois to begin training as a Hazardous Waste Disposal Specialist."

I should not have been surprised to learn that the so-called aptitude testing I underwent as an airman returned a similar result as my civilian experience with the pencil necks in Illinois. State and federal agencies were obviously cut from the same cloth. I guess there is no way to escape one's fate. Here I was anticipating seeing the world and I wound up right back where I started.

At the time, the title did not seem terribly bad. The true meaning behind my training instructor's disdain for my assignment became painfully obvious after my first three months of duty. Apparently, those privileged souls better served than myself referred to my lofty station by the euphemism of 'Division Dumpster Diver'. Not flattering, perhaps, but preferable to 'Bedpan Commando' or 'Skivvy Sorter'. I was the envy of indigent and homeless people everywhere. My poor attitude went south after that.

I employed every callow tool in my revolutionary arsenal; drinking, drugging, slathering my non-regulation length hair with pomade and a hundred other minor infractions. I did not possess the nerve to attack the machine with full frontal fury. I was not old enough to know better, but I was too young to care. Hell, I was just a kid; one kid against the United States Air Farce (U.S.A.F.), or as I and those of like mind fondly dubbed it, 'U Sure Are Fucked'.

Still, being a man in uniform had its advantages. I got to fly places for free, providing I located a 'hop' going my way at the prescribed time. There was never any shortage of booze, 'scripts', or weed, and I availed myself of all three more times than I can remember. In year four of my enlistment, I was practically comatose. I antagonized officers, smoked dope on the base hospital roof and bedded as many WAFS as was inhumanly possible.

On one painfully memorable December weekend, I was due to report to the base barracks for `dorm guard duty`, a rather piss poor excuse for monopolizing an airman's off-duty time. The idea of 'guarding' a dormitory was ludicrous. This dismal tradition was, no doubt, the brain fart of some past Napoleonic wannabe, but Chanute (*mi hogar lejos del hogar*), like all suck-ups, blindly followed suit.

I celebrated the occasion by polishing off a fifth of MD20/20, known affectionately as 'Mad Dog' by those in the know. I had been saving it for an auspicious occasion and this one seemed to fit the bill. It was not long before I was salivating like a mad dog, as advertised.

My "roomie", being the military brat of a lifer, dumped me onto the curb near my assigned station where I spent several lost minutes squatting on my haunches and cursing incoherently at everyone passing by. A noble two-striper overheard my ranting and kindly ushered me inside the hallowed quarters I was to guard, where he introduced me, clothes and all, to a cold shower. Hoorah, dipshits.

The airman-of-the-month I was relieving that weekend notified the unit commander of my condition, like good little boys do, and there was hell to pay come Monday morning. The good major handed me an Article 15 for "failure to adjust, non-conformism and dereliction of duty and actually threatened my stripes. Granted, there were only three, but I had endured a relentless shower of bullshit to earn them. Never-the-less, I pigheadedly resisted assimilation by continuing my one-man crusade against "the man" and refused to accept discommendation over a minor lapse in judgment.

It was to my great relief that an early release program would set me free a full three months before my enlistment expired. I applied, and my "superiors" eagerly granted my request. I counted the days and began to realize that maybe Dad was almost right. My experience did not kill me, it just made me wish I were dead; but I did feel a good deal stronger for it. My world, for better or worse, was about to change again.

The years following my four-year hitch were rambling, rootless years. The occasional girlfriend never seemed to mind my average qualities, and I, in turn, forgave them for falling short of my ideals—a fair arrangement all around. The easy attainment of my less-than-lofty aspirations provided no incentive to excel beyond the reach of the desire de jour and reduced my lifestyle to the lowest common denominator, which was, in my world, very low indeed.

I hoped all that would change when I met Lily Brown. Lily was a firebrand, scrappy and levelheaded; the kind of no-nonsense gal I needed to push me towards accomplishment and success. We were both twenty-five and filled with passion and promise. But splendiferous achievement was a concept foreign to me, and our initial attraction and infatuation sadly faded into an uninspired stream of Saturday night revelries and Sunday morning hangovers. Fights over missed opportunities and unrealized plans kept things interesting, if predictable.

It was not long before I began sleeping around, and Lily bedded a bottle. After two lackluster years, Lily left for Bermuda with her employer—a man of considerable wealth and means far beyond my own station—and I never saw her again. When I finally accepted the fact that my last chance for a better life had escaped me, I stopped aching for Lily and consoled myself with the reaffirmation that 'we can't all be dentists'. I bid adieu to love and resumed my rounder habits; c'est la vie, que sera, sera, etc., ad nauseam.

I became more cynical and insouciant, (a virtual impossibility to those who knew me), living for the moment and at home in Los Angeles or Boston, Miami or Chicago and all points in between. The country was my oyster, and I liked it that way. I fancied myself a gypsy and chose private investigating for the potential travel opportunities inherent in that profession.

Success at my newly chosen occupation facilitated rising in the morning, but the reality of an investigator's routine was anything but glamorous and exciting. The endless procession of wayward husbands and unfaithful wives cemented my notions of the infeasibility of honest trusting relationships and left me dull and uninspired after a time. Then the shit hit the fan.

One of my female clients became embroiled in a murder for hire scheme. The victim was my client's husband. I was the patsy. The fact that my client and I were also on intimate terms sealed my fate. I foolishly agreed to burglarize her husband's office for incriminating evidence that might compromise their pending divorce settlement.

My lawyer, bless his heart, had the golf course connections and country club standing to beat the system and help clear me of criminal liability—except for the burglary charge. The judge, in his infinite wisdom, suspended the sentence but demanded I surrender my P.I. license under recommendation from the Association of Investigative Services Board and the local District Attorney in and for the County of Los Angeles. My peers justifiably criticized me for 'thinking with my other head', and I had great difficulty living the episode down.

One thing was absolute; I could never again apply for a private investigator's license, or any kind of license for that matter, in the great state of California. Big deal, I despised the place anyway. Better to leave pretentiousness and status seeking to those who covet it the most. If ever there was a poster child for self-absorption and deceit, L.A. was it.

CHAPTER XVI

Los Angeles was stagnant that summer. But unlike a stagnant stream's existence— dormant and drowning in its own stink—L.A. moved, if only in a linear direction. Money fueled the engine. The smoggy megalopolis, muscled by ambition and greed, had an unquenchable thirst for notoriety. The same brandished desire for fame dripped from everyone's Carmex-craving lips and passed from wannabe to wannabe like a social disease through indigenous fish-fingered handshakes. Celebrity ruled there and painted the once attractive area with broad superficial strokes from human nature's putrid palette.

The haves and the have-nots were constantly at odds. The privileged side flaunted status and wealth; the envious others lived on the fringes of the economy convinced that their 'golden spoon' was torn from their mouths while they slept and used illicitly to fill the noses of the social elite. Yes, Los Angeles was stagnant all right, especially for the have-nots. The only change the lower classes ever noticed was the marquee at Grauman's Chinese Theater.

Christ, even the weather was ridiculously predictable—a plethora of cloudless, listless, breezeless days. Invisible pollutants belched from the pipes of countless conveyances mingled with the sea-heady atmosphere and exacerbated the daily respirations for the clueless citizenry. Millions inhaled the appalling hallmark soup that passed for breathable air, all the while professing an undying devotion to healthy living and touting their enviable lifestyle.

Granted, Southern California was not as stifling in winter. On clearer mornings, the ephemeral natural skyline of the San Gabriel Mountains lent the area great presence, if only for the briefest of times. But like the rise and fall of a promising but limited stage persona, the massifs strutted and fretted beyond downtown's man-made stage until the stench of civilization asserted its dominance and the environs reverted to tacky normalcy.

Yes, if it were not for the people, Los Angeles would be a great place to live. I counted myself among the teeming millions and was just as shallow and money-grubbing as the rest of my wretched neighbors, despite my nobler assertions. Why else would I be here? Rubbing shoulders with all the vermin associated with the "entertainment" industry offered endless opportunities for a man of my vocation to turn a buck, and I often made off like a fat rat.

I set myself up as a private investigator—the emphasis on 'private'—and delighted in finagling and dissecting the sordid details of the lives of the "beautiful people" that sought my council. 'Soulless' would be a more apropos description of my clientele; but God is the wiser judge. Any adjudication concerning deserved inheritance in the hereafter is better left in his capable and almighty hands.

I busied myself with concealing the facts as quickly and quietly as I uncovered them—for a price, of course. The grimier and grittier the situation, the higher the fee. That was only fair. The vulgar species that inhabited the concrete abomination from Long Beach to 'the Valley' knew the price of their behavior and were willing to share their wealth as the cost of doing business. It was better to pay out the nose for protection than to curb one's sybaritic habits. Go figure. I could not make them curtail their hedonism, but I often made them wish they had.

On one particularly soulless day, the blue-grey smog hugged the choking coast to its breast and refused to let her go. The air smelled like the reviews of the last movie I suffered through, but that alone could not stop me from attending my appointed rounds. I was at the office at the ungodly hour of eleven a.m. sharp, when *she* walked in.

You get used to beauty and glamour in this town, but not to class. Class is a commodity Los Angeles could use in spades. I could tell in a heartbeat that she was an out-of-towner. I feasted my eyes for a good thirty seconds before rolling in my tongue and offering her an obligatory seat.

She was the 'dishy' type, used to spending money hand over fist and stepping over men, but what did I care. The other men in her past and present had nothing on me—aside from looks, charm and money. I represented her future, and I deceived myself into believing such a lofty goal was obtainable the minute she removed her Foster-Grants and dazzled me with her emerald stare. She was dressed to the nines like most women of her station, and I forgot my train of thought when the hem of her yellow-silk Halston skirt hitched a ride up her honey-tanned thighs.

"Mr. Case..." she began. Her sultry voice shattered my stupor and left me red-faced like a naughty child caught with his pants down. She expertly placed a Virginia Slim between the folds of her berry-red lips where it hung impatiently waiting for the opportunity to indulge her. "Got a light?" she purred coyly, knowing full well I would scour my office and the entire building until I found one.

As luck would have it, my previous client had left his gold-plated Dunhill lighter a month before when hastily departing my office. I intended to return it, of course, but it was such a pretty thing. Given the elegantly engraved initials on its eighteen-carat surface matched my own, I saw no harm in keeping it until such time I could return it to its rightful owner's vest pocket.

I leaned over casually, holding the lighter inches from her slightly upturned nose long enough for her to assess the article's quality and value. With a flick of my thumb, the butane flame roared to life nearly singing her eyebrows in its fervor. She was cool as a bottle of Coke and never flinched. Taking my jittery hand in her own, she guided the dancing flame until it kissed her cigarette. Her touch was alternately calming and exhilarating. She drew a mouthful of smoke into her ample lungs, inhaled it French-style through her nose and directed the remnant cloud in my direction with playful contempt and a wicked smile.

A pulse of pain in the web of my hand between thumb and forefinger followed the sharp snap when I flicked the lighter's case shut. Embarrassed, I masked my discomfort and surprise in a pivot away and returned to my desk. I speedily deposited the offensive device in my trouser pocket. I left my hand therein. Where I surreptitiously rubbed it gently across the pocket's flannel inner lining to sooth any mangled tissue.

"Sorry..." she said with a half-smirk. "Thanks for the light."

"It's nothing," I lied. "What brings you to see me today?"

"It's my monster husband," she answered with a pout after

dragging in another mouthful of carcinogenic vapor. "He doesn't appreciate me anymore."

"I find that hard to believe. What is he, deaf, dumb and blind?"

"He might as well be," she cooed. "He wants a divorce. He says I am only after his money."

"Well, are you?"

"Of course I am, but that is beside the point. I have been with him for six months now. I deserve something for that, don't I?" Her arched eyebrows and batting lashes accentuated the sparkling depth of her jade-green peepers.

"I would think so," I lied again. "But we all have a little monster in us, don't we? What makes me any different?"

"I think I can trust you," she answered. The lying was getting contagious. "If you buy me dinner tonight, I'll fill you in on the whys and wherefores."

"I'd like nothing better, but won't your husband object?"

"The old goat's out of town this week...for the whole week. That's seven days for those of us who can count—plenty of time to get acquainted. I'll call you with the details of where to meet, if you're interested." With that, she rose and glided to the door.

Her frankness was refreshing and the possibilities intrigued me. I said what I always say when caught off guard. "Ok, when do we start?"

"We already have," she teased, blowing me a kiss.

Ok, she had opened the door, and I blundered in. She left me with an emptiness inside and a gnawing hunger. I chewed my pencil to bits while I digested the fruits of our impromptu meeting along with the pencil's eraser. Staring wistfully out the window of my second story suite, I watched her emerge from the building and climb into the back of a silver Jag. She glanced up at me as she swung her sinewy legs into the back seat. Even from here, the sight of her made me weak in the knees. She was smart bait for sure, and I was one shark that just had to take a nibble.

She called later that evening. We met at a jazz club called Wiggy's on La Cienega and Melrose. She wore black—an obvious sign that I was in for trouble. But 'trouble' being my middle name (born standing up and talking back, and all that) I was game for a dame, if you catch my drift.

The joint smelled of cheap cigars and cheaper cologne, but the music was tight. A tough little torch singer was scorching the crowd with a love-lost number and the trio behind her had no trouble fanning the flames. I sat down beside my date realizing I had no recollection of her name. So struck was I during our first meeting, I failed to ask.

"Misty," she whispered, as if reading my thoughts.

"I beg your pardon," I stammered.

"My name is Misty; in case you were wondering."

"Well, hello, Misty. I *was* wondering," I admitted.

"It's short for Mistral. I'm named for a cold wind in France."

"Then you're French?"

"No, I'm from Toledo."

"Oh, very pretty name," I replied, "but it doesn't do you justice."

"Thanks," she said dismissively, as if compliments bored her to tears. "Let's dance."

She slinked to the dance floor like a snow leopard in heat. I followed puppy-like and soon fell into the swing of the crowd. The syncopated music swept us away with its suave melody and dropped us on the verge of an inescapable embrace. As she swayed, the spun silk fabric of her dress caressed her curves like lathered soap. I had no claim on the real deal underneath, but I had a chance if I played my cards right. As conjectures go it was a long shot, but I was bound to test my theory just the same.

After imbibing several more stiff drinks and cutting the rug to pieces, we agreed to reconvene at her estate in Palos Verdes to discuss the particulars of our arrangement. She insisted we leave separately. She employed a waiting driver and I was to tail her, inconspicuously, of course—a chance to prove my mettle as an undercover operative. I accepted the challenge and arrived at her place around midnight just as her chauffeur pulled the silver Jaguar out of sight.

She told me to use the side entrance and I obliged. Her lips met me at the door and after she kissed me, I stood with eyes closed waiting for the rest of me to arrive. When I opened one eye, she was flirtatiously ascending an open staircase across the room, dragging her evening wrap behind her. This puppy was on a short leash, and every step she took compelled me to follow.

A short while later, 'short' being the operative word, I was nude and lying languidly across the velvet covering on her bed wondering what had just happened to me. She rose unexpectedly and I reached out in panic lest I lose her forever.

She brushed my eager arms aside and drifted like a lioness on a cloud to the open window overlooking her private garden. I was under her spell now, and every nuance of her feminine mannerisms hammered the message home. I was hers and she knew it. Now it was time for the real fun to begin.

"He's going to destroy me," she lamented. A sheepish glance in my direction told me she expected an immediate response. When I remained silent, she elaborated. "I haven't always been a good girl," she explained. "Two years ago, I did some things I'm not very proud of. He has proof—a letter I wrote. I was stoned most of the time back then, and I needed money. Anyway, he has it. It's in his office safe. If I don't get it back, he'll use it to discredit me during our divorce proceedings." She began trembling as her voice quivered with believable emotion.

"Hold on," I interjected. "Tell me what happened."

"I got involved with a hooker named Kenzie who was trying to extort money from a financier she was dating. She said he owed her big time, and I could have half of everything she got if I sort of set him up to be embarrassed."

"What do you mean by 'sort of'?"

"Will you let me finish, please?" She paused briefly and pinched the bridge of her nose between thumb and fore finger as she collected her thoughts. "I agreed to help her", she continued, "and went with her to his house that night. I've always looked young for my age, and Kenzie wanted me to pretend to be a runaway. If he let me in, which was likely, I was to seduce him. She was supposed to be there to record our little escapade. Anyway, she was there, all right, but he was dead. She shot him with his own gun and threatened to blame it on me unless I helped her clean up the mess and make it look like a suicide. I was scared and had no clue what to do, so I helped her. She made me write the suicide note. The police arrested us a day later on suspicion of murder.

I met Arnie, that's my husband, through my attorney. Arnie somehow bought the suicide note from the police, I don't know how for sure, and managed to get the charges against me reduced for lack of evidence. They charged me with being an unwitting accomplice and placed me on probation. I've been living with him ever since. Now he's met someone else and wants me out of the picture."

I moved in behind her and caressed her ivory shoulders as the tears flowed. Her seeming sincerity touched me, and the fact she had chosen to tell me the most intimate details of her past moved me deeply. Despite our brief interlude, or perhaps because of it, I vowed to do all in my power to help.

Afterward, we engaged in a long night of merry making that reinforced our bond and cemented my loyalty to the cause. Breakfast came and went. Over a second cup of Cuban espresso, she laid out a well-conceived plan to retrieve said note in light of Arnie's importunate absence. We were to enter his office on Wilshire Boulevard after nine p.m. She assured me she had visited the premises many times at that hour and the guards would not be suspicious. I knew she was taking me for a ride, but what did I care? I had been on lots of rides lately and they all led to the same place—nowhere. Maybe this time would be different and I would finally wind up where I longed to be.

We arrived at the old fart's domain at nine p.m. The guards practically tripped over themselves trying to resolve who would open the door for Misty this time. She laughed good-heartedly and thanked them for their trouble. They escorted us to the elevator. Actually, they escorted her. I just played caboose. We ascended in silence to the penthouse suite. She smelled incredible.

When we arrived at Suite A-1 (named in tribute to the occupant's ego, no doubt) we found the door unlocked. Misty cast a cautious glance my way, then turned the knob and entered warily. The office appeared to be unoccupied.

"Over here," Misty directed, stepping silently to an area behind her husband's desk. "The safe is behind this painting."

"How clever," I scoffed. "No one would ever think of looking there."

She pulled the stylized velvet image of Elvis from its mooring to expose a square safe recessed into the wall.

"Great," I scoffed again, "now all we have to do is get in."

"I've got the combination," she offered, slightly annoyed. "I'm not stupid, you know."

Actually, I had no clue whether she was stupid or not, but I thought it better to hold my tongue before casting aspersions and did so as she whispered the first number. At that moment, I heard a distinct double-click. I thought it unlikely we had gained entry with so little effort, but I paused just the same and tried the handle.

"Find what you were looking for?" A sarcastic baritone edged the darkness aside before the green-hooded desk lamp had a chance.

We turned simultaneously in the direction of the voice and met the barrel of a .38 caliber Smith & Wesson revolver head on.

"What are you doing here?" Misty exclaimed before realizing what she had said. Then, in an attempt to mitigate her blunder and construct a ruse, continued: "Oh, Arnie! I'm so glad to see you. This man forced me here! He said he would..."

"Stow it, baby. I'm not interested in explanations." Arnie spat, cutting her off at the knees. "I thought I would come back early and surprise you. Looks like I did."

"Arnie, please," she pleaded, gravitating to his side.

The distraction was all I needed. I rushed him, eyes fixed on the weapon in his hammy fist. Our collision knocked him back against his desk and caused the gun to fire. Misty ducked away while I struggled with her husband for control of the revolver. The heater's three-inch-long barrel afforded me adequate purchase to wrestle it from his grasp.

The tables had turned. I held him at bay while I glanced into the room for my partner in crime. "Misty!" I strained through clenched teeth. "We've got to get out of here. The guards had to have heard that shot. They will be here in minutes!"

There was no answer.

"Misty!" I reiterated more loudly.

From behind her husband's head, I saw rise an enormous silver and black object. I had admired the freestanding ashtray earlier near the desk. I sensed an ominous conclusion and shouted, "No!" It was too late. The object fell with deliberate intent across the man's skull, splitting it like a melon. He slumped to the floor.

Misty's trembling body appeared where her husband formerly stood. A deranged, homicidal rage distorted her classic features into the raging mask of a demon. Her breath came in shallow staccato gasps and her arms remained raised even after she dropped the murderous weapon upon what was left of the man's skull with a sickening thud.

"You crazy..." Before I could complete my latent admonition, two uniforms burst through the office doors and centered us in their gun sights.

I looked down at the crumpled mass before me that moments before had hopes, dreams, memories and life.

Misty walked casually to the window as Barney-1 picked up the telephone receiver from the floor where it had fallen. Barney-2 disarmed me and kept us covered. "I want to report a murder," Barney-1 disclosed to the 911 operator on the other end of the line, "and a break-in...900 Wilshire Boulevard. Suspects in custody... repeat...suspects in custody. Get here, pronto...over."

I sank into Arnie's executive chair. His splattered blood writhed upon the red leather upholstery as if the maroon liquid was a host of living, breathing organisms. Dizziness and disbelief overwhelmed me. My discombobulated brain sloshed from side to side inside my skull like a bucket of frogs atop a spineless fleshy column. I closed my eyes and quieted my nerves with assurances that the nightmare would soon be over. This was one place I definitely *never* longed to be.

CHAPTER XVII

When it all blew over, I vowed again to give up women (yeah, right…good luck with that). I moved back east and took up residence in Ohio, where I rekindled a childhood interest in writing. My hope was to earn my keep as a journalist. Although hamstrung by a lack of formal education, my natural talent for detail and description honed keen through dedication to my former craft held me in good stead with my contemporaries. I found smaller newspapers and magazines eager to enlist my services and publish my work and, through unprecedented dedication and focus, managed to sustain myself comfortably from gig to gig. Still, after the novelty of whacking out deadlines wore off, that, too, became stale and repetitive.

It was on Groundhog Day, February 20__ that I found myself on business of a nature quite different from the usual tiresome and banal endeavors I had grown accustomed to and, I must say, I found the departure refreshing. A small newspaper, *The Village Clarion*, several miles south of the town in which I currently resided rescued me from my baneful existence to investigate the disappearance of the publisher's goddaughter.

The lass had obtained a cooking scholarship to attend a small, but renown, culinary institute in New England for the fall and had simply vanished before the semester's end. The young woman's mother, an employee of my client, was convinced that some ill fate had befallen her daughter and had emphatically entreated upon her employer to initiate a search effort.

The publisher, Mr. Bernard Biggs, passed the affair off as an impulsive act of youthful rebellion and was certain the young woman had met a dashing freshman and put her culinary ambitions on hold while she pursued interests of a more discreet and personal nature. Nevertheless, he acquiesced and assured the distraught woman that he would launch a full-scale inquiry into her loved one's whereabouts and spare no expense finding and returning her to the bosom of her loving family—should his agent uncover anything of sinister note or facts that intimated something ominous was indeed afoot.

The publisher's apparent lack of conviction concerning the seriousness of the matter prompted him to dispatch no greater qualified investigator than myself. However, in my defense, let me state that my talents were not without merit. My investigative background served me in good stead and I proved myself reliable on previous assignments. I had worked before for Bernard Biggs on a number of occasions on matters of lesser import. My fees were quite reasonable and I garnered results commensurate with my efforts.

Mr. Biggs, being the sort who preferred attending to his own affairs as long as he could find others to do the dirty work, felt confident someone of my credentials could handle any preliminary inquiries. The authorities would always be there, if needed, and he could ply their resources should my own investigation prove unfruitful.

Our meeting took place in Biggs' private office the following day. It was a cold, grey morning with a smattering of snow vacillating weightlessly in the chilly air.

"Just find her, Harry." Biggs demanded. "Her mother is worried sick, and I haven't had a minute's rest in weeks."

"I'm a journalist now, Biggs, or at least that's what I tell myself and anyone who asks. I haven't done any personal investigative work in years…and I'm non-licensable."

"You don't need a license to ask questions," Biggs answered immediately. "You just find my goddaughter." His ruddy face deepened two shades and his knitted brow betrayed his Neanderthal ancestry.

"Relax, Biggs, I'll find her. What's her name again and what does she look like?"

"Everything you need is in here," Biggs replied, tossing a manila-flavored legal envelope in my lap.

I rummaged hungrily through the assortment of papers. "What, no eight-by-ten glossy? Wait a minute...here it is."

Biggs looked annoyed.

I pulled the photograph from the envelope and practiced an anemic wolfish whistle through my thin chapped lips. "Not bad," I exclaimed admiringly.

"I hope you don't think with your groin on this one," Biggs spouted in his trademark accusatory tone.

I smiled and fed the photograph back into the quickly warming envelope. "I'll read the rest later. Look, you called me here because you know I can do the job. Am I correct? So quit worrying."

"Her name is Clara Connor." Biggs resumed, "Everyone's called her Kim since she was a baby, but she prefers Clara now. She is my only godchild and more precious to me than life itself. You follow? Her mother sent her off to some cooking school they call a "culinary institute" in upstate Vermont. I tried to persuade Kim, er...Clara...to attend Ohio State University in Columbus, but she would not hear of it. You know how kids are?"

"Yeah, I know how they are," I answered not really knowing. "And that's quite a statement considering I've never had any of my own...at least none I know of."

Biggs dismissed the comment as irrelevant, immaterial, etc., etc., and continued. "And now, there's a hole in the screen door. Do you know what happens when you fail to fix a hole in the screen door, Harry? Not only do you let the canary out, you let the flies in. The girl's mother contacted the police without my knowledge and filed a missing person report, and now my offices are swarming with every two-bit reporter from Baltimore to Pittsburg; flies, all of them."

"Yeah, I know about flies, too. I'm one myself."

"You're different," Biggs corrected. "I asked you here."

"You know, Biggs, a missing person report is a smart move. You can never have too much help or too many eyes looking for the prize." I tried to assuage the worried man's fears with some positive rhetoric and thus assure him that my concerns were aligned with his own.

Biggs walked to his mammoth office window and gazed from the superiority of its fourth story prominence upon the streets he felt he ruled by divine right. After a moment's reflection, he seated himself in his black, brass-studded, leather chair and squeezed behind his Italian designed mahogany desk. Closing his eyes seemed to quiet his racing mind and calm his inner angst before he continued his presentation. He locked his fingers behind his over-sized head and glanced around his capacious office at all the trappings of his fruitful life.

He picked up a bronzed, miniature golf-club paperweight and held it lovingly in his hands while he read the inscription for the umpteenth time: *'Keep Swinging'*. "My wife gave this to me before she passed away. We were married for twenty-seven years."

"Look," I interrupted. "If you're gonna tell me your life story, I'm gonna need a drink."

Biggs snorted through his nostrils dispelling all traces of sentimentality and placed the object back in its revered spot near his wife's photograph.

"You were married once, weren't you? What was her name?" He asked, snapping his fingers repeatedly, as if the ritual would excite his memory.

"Lily."

"Lily, that's the one. She was some gal, a lot of upkeep, though. You should have kept her, Harry. What happened anyhow?"

"Who knows? She got tired of my habits, I guess. The first two years were great. Then something happened. She became shrill and demanding...and critical." I paused as I felt my mood dampening and the old familiar veil of unhappiness descending upon me. "I suppose two years were all I deserved."

"Maybe you didn't satisfy her as a man?" Biggs commented.

I looked up with a wince in my eye and deduced from the man's body language and anticipatory glance that the bastard was baiting me.

"Hey, look," Biggs explained. "It happens. It has nothing to do with how much lead you've got in your pencil. Women need more. More than a schmuck like you or I could ever give them. Which reminds me of a joke that seems fitting: *What four animals does every woman wish she had around the house?*"

I reeled in my impatience. "I couldn't begin to guess."

"*...A Jaguar in the garage, a mink in the closet, a tiger in the bedroom, and a jackass to pay for it all.*" Biggs exploded with laughter.

I managed a small guffaw and added, "Yeah, I can see how that would be fitting in your case, but I don't have any trouble with dames. So, speak for yourself."

"Listen to you…'dames', he says. Who do you think you are—some hard-boiled gumshoe in a Mickey Spillane novel? This is the sensitive century, Harry. Haven't you heard?"

"Mickey Spillane? I didn't know you could read, Biggs. You're a fine one to talk about sensitivity. Your only godchild is missing and you won't even spring for airfare. I've got to take a stinking bus to some stinking berg in the stinking sticks because you're too stinking cheap to send me first class by air."

Biggs perked up. "Does this mean you'll be going?"

"I guess it does, but I'll need a gun."

"A gun...what on earth do you need a gun for? You're going after a teenager, Harry, not a goddamned drug lord."

I slipped a little further into another of Biggs' fine leather upholstered chairs and kicked my feet out in front of me. Crossing my legs at the ankle and folding my arms underlined the firmness of my position. I felt ridiculous.

"That may be true…but there are a lot of unsavory types out there, and I have an uncanny way of meeting up with them. No gun, no go."

"Alright, Harry, you'll get your gun. Any particular make or model?"

"Of course...Walther," I answered without hesitation…"PPK and an extra magazine...plus two boxes of jacketed shells, .380 caliber, in case you didn't know."

"Anything else, Mr. Marlowe," Biggs asked sarcastically, "or is it 'Bond', now?"

"Hey, you really can read, but Marlowe was Raymond Chandler, I'm more of the Mike Hammer type. Bond? Yeah, you can call me Bond...Harry Bond." I laughed at my cleverness, but I knew I would never make it in stand-up and reminded myself not to quit my day job. "I want a place to stay when I get there for as long as I need it and a couple hundred to get me started on my merry way. I'll wire you when the money runs out and you can send me more."

Biggs laughed. "That's what I like about you, Harry. Straight up and to the point. I'll make sure you have everything you need. You just make sure you find my goddaughter."

I rose and stretched before donning my tan, English Fog trench coat and brown fedora.

"That's what I like about you, Biggs," I replied, reluctant to let the opportunity pass. "Always willing to pay someone else to do what you should be doing yourself." I leaned in his direction and waited for my remark to have its intended effect.

Biggs did not flinch. He turned again to his office window and stared down upon the slate-grey world beyond, his hands buried deep in his trouser pockets. He called me back before I hit the door. "Harry, one more thing...I love my goddaughter deeply. She's a very attractive girl...young and impressionable. I don't want to hear of any shenanigans when you find her. You follow?"

I felt insulted, but I admitted to myself that shenanigans were not that far outside the realm of possibilities. "Don't worry, Biggs," I answered as convincingly as my poor acting ability could convey. "You'll know the minute I find her...as long as your checks don't bounce."

Biggs chuckled again. "That's what I like about you, Harry. You are such a mercenary. Now get out of her, I have work to do. And see that you don't waste my money." Biggs stuffed his bellicose behind between the puffy arms of his studded chair again and shuffled some papers around in pretense of attending to urgent affairs.

I opened the office door and turned for a last look back, determined to get in the final shot. "That's what I like about you, Biggs," I reciprocated. "You're such a bastard."

CHAPTER XVIII

I always considered midnight the best time to begin a trip. By the time day breaks, a major portion of the tedious beginning miles have eroded away leaving any negative preconceptions behind you.

It was pouring rain, but I was in good spirits and optimistic of concluding my assignment in gloriously non-dramatic fashion. The venerable Biggs had dispatched a car and driver to see me to the Greyhound bus depot. Without further ado, I was off.

Before the first hundred miles had transpired, I fell into a deep slumber and was quite surprised upon awakening to discover how much of my journey had transpired since my embarkation. The dawn of day restored my vigor, and I was reassured to find my effects still situated upon my lap as they were when my journey and nap began. My destination was closer than I thought possible and the realization filled me with anticipation.

However, the next several hours were an endless stream of non-descript All-American towns, bathroom breaks and squalling babies. I was understandably relieved when the bus passed across the Vermont state line. After a time, the landscape took on a stark, surreal quality quite out of step with my former observations.

I began to notice a distinct change in the atmosphere, and an uneasiness rising from the pit of my stomach settled over me like the dust that caked the bus's tinted sliding windows. My apprehensions escalated. Hot flashes and cold sweats alternately required me to either loosen my collar to reduce my fever or clinch my crossed arms about my torso to escape the chill.

My mind felt stunned as if blasted by a powerful ray and my thoughts were peppered with darkness and despair. I grew emotionally detached from myself, as I had after learning of the sudden death of my mother when I could only ingest the enormity of what had happened incrementally and in tolerable doses.

It was during this unnerving episode that I first noticed an odd dwelling a half mile off the highway. The house seemed cold and unapproachable as anything I had ever seen. I glimpsed it only an instant, for the bus rounded a sharp curve just as the old place appeared to me through a break in the trees. The fleeting image impelled me to swivel backwards. I narrowed my gaze and maneuvered to best advantage to prolong the moment. A dense mist enveloped the old house and chased the miserable impressions from my mind.

Fellow passengers apparently found my actions queer and punctured me with disquieting eyes until I resumed a respectful frontal posture. The distinct presence of the estate was ominous and moving, and I could not explain why my fellow travelers conveyed no similar intrigue or emotion while passing it. My discomfort faded coincidentally with my relative distance from it. Aside from this singular occurrence, my pilgrimage was odiously benign.

When my bus arrived in Milford, I paused briefly on its lower step while disembarking. The folding doors clipped my rear when the nervous driver sped off with no regard for my safety or proximity. A noxious cloud of black diesel smoke belched from the transport's rattling tailpipe. With a gut-straining cough, I jumped to the curb. The brutish conveyance bullied its way down the narrow street and disappeared from view.

I held the dubious distinction of being the sole passenger to claim Milford as his destination, but I was unprepared for the peculiar nature of the local citizenry. Perturbed as I was at the bus driver's inconsideration, I gathered my thoughts and proceeded along a ragged canopied platform to a small café. There were few customers inside. I preferred sitting at the counter, and did so, laying my briefcase and jacket on the stool to my right. A limping waitress half-heartedly wiped the counter in front of me with a soiled cloth without a word or glance of acknowledgement. Wiry fuses of hair accented the sides of her misshapen head and a mop-like profusion gathered with an elastic sprang from the top of her scalp like a clump of liriope.

"Excuse me," I interjected impatiently, still irritable from my travels. "I'd like to order something, if I may?"

The apathetic matron dropped her oily dishrag near me as she hobbled around the corner of the counter and into what appeared to be the kitchen. I stared after her in disbelief and turned to catch the reaction of my fellow patrons. No one seemed to notice the impertinence directed toward me and went about their idle conversations as if nothing was amiss.

"Did you see that?" I asked no one in particular. No one in particular answered. When I turned around again, a cruel looking young man stood startling close before me.

His ginger hair hugged his scalp and his dull, rheumy eyes presented an unhealthy appearance due to fatigue, eye shadow or both. A dingy white apron hung shabbily about his torso and smears of dried blood or oven grease decorated its front. My face reflected from an ebony-handled cleaver held chest-high that cried out to me as if my name were engraved upon it.

I blinked several times before his image reconciled itself and I found my voice. "Oh, uh, hello," I stammered. "Do you serve ham sandwiches?"

The boy nodded.

"Could I have one of those, please, with a cup of coffee? Oh, and hold the mayo."

The boy nodded again but did not move. He stood staring at me and I at him until a shrill voice demanded his presence in the kitchen. He turned slowly and ambled off. I shook my head in disbelief. "Locals," I muttered beneath my breath. I retrieved my briefcase, pulled some papers from it and spread them carefully before me on the counter. The picture of the subject of my investigation was on top. I re-examined the portrait once more and admired the comely lass until my meal arrived.

"Hey, watch it," I reprimanded curtly, when the server tossed my order in front of me with a pronounced thud. He stared at me with the blank expression of a drugged mental patient. "That'll be six-fifty," he demanded with an outstretched hand.

After moving the plate of food and securing the papers back in my briefcase, I gave the youth the exact amount and thanked him for his efforts. "What's with these people?" I growled rhetorically, not caring if anyone heard. Common sense suggested I examine the preparation before ingesting it. I discovered between the stale slices of bread an appalling wrinkled "pigskin" wallowing in a heavy smear of yellowed condiment. I shot a reproving glance towards the kitchen as I vigorously scraped away the offensive substance from my sandwich with the plastic fork so thoughtfully provided.

As I was starving, I took a bite despite my misgivings. The entire portion of meat, and I use the word 'meat' lightly, slipped from between the bun and dangled like a swollen tongue upon my chin. A corpse-like odor enraged my nostrils, and I spat out the malodorous matter immediately. A quick rinse was in order to remove its sordid aftertaste, but the coffee I followed it with only heightened the foulness. My typically hardy appetite evaporated into oblivion, and I gagged when a cockroach clambered defiantly across my plate.

I jumped to my feet and glared with outrage through the kitchen pass-thru that punctuated the back of the wall opposite me. The reflection in a mirror left of the pass-thru informed me that I was now alone in the establishment. I marched determinedly down the length of counter and entered the kitchen. The stench of singed meat and hair assaulted my olfactory nerve as I entered. Slimed pots blotched with grey fuzzy matter festered on counters and food scraps and drippings soiled the once proud floor.

The area was trapezoidal with an opening at the narrow end that dissolved into blackness. A spark of fear appended my outrage as I approached the darkened recess. I sensed moving shadows beyond. A scarcely audible scratching sound drew me forward. I could feel rivulets of sweat dribble down my back despite the kitchen's dominating clamminess. When I stopped less than a dozen feet from the end of the space, a pair of disembodied eyes red as embers and two rows of ivory dagger-like teeth sprang in my direction.

A rush of adrenaline flooded my veins. Terrified and off-guard, I deflected backwards and tripped. I twisted as I fell and glanced toward the well-lit area I now coveted. It loomed miles away distorted by a dreamy, translucent curtain that rippled uncannily before my eyes.

Just as suddenly as the threat materialized, it vanished. I regained musculature control and struggled back to relative comfort. I collided with the obnoxious waitress as I transitioned from darkness to light. The dim, witless face of the cretin server lurched over her shoulder like a hunchback's defect.

"What are you doing back here?" the crone demanded.

The top-cropped teenager stepped to the side still brandishing the cleaver, his obvious weapon of choice. "No one's allowed back here," he stated defensively.

With excitement and disbelief, I turned and pointed to the black hole from which I had just escaped. "There's an animal back there!" I exclaimed. "It came after me!"

"Animal?" The woman questioned, "What animal? The only animals here were killed and quartered days ago."

"It attacked me," I implored. "It was in the back. Surely you've seen it."

"There's no animal here," she reiterated.

"You better get going, mister," the boy added aggressively. He raised the cleaver slightly, reaffirming his grip on its ebony handle.

With a groan of incredulity and a third glance into the void, I brushed the unusual pair aside with my elbow as I passed. My briefcase lay on the floor. I may have knocked it unknowingly from its pedestal before, but its inverted position posed a different theory.

I picked it up and brushed away the scraps of food clinging to its leather surface. The gold latches bore several visible scars as if someone used considerable force with a prying instrument to compromise the locks. However, the papers inside were intact, so I concluded the case must have been damaged from the fall from the stool.

A backward glance at the two bizarre people inside convinced me that leaving was my best and only option. I gathered my belongings and left the dreadful spot immediately. Once outside, a revitalizing spurt of February sun worked wonders in dispelling the lurid oppressiveness of the café.

I then set about procuring suitable lodgings for the duration of my stay in this strangest of communities. I foolishly neglected to reserve accommodations before my departure. If the first day of my adventure was typical of the remainder of my time here, I had possibly bitten off more than I could chew.

Between the cursed café and the Ambloy Hotel, I saw no one. Evening was settling in and the streets were deserted. The downtown itself was a collection of staid, red-bricked structures, each remaining true to a parent design of colonial interpretation. The white trimmed windows and black shutters were consistent from storefront to office building and held a pleasant contrast to the uniform blood-hued exteriors and grey-shingled roofs.

This congruity ended abruptly where the main way crossed an abandoned railroad track that bisected the business district. On the far side of the tracks, sordid structures in varying states of disarray struggled to retain their footing along narrow passageways of broken pavement. Refuse buried the sidewalks two layers deep. Newspapers, plastic bags, paper cups and articles of castaway clothing blew helter-skelter up and down the alleys and into the streets. The air stank of urine and animal waste and, now and again, rodents scurried from gutter to gutter searching through the litter for edible offal or a pool of potable water to defile with their presence.

It was difficult to continue along this abhorrent route, but the Ambloy Hotel shown ahead with its flickering neon marquis dancing seductively. The establishment, being quite possibly the only accommodations in town, would have to serve as a headquarters from which I could expand my inquiry.

The thought occurred to me as to why any school, culinary or otherwise, would invest in such a deplorable region. The answer, of course, was that the mission statement of the State College Board and the wise regents responsible for regulating such matters was to spread enlightenment and prosperity to those regions of the state most sorely in need of it. Regardless of the obvious irrationality of their conclusions and mitigating circumstances aside, the overall repugnance of the area alone should have signaled concern.

At any rate, it was here my investigation would begin. The college where the subject of my search had enrolled lay beyond the outskirts of town, but the subject's last verified credit card purchase placed her in a tiny, north-side boutique. Prudence argued to pursue the more recent lead. Theoretically, the trail would be warmer and a wiser bet...theoretically. I would visit the boutique on the morrow. For now, my foremost concern was securing a bed and a bath.

"Greetings," the clerk shouted from behind a chest-high counter as I entered the lobby, scarcely waiting for the door to close behind me.

The loudness of his perfunctory address startled me and the intensity of his gaze fixed me like a bayonet.

"Hello," I answered circumspectly. "I'd like a room, please." The strange looking man's countenance held my stare longer than I liked.

The clerk was a wiry man of around thirty years of age. Centered on his face and confined by a donut of hair that circled his head like marauding Indians, a demonstrative snout protruded like a shark's fin. Parted mercilessly by this cartilaginous fin, two widely-spaced, amblyopic orbs contended with each other for dominance. When the man spread his gaping wound of a mouth to speak, an inordinate number of king-sized, irregular teeth presented themselves for extraction. This was not the first time I had seen teeth in a horse's ass, I thought.

"For how long?" he droned.

"For as long as I need it," I snapped.

"Very good, sir. Please sign here." He spun an ornately bound ledger filled with discolored brittle paper and pushed it across the counter. He handed me a black pen with a peculiar feather attached to its non-business end. "We only have one room," he instructed, "top of the stairs…end of the hallway…Room 18."

"That's funny," I observed, "the place looks deserted."

"That *is* funny," he smirked menacingly. He extended a gold skeleton key that protruded from a fist of fleshless fingers that gathered at the terminus of his bony arm. The key's large head was an ornate affair of well-conceived design, and consisted of mirrored birds with the number eighteen held fast between their breasts. I plucked the item from his grasp and offered it a second glance to confirm one of his skeletal fingers did not detach along with it.

I then became aware that a mottled collection of pale blue fibers covered every surface in the lobby. Closer inspection revealed the substance to be similar in texture and appearance to shredded fiberglass matting, yet it was feathery and light enough to disperse with a footstep. Interestingly, the only visible footprints in the azure snow were my own despite the clerk's implication of a full house.

The staircase ascended in an arc along one side of the lobby. The blue fibers fled before my footfalls. The staircase treads and risers, carpeted in threadbare maroon wool, were scarcely discernable beneath the layer of filaments. I displaced a square yard of the fibrous material at the foot of the stairs with several waves of my hand to reveal a spiraling pattern of winged cherubs and surmised the pattern logically repeated throughout the carpet's length and breadth.

At the top of the stairs, bare bulbs of low wattage alternately placed at intervals along each wall dimly lit a gloomy hallway. The corridor advanced some eighty odd feet to a green door with the number eighteen thereon in tarnished brass. No other doors had numbers, nor was there any sound or sign of occupation therein. To compound my confoundedness, the knobs on all the doors but room Number 18 were missing.

My new home away from home was about twelve feet square and sparsely furnished. A wafer thin mattress on a frame of brown tubular steel construction dominated the space. A catty-cornered chair and tiny dresser of black wood topped with a fractured mirror occupied the far end. Above the bed hung a poorly framed, darkly-paletted oil painting—its crazed yellow varnish bespeaking great age. I could not help but admire the artist's deft hand and imaginative composition, although I found the depiction quite disturbing—a dismal farm scene with an upset cart surrounded by the sprawled bodies of injured passengers. Sleeping beneath so graphic a depiction of possible death and certain injury might prove unsettling under ordinary circumstances, but the difficulties of my journey so far overruled its disquieting qualities.

A dingy but adequate bathroom complete with sink, stool and shower offered me opportunity to settle in and unwind. I availed myself of all three amenities and soon felt vital enough to review the photographs and documents I had brought with me. I placed the items carefully along one edge of the bed and committed the information to memory.

There were several photos of the girl, each showing her in different light and attire save for a distinctive red jacket with white sleeves that she obviously held in high esteem. The girl wore or carried it in every picture. She apparently loved the jacket and could have worn it the day she disappeared. It was my only solid lead so far and an important one. An article so singular would surely spark a remembrance in a town as small and insular as this one. The young woman's features were memorable as well. She would not be just another 'pretty face' to most observers and likely to ring some bells.

My search would commence as early in the morning as my body

would allow. I would begin with the purple-lipped clerk and branch out from there. I could accomplish little else tonight, so I swept the documents from the bed, except for one eight-by-ten glossy and squeezed beneath the covers. The room had grown quite cold since my shower and a chill swept over me. I slid deeper beneath the cover sheet and white crocheted spread. I lay there for some time willing my mind to etch the lines of the young woman's visage upon the backside of my drooping eyelids. I could still see her face when sleep at last sealed my eyes and I drifted off.

CHAPTER XVIX

Several hours of fitful tossing and turning marred my sleep that first night. I lay transfixed in a curious state of disembodiment. Unpleasant and confusing dream fragments occurring in abundance kept me on the verge of wakefulness, yet my eyes were glued shut and I could not will them open.

In one sordid affair, I am dozing on a bench in a bus terminal awaiting the arrival of a connecting bus. A woman in a red tunic with white sleeves awakens me. Her face is featureless and held scarcely four inches from my own. She unexpectedly insults my appearance and insists I get a haircut. When I protest, my dead mother appears behind the woman and convinces me to do as instructed.

The bus station morphs into a salon and the woman limps behind me with scissors in one hand and clippers in the other. Her red tunic flows in slow motion as she moves, and I am convinced she is nude underneath. In the corner stands a shadowy figure stropping a meat cleaver back and forth across a wide strap of black leather. I sit uncomfortably on my hands.

The stylist offers me food and drink, which I refuse. She tucks a heated blanket over the lower portion of my body. My clothes miraculously disappear beneath the covering, and the chair in which I am sitting suddenly reclines. The woman straddles my torso, grinding her loins suggestively against me. I can feel her hot flesh through her tunic. A warm wetness floods over my now exposed hands and I am convinced the woman has urinated on me. However, when I inspect my hands to dry them, I realize the wetness is blood.

The stylist dances seductively and slinks behind me. She enables the clippers and presses them to the back of my neck. The vibrating clippers sear my flesh like a branding iron and I am terrified they will sever my spinal cord, but I cannot escape. My eyes strain at their sockets like those of horses in a burning barn. She concentrates her efforts solely upon the left side of my head. She presents a dragon-handled mirror before me and laughs at my shocked expression. She holds an open scissor to my throat while she buzzcuts the right side of my head, as well, leaving a startling unconventional strip of hair roughly centered on my skull. "That will be eighteen dollars," she whispers before vanishing.

Suddenly, the chair spirals a hundred feet into the air, and I find myself atop a tower of steel scaffolding. I grip my tenuous seat as a hidden theatrical light scans the scene and isolates me from the surrounding void. I pray for a familiarity to cling to before a terrible blackness pervades my senses. The blackness lifts to reveal a dense fog suspending a host of swirling phantasmagoria.

The chair in which I am reclining mutates into a revolving stool. As the stool and I spin around, several gnome-like creatures ascend the steel structure. When they reach my level, they perch like gargoyles on the scaffolding's four corners. Their eyes follow me and the flickering light reveals creepy, wanton smiles upon their faces in stark succession. They inch closer with each rotation of the stool, their reptilian tales wagging in anticipation of an attack.

I spring desperately from my seat and jab an iron finger at each in turn while screaming. "Be gone!" They fall from off their tottery perches to the earth but land like cats and scamper off to their respective lairs.

The spot light extinguishes as quickly as a snuffed candle. The scaffolding crumbles beneath me at an accelerating pace. I hurtle down through the inkiness of space. "Please God, let there be light!"

The scene changes before I hit the ground. I am now in a car speeding through the night on a deserted highway. Rain, like piss from a race horse, tamps visibility to near zero and reflects light back into my tired eyes with alarming precision. My vehicle's headlights flicker and dim to nothing. In the distance, several luminous orbs dance like fireflies. Their numbers multiply and their perceived direction is lost to me. The orbs increase in size and their dancing energy explodes to a frantic level. The intensity becomes blinding. I gasp in fear as the orbs swirl around me.

"Please God, let there be light!" The scene fades to unbearable brightness, then…nothing.

#

I awoke on the floor and fumbled blindly for the switch to the small lamp I knew to be on my nightstand. (Please God, let there be light!) I found it beneath the bed. I was relieved to discover it still functioned. I held the lamp aloft and used its cock-eyed shade to direct the rays around my quarters, which I found to be remarkably upset.

Tattered drapes dangled from broken rods. The mattress I initially slept on lay atop the overturned bureau and my belongings littered every corner of the room. My thoughts were scrambled and unclear as to how I slept through what must have been an incredible ruckus. The light from the damaged lamp flickered and died just as the welcome sun entered through the denuded window and foretold the break of day.

The nightmare had shattered my composure. With trembling hands, I wiped the profusion of sweat from my face with the bed linens. "Jesus," I gasped, fighting for breath. "Welcome to Milford." I attributed my nocturnal disturbance to the experience at the diner the day before and dismissed it as an unfortunate happenstance, but the shambled room was quite perplexing.

In a moment, humor lightened my predicament and my mood. I stretched and began the arduous task of assembling my belongings and tidying the room. When things were again in order, I left with a list of questions a mile long and sought the council of the purple-lipped attendant. "I will throttle him after draining him of information," I said aloud in half-jest.

The awful little man was just where I left him. "We trust you had a good night, sir," he whinnied without even looking up.

"No, I did not have a good night. What happened anyway? Did I sleep through an earthquake?" I snapped sharply.

"I wouldn't know, sir. I only work here." He added, shit-eating grin proudly displayed.

My disdain for this repulsive pipsqueak was growing. "What *do* you know?" I asked. A nebulae of sky blue particles arose when I dropped my briefcase atop his antiquated ledger.

"The man lifted his eyes and responded with the air of a priggish butler. "That would depend, sir, on what it is you are specifically asking?"

"For starters, what is all this pale blue powdery crap covering everything?"

"We don't know, sir. It drifts in from outside, I suppose. We clean it up and it reappears the next day. It looks like the ashes from a house fire, does it not? Or, perhaps, flakes of skin?" He suggested.

"What it looks like is the maid has the week off." I spat. I opened my briefcase and showed the man the portrait of Clara Connor. "Have you seen this young woman?" I held the photograph directly in front of the idiot's face.

The idiot grimaced as if my proximity caused him physical pain. He deflected his head in disgust as he reviewed the picture before him from the corners of his eyes. "Yes, she was here...about three weeks ago."

"Who was she with when you saw her?" I probed.

"No one," the man answered. "She was alone."

"Well, how long did she stay and when did she leave?"

"As I said, she was here about three weeks ago...stayed one night." The man was growing increasingly nervous. He picked up a pen and pretended to fidget with his work.

"Do you know where she went or why she was here?" I reiterated.

"No, sir,' he answered. "I've told you everything I know."

On impulse, I turned and glanced up the stairs. When I readdressed the matter at hand, the attendant had disappeared. I hopped the counter and peeked behind the heavy drapes to the rear of the clerk's station. He was nowhere in sight. While browsing the pages of his ledger for confirmation of his claim, my eyes came to rest on a familiar name. There on the page dated 7 January was the signature of Clara Connor. She had stayed in Room 18.

My eyes again averted to the stairs, and I distinctly saw the fleeting form of a woman wearing a red, white-sleeved jacket turn into the hallway at the top of the staircase. I tore the page from the book and sprinted to the second floor. As I cleared the last step and faced the long hallway, I saw the figure vanish through the door of my room.

I remembered locking the door earlier when leaving and could only re-enter the room with the skeleton key. All was as I had left it except for a crimson discoloration now evident on the wall beneath the painting that hung above my bed. The pattern of the stain evoked a striking similarity to the jacket Clara wore in the photograph I held before falling asleep the night before.

A feverish chill thrilled me as the crimson discoloration began to creep up the wall. A pound of anxiety filled my throat as the stain spread across the canvas and dissolved before my eyes. With a surge of renewed interest, I examined the painting's background and noted the singular lines of a crumbling structure I had overlooked before. In astonishment, I relived the impressions of the old manor that had so disturbed me and riveted my attention on my bus journey to Milford.

The realization that the coincidence might not be just a coincidence set my blood on fire. I was hot to go and started out the door before realizing I had not seen the Walther since boarding the bus more than thirty hours ago. The fact had not occurred to me as I straightened the room, and the panic of losing the weapon so carelessly weighed on me.

I instinctively patted my jacket pockets then rifled my suitcase and briefcase. I found it in neither. I canvassed the room corner by corner, looked under the mattress twice, under the bed, in the bureau drawers...nothing. I was ready to leave without it, when a glint in the bureau mirror caught my eye. I could see in the mirror the reflection of the semi-auto on the bathroom vanity.

The muzzle pointing right at me was, even as a reflection, remarkably intimidating. I spun around to find my pistol next to the leather in-the-pants holster. I had not remembered laying it there, but admitted that it was possible given the confusion of the preceding day. Why I had overlooked it earlier when cleaning up confounded me. No matter I thought, fixing the holstered gun discretely inside the waistband of my trousers. It was good to have 'Old Betsy' back where she belonged.

I forgot about the boutique. My revised order of business called for securing passage to the old house. I could not wait for another bus to stray this way again, and I handily dismissed the chance of locating a rental agency in this miserable little berg. Walking was not out of the question, but my destination lay a healthy fifteen miles or more by road, and I was no Daniel Boone. My best option would be to bribe a local to deliver me to my destination.

Those citizens willing to converse with a stranger seemed eager to assist until I informed them of where I intended to go. I had no idea what to call my destination, but my description of the place left no doubt in anyone's mind that the object of my interest was Lovingdale Manor. Word magically spread throughout town and, in a matter of minutes, residents were whisking away when I approached even before I could speak. Noon was nearly upon me and my luck seemed in short supply.

"To Hell with them," I scoffed after watching the last in a long line of cowards desert Main Street. "If I have to walk, I have to walk."

I copped a bottle of water and an apple before leaving town. The streets were deserted, but I sensed the eyes of the citizens dissected me from every corner and window as I passed their storefronts. The twisted town was soon behind me, and I felt better knowing it. I walked for an hour or more and reasoned that it would take until nightfall to achieve my goal unless I increased my current pace.

It figured that the sky would darken on my way, and it did with increasing threat of rain. There was nothing to do but continue. 'Damn the torpedoes, full speed ahead,' I reminisced, remembering a worn out adage from my middle school years.

Another two hours passed, when I heard the advancing sound of a motor car to my rear. Hoping my desperation was not overtly apparent, I turned facing the approaching vehicle and offered my thumb with the most congenial smile I could muster. To my surprise and relief, the red truck whined to a halt and the door sprang open invitingly. An elderly farmer manned the wheel. He said nothing nor looked at me as I scooted in beside him. The truck was an older model International that had seen great care over the years. It was obviously a source of pride to the owner, so I used my astute observation as an ice breaker.

"Nice truck," I began rather feebly. "What is she, a '59"

"'58," the farmer corrected.

I nodded as if the difference should have been obvious. "I'm headed up to the Lovingdale spread," I admitted. "Do you know the place?" I asked naively.

The man turned and looked at me for the first time. His face was drawn and curiously asymmetrical "I know of it," he answered. "What in tarnation are you going there for?"

"I'm looking for someone," I replied, "a young girl, college age, blonde, very pretty. She might be wearing a red jacket with white sleeves. Have you seen anyone that fits that description?"

"Mister, nothin' fits 'round here. Yer about to find that out fer yer ownself."

I looked at the man until the gist of what he said sunk in. For the remainder of the ride neither of us spoke again. He let me out at an intersecting dirt road, pointed his arthritic fingers in the direction of the old house and sped off. The storm was practically upon me now, and I turned up my collar in anticipation as I headed up the narrow dirt lane.

The apple I brought with me called my name, and I retrieved it from my jacket pocket. I tossed it playfully in the air a time or two then dug my fingertips into either side of the stem. With a customary display of machismo, I halved the fruit with the sheer force of my hands. The need for bravado usually presented itself whenever my manhood felt threatened. The macho act was impressive when witnessed; comparable to popping the bottom from a coke bottle by slapping one's palm over the mouth of the bottle after consuming ninety percent of the contents. The granny-smith was tart and sweet, like all good apples and tasted better for my exertions — just as stolen watermelons taste far better than the store bought kind.

The sporadic sprinkles of rain quickened my pace. I patted my waistband to insure that 'Old Betsy' was still riding along and watched the swirling mass of grey goo in the sky coalesce into a frighteningly real possibility. It was barely five o'clock but twilight was commencing. Despite the dimming light, I could identify the manor's signature lofty spires through the naked branches whenever the treetops permitted.

The wind had felled a sizeable, moss-covered oak across the drive just before a rusted gate that barred entrance to a narrower continuation beyond. I circumvented the hazard as best I could. The mass of the toppled giant was such that it compelled me to enter the tangle of limbs at their outermost reaches. The girth and stature of every limb seemed a tree in itself.

Once clear of the formidable obstacle, I pressed on in earnest. I had not considered spending the night and I was customarily unprepared for the worse, but my jacket was warm and the weather unusually so for February. Winter thunderstorms were not unheard of, but they were rare. In any event, I believed I could rest comfortably overnight providing the old house offered adequate protection from the wind and rain.

Countless wagons and carriages from a past age had carved the defile four feet lower than the surrounding terrain. The trees lining the rotting banks loomed overhead and leaned inwards in haphazard and threatening fashion. The roving path inspired in me waves of nausea that I attributed to nervous tension or fatigue. I found myself yearning for higher ground or an open space from which I could see and breathe more easily.

The determined rain caused my clothing to cling like starving children to my blanched, tingling skin. Red mud caked the treads of my shoes, and the uncomfortable chill that entered the equation set my mind on a course for shelter.

Minutes later, a dim glow ahead in a treetop stopped me in my tracks. I paused to ponder the phenomenon in hopes of determining its source and character. The swirling gaseous cloud, blue-white and translucent as smoke, seemed driven not by the prevailing west wind but by an innate alien energy. The billowing cloud impressed upon my mind the semblance of a woman's figure; obscure, to be sure, but undeniably female. The whipping tentacles of ethereal light mesmerized me and beckoned me towards it. Unsure of what to do or expect, I stood my ground; my reluctance fueled by apprehension and the uncertainty of what I was beholding.

The cloud, or whatever it was, seemingly grew agitated at my dithering and expressed its harkening behavior more urgently. Without warning, the spectre swooped from its treetop nest and descended upon me with such drama and speed that my heart stopped. A shriek emanated from the entity—harsh, high-pitched and horrible—like the scream of a murdered woman.

I fell to the ground in terror. I sought to speak, but could not find my voice. Had I found it, I quite possibly would not have known what to say or how to say it. My continued inaction spurred the haunting image to surge over me again in renewed fury. Driven to my feet, I stumbled clumsily forward. I fell several times but arose quickly as the nagging horror urged me on. I finally broke free of the confines of the forest edge and into the unkempt space surrounding the main house. The apparition vanished. I found myself standing several yards away from an imposing set of double doors fitted with large stylized handles and hinges lapping at the door's sturdy edges. I backed off from the entrance as if knowing better, but a glance over my shoulder reminded me that greater terrors awaited me from whence I had come.

I approached the gothic dwelling with great trepidation. The now incessant flashes of lightning caused the skin of the building to shine like mica. Terrific streaks of blue white light tore paths through the firmament and the resounding objections of thunder boomed even before the ragged scars had healed.

With each flash, the frightening silhouette of a stoop-shouldered figure shown upon a singular window that alone allowed the eastern facade of the stoic structure to breathe. The figure, glaring and menacing as the lightning that gave it life, was convincingly real and projected an undeniably dreadful presence. The vision was stark and motionless against the dying of the day.

I sensed the same evil force that colored my dreams. Something told me I was in the presence of a great demonic threat that birthed and nourished whatever deviltry infested the ground on which I stood. With considerable difficulty, I navigated the perimeter in search of an alternate entrance. The lightning provided sufficient illumination, but the brambly understory of nasty vegetation fought vociferously as I dragged through its virgin entanglements.

I circled the house several times to no avail. The obstinate monstrosity seemed to revolve on an unseen central axis. The premise was ridiculous, but how could I explain it otherwise? I was certain I progressed in linear fashion, yet, every emergence from the undergrowth found me back where I started.

The eeriness I experienced could not be overstated. With each burst of light, the shadow etched upon the glass of the singular window beguiled me to venture willingly into its unknown dimension. I paused before the edifice wondering if I possessed the courage to explore my deepest fears or the strength to confront and conquer the noir nature of my imagination.

CHAPTER XX

Day turned to night. I had been wise enough to carabine to my belt a small flashlight, which I now employed to great use. The slender shaft of light fled from my hand and rested on the ornate metal handles fastened to the foreboding front doors of the massive ruin. I seized the cold iron in my hands and pulled. The doors opened with a tortured sigh.

Inside was cold and damp as a tomb with every nook and cranny covered with decades of dust and cobwebs like every picture of every haunted house I had ever seen. Remarkably, there was no foyer or anteroom beyond the door. Instead, a dank hallway led into a vacuous space with vaulted ceilings.

An elaborate staircase adorned with art deco volutes and balusters crawled up the wall on one side and turned sharply towards some unimaginable obscenity as it neared the top. Draperies rent by a thousand clawing fingers hung like executed felons from oversized windows, and the skeletal remains of the sashes beyond the rotten coverings revealed their true selves when lightning flashed.

The staircase had a forbidden and threatening aspect that both attracted and repelled me. I approached it guardedly and glanced about me to assure myself that I was truly alone. I took the first step. I climbed by degrees, riser by riser, tread by tread. An exceptionally prolonged flash from the heavens fully illuminated for the first time the decadence and decay surrounding me.

My eyes swept the room absorbing details that might serve me later. The flash ended, but not before the ghostly image of Clara Connor materialized near the top of the stairs. I blinked my eyes in disbelief and the vision dissolved.

Although composed of the same pervasive and elemental substance as the night itself, translucent and weightless, the vision was as real and convincing as an imminent threat. There was no doubt that I had seen something. Perhaps my mind was tricked by the deep shadows and shifting light. Hesitant to proceed yet bound to continue, I inched cautiously forward.

My heart raced wildly within my chest, incensed that my body refused to release it from its designed obligations. One step...two steps. Slowly, I ascended the imposing staircase into the gloom. "Clara?" I whispered. "I'm not here to hurt you. I want to take you home."

At the upper landing, another hallway paralleled the lower one. Two rooms with their doors partially open adjoined one side. Another room anchored the hallway at its terminus, but its door hid behind several planks nailed fast to the jam.

I stopped at the door of the first room and cautiously pushed it open with an outstretched hand. The shriek of creaking hinges knifed through me and ricocheted from wall to wall throughout the empty house. There was nothing inside but a single metal bed frame with a naked bedspring still upon it. The bed's mattress lay upon the floor; the ticking ripped by beast or squatter searching for food or the proverbial nest egg. Rough-hewn timber slats, darkly browned with age, lined the interior of a doorless closet that occupied the corner of one wall.

The subsequent room near the shuttered one had a different character altogether. This door was more difficult to open. I encouraged it with my shoulder. My flashlight's dim circle of light revealed no bed frame or furniture in this room, just a similar mattress foully stained and repulsive. Again, a solitary closet with no door guarded the corner. It dawned on me that it shared the structural elements comprising its back wall with the closet in the first room. The slats were generous in their proportion and widely spaced. With the aid of my flashlight and despite the raging storm outside, I was able to look between them and confirm my suspicions.

As I peered past the wooden barrier, a shadowy blur in the adjacent room triggered a shock that surged through me. I sprang back striking my head on the doorway jam. My torch hurled from my grasp, careened across the hardwood floor and sent searchlight spirals of illumination across the walls before dying out. The impact of my injury caused a blackening aura that nearly subdued me. I regained my senses and turned just as light from outside revealed a maniacally grinning face not three feet from my own. The creature was upon me in an instant, clawing and tearing at my throat with surprising strength and tenacity.

I fought to free myself, but the thing was intense and determined to do me great harm. Instinctively, my knee shot forward and met with resistance upon my attacker's groin. The monster released its grip immediately and burst through the window, shattering it into a thousand shards. The second story opening was a good twenty feet above the sloping ground below. I was convinced a fall from such height meant certain injury or death. I was flabbergasted to spy the beast limping creepily into the dense folds of the forest.

I flailed my arms in front of me in panic, using blind sweeping gestures to search for my lost torch. The unit had come to rest against the side of the repugnant bedding. I picked the flashlight up and clicked it on. A repulsive, red-black liquid resembling blood oozed from the mattress's filthy ticking. It was impossible to determine a source or explanation for this phenomenon in the death-dark room and the sight of it made me grow sick and faint.

The horrible substance covered my hand while it rested on the mattress edge. I jerked away, my mind reeling. I struggled towards the doorway. My knees buckled and I crashed back to the floor. My dimming eyes discerned the vaporous form of Clara Connor pass unimpeded through the shuttered door to the little room at the end of the hall seconds before unconsciousness overcame me.

I awoke as the morning sun painted the interior of the somber room with dabs of optimism. A small wren perched on the shattered sill of the window through which my assailant had escaped. The bird chirped merrily until my stirring movements startled it into flight. I was in considerable pain and the pounding of my heart and brain unsettled me terribly. I felt both would explode should I fail to lessen their excitability. I sat up slowly, gathered my thoughts and rubbed my head.

My last recollection of the previous night was of the curious shuttered door. I stood in front of it for a moment before pulling at the wooden barriers hastily nailed thereon. I say 'hastily' for the nails were poorly spaced and only partially driven in. To board the room up from the outside, logically, was to keep someone...or something...from escaping. I easily breached the barricades rudimentary construction and freed the doorway with minimal effort.

Inside the depressing little room, I found nothing more than a well-built rocking chair of Amish design situated near the room's only window. I realized that this window was the exact one from which the apparition glared at me the evening before whilst I sought entrance into the mansion. Near the rocker, a Chinese pitcher of blue and white porcelain occupied a three-legged pedestal with a faux marble top. The vessel was half filled with water that swarmed with a plethora of large purple flies. A tsunami of nausea surged up from the pit of my empty stomach and I turned away to face the wall.

Newspaper headlines, pinups of movie stars, advertisements for assorted household appliances and leaves from fashion magazines plastered the walls of the minute chamber. However, my trained eye noticed the date on the front page of a newspaper glued to the wall to be no older than one month past. Someone had been in this shuttered room not thirty days before.

Nothing was gelling, and I would glean little more by remaining here. I decided to return to town and renew my investigation along a more conventional path. All I had learned thus far, was that someone, possibly a transient, was inhabiting this wretched place and had shuttered a small room in the house for unknown reasons. Still, the vision of Clara Connor during the night left me hesitant to quit the property altogether before I explored the premises more completely.

Outside, I discovered a faint blood trail beneath the window from whence the beast had fallen. Why the storm had not obliterated it was yet another mystery. I followed the congealing blood for some way but soon lost it amidst the tangle of vines and brambles. I was convinced my investigation would lead back here and equally certain that the creature that attacked me would not abandon its lair due to my presence alone.

The journey back to town passed pleasantly enough. The morning sky was on fire and imbued prodigious numbers of leaves carpeting the road edges and stream bank for as far as I could see with the same warm burgundy and sienna glow. Few motorcars passed by, but it only took one supportive soul who did not pass to transport me safely and soundly back to my point of beginning, the Ambloy Hotel.

As luck would have it, the one who stopped was none other than the farmer who picked me up the day before. "Are you my guardian angel?" I quipped, thankful for the ride. The driver stared straight-ahead, typically tight-lipped and unresponsive. I smiled to myself, shrugged and turned my attention to the passing landscape. Feelings of déjà vu underscored my thoughts again. Such uncanny duality of circumstance was rare, yet a recurrent theme since undertaking this assignment. My instincts and intellect were polarizing, and the increasing distance between them led me to question my judgment. I doubted my senses for the first time in a very long while.

I was tired from my exertions and appreciated the lift, none-the-less. I sat with my head partially outside the open window, letting the cool rushing air chase the cares from my conscience. I thanked the taciturn fellow when we arrived in town and we parted company.

The bitchin' winter wind had returned to scour the streets and alleys with fiendish delight. Each bitter blast caused lighter trash to hover in the air like drunken wraiths. The stratospheric layers that blazed so brilliantly earlier that morning foretold the pregnant cumulonimbus clouds that now hung like ripe eggplant in the western sky. The agitated atmosphere was frightening and the potential threat undeniable. It was just as well. The town could use a good antiseptic cleansing. It would take a storm of storms to bleach the bones of this cursed spot…and Lovingdale House as well.

The town literally buzzed with activity today. Trucks and cars, buses and wagons lined the streets. Storekeepers and homeowners scampered about like chipmunks loading personal vehicles with valued possessions and cargo. The entire community seemed collectively engaged in a mass exodus for a purpose foreign to me.

Perhaps violent extremists had unleashed a deadly virus into the local water supply. Or an up-wind nuclear reactor had melted down and threatened to annihilate every living thing for a hundred miles when the radioactive plutonium reached the water table. Or war had been declared over the premeditated acts of resident terrorist cells and an invading army was crossing the Canadian border into the United States even as I watched the confusion unfold.

No one would cease their consuming activities long enough to acknowledge my presence, yet alone indulge my conspiratorial theories. In a matter of minutes, the streets were empty. I stood alone outside the entrance to the Ambloy hotel disbelieving what my own eyes had just witnessed. It seemed my investigation had taken a new twist. Everyone I intended to question had now dispersed to the four corners of the Earth. The grim abandoned storefronts met my gaze with the forlorn enthusiasm of disenchanted clowns.

In lieu of what had transpired, I thought it best to check in with my employer and inform him of what little I had uncovered. My cell phone battery had died, and with no way of recharging (I forgot to pack its proprietary cable) or procuring another battery, I cursed the useless contrivance. Fortunately, I spotted a rare pay phone outside the drugstore entrance and was delighted to find it in good working order. Biggs' personal secretary answered the call.

"What do you mean he's unavailable?" I argued. "Tell him Harry Case is calling? He'll want to speak with me."

The secretary was unrepentant. "I mean he's unavailable," she repeated, "as in not here. He left for Vermont this morning...some business concerning an estate purchase, I believe. He was quite secretive about the whole thing."

"Biggs is here...in Vermont? What's he doing here?"

"I just told you, sir. Would you like to leave a message or call back number in case he should check in?"

"That won't be necessary, thank you. Just tell him I called and that I am onto something promising. He'll know what I mean. Maybe I'll run into him here." I hung up the phone and walked back across the street to the hotel with more questions than answers...again.

I had no choice but to revisit my room at the Ambloy and hoped more productive resources would avail themselves to me in quick order. To exacerbate my befuddlement, I discovered the purple-lipped desk clerk busily defending his station as if nothing outside his immediate world was amiss.

"What are you doing here?" I asked in amazement.

"I work here, sir," he replied scarcely looking up.

"I realize that," I explained. "Why aren't you leaving town with all the others?"

"Others, sir?" He commented blandly.

"Don't play dumb with me," I threatened. "You know damn well what I'm talking about. Where is everyone going? The whole town is packing up and leaving, and you're telling me you don't have a clue what's going on? Why aren't you leaving with them?"

"Leave, sir... me? Oh, no sir, I could never leave. I intend to die here, just as you will. Why did you come here, sir? You've stirred everything up again. It was quiet until you came."

I could not believe what I was hearing. "Listen, you jerk," I demanded, grabbing him by the lapels of his cheap mortuary suit. The fellow offered no resistance at all, but signaled me intently with his darting eyes that we were not alone in the lobby. When I turned in the direction of his gaze, the flat side of a meat cleaver smashed squarely against the right side of my skull. The bludgeoning knocked me cold as my world spun out of control.

#

The next thing I knew; I was walking down the gravel road in the town where I grew up. 'Old Cooksie', a kind elderly neighbor I knew as a youngster, stopped to give me a lift in his blue Chevy truck, just as he would have in my youth. I and a group of lads I ran with hung that handle on the old gentleman for the platter of confections he always provided our gang whenever we frequented the swimming hole that fronted his property.

There was a great culvert at the juncture of his driveway and the main road. Whenever soaking rains raised the water in the stream to flood stage, the 'hole' on the downstream side of the culvert scoured out to a considerable depth. That recurrent event made it a prime spot for summer games of 'chicken'; particularly, daring one another to jump from the culvert top to map the murky channel's reconfigured bottom. I was always the first. My near drowning marked my last time.

On that occasion, I inhaled a large quantity of sediment-heavy water after jumping in, and I panicked when my lungs seized. I remember my swim mates' 'oohs' and 'aahs' when I disappeared for the third time beneath the chocolate emulsion. I barely survived by pushing off from the bottom each time I sank, thus propelling my body to the surface and shortening the distance to the shore until I was able to crawl out on the muddy bank.

I tried not to think of this frightening episode as Cooksie and I rode along, but it was nearly impossible. My destination was unknown to me. In fact, I did not know whom I was visiting, or why, but it did not seem to matter. The old grain silos, train tracks and the smell of cow manure struck a familiar chord. I leaned back in my seat and smiled, content in reminiscent wonder. It felt good to be home.

A bit later, my eyes rested on the sashaying behind of a young female in white hip-hugger slacks and a sky-blue striped, jersey knit top that clung to her curves like a Porsche 911. Her caboose looked quite familiar to me, but it was not until I saw her face that I recognized my ex-wife, or at that time, my wife-to-be, Lily Brown.

I was in awe and bade Old Cooksie to stop and let me out. He did as I requested, and when I leaped from the truck the main drag of my youthful home widened into a Los Angeles thoroughfare. I stood staring at the post-modern Capitol Records office building on Wilshire Boulevard, where I worked briefly as a janitor after my military discharge.

I saw myself leave the building through a side entrance after my shift ended at around four-thirty in the afternoon. I ran to catch myself. When I spun my doppelganger around, I faced Staff Sergeant Juan Jose Padilla, the ornery, sadistic training instructor who presided over my basic military indoctrination.

What was happening? My mind whirled like a dervish and swept me up in its spiraling vortex. Memories churned through my head in ever-resolving clarity and numbers—things I had long ago buried; things I had hoped to forget.

Suddenly the vortex faded, and I plunged headlong into an abyss. A pinprick of light appeared far below me but magnified exponentially as I fell. Ultimately, the light and I collided with an explosive burst of brightness and my eyes sprang open like switchblades.

I now could see nothing but an intense thread of light. At first, I believed myself to be blind, but as my eyes adjusted I recognized the thread to be the sun leaking through a pinhole in a tarpaulin suspended a couple of feet above my head. There was adequate light for me to discern the stenciled letters 'LRL' imprinted in an old English font upon the material's inner face. Someone was transporting me in a vehicle to a destination unknown. My ankles were bound together and my hands tied behind my back. I was 'fit to be tied' (no pun intended), for a third rope attached to the others encircled my neck. I discovered to my dismay that the noose tightened when I made an effort to free myself. What manner of treachery was this?

With great care, I manipulated my body to where I could spy on the occupant, or occupants, in the vehicle's cab. A lone person sat behind the wheel. I recognized the culprit immediately. The same Mohawk-headed moron that confronted me in the diner had now kidnapped me and trussed me up like a wild pig. I recalled a flash of the baboon's demented face before the blow from his cleaver knocked me silly in the lobby of the Ambloy Hotel. What did he want with me? Where was he taking me?

I maneuvered again with similar caution and managed to right myself upon my knees. In this position, I succeeded in lifting the tarpaulin with my head and peered out from beneath its ragged edge. Another sinister sight rang true as the Liberty Bell. Lovingdale Manor was gliding by in the distant haze. Even though the ancient estate and I were now on terms more intimate, it still evoked feelings of doom and terror in me every bit as powerful as it had the first time I saw it from the bus window.

Worried and confused, I sank back into my former position. The noose constricting my throat made breathing a chore, and my better sense warned me to cease my exertions until I found myself more safely situated. It was clear my destiny was somehow tied to Lovingdale Manor. I prayed that Clara Connor had not become entangled in its unholy web as well.

CHAPTER XXI

Harry's contract to pursue the case eased Ellen's concerns a little, but fear and worry still lay just beneath her skin. At least somebody was doing something. Nevertheless, Ellen informed her employer that if Clara was not located within the week, she would be off to Vermont herself. Biggs entreated upon her to give his associate time to produce results. He promised that he would forward the matter to the FBI and spare no expense in finding and bringing Clara home, should his investigator's efforts prove fruitless.

Whoever said 'no news is good news' obviously never spent a night alone worrying about a loved one half a continent away. Ellen slept little and ate less. Her frame was thinning and her once delicate skin was slowly eroding away to lines and creases. She spent hours wandering about her apartment and staring out her kitchen window at the petite concrete birdbath Clara helped her place the previous spring. Whenever a cardinal or bluebird visited the outdoor display, the burden on Ellen's heart would lift ever so slightly and a glimmer of hope would brighten her eyes. The moment was fleeting, like the avian visits, but she longed for those moments and watched for the returning birds throughout each day.

When a package arrived at the Clarion Building bearing a Vermont postmark, Biggs hastened to his private office before opening it. He feared it was from Roger, and wanted privacy before exploring the dreaded contents. Perhaps, an ear was inside or a finger from the delicate hand of his beloved Clara. One should expect monstrous things from monstrous persons.

Biggs sat the package on his desk and seated himself before it. He stared fearfully at the plainly wrapped box for several minutes before removing the string and brown paper. The container was fashioned to resemble a tiny coffin. A crudely drawn cross bisected the cardboard lid. Cotton lined the inside; a thoughtful touch, if one is the morbid type. Biggs removed a folded note and placed it aside absent-mindedly as his eyes fell upon the remaining article.

Curled into a spiral at the bottom of the box lay a lock of blonde hair shimmering with a hint of strawberry. Biggs removed the item from its unworthy container and held it unnervingly before his face. Binding the purloined tress was a sheer gold chain from which a delicate horse charm dangled. Dried blood besmeared the charm and a minute, foul glob of scalp tissue clung tenaciously to the end of the golden strands.

His heart stopped when the implication became clear. He slumped forward over his desk and dropped the item in shock and disgust. Someone had apparently torn the hair mercilessly from the head of the victim. That someone was Roger Perry and the victim was certainly Clara. A cold sweat beaded his taut, sallow face.

Resolution quickly supplanted his dismay, and his mind snapped back to attention. He would destroy Roger with no delay. He would find this heartless, loathsome creature and show him what real terror is all about. He picked up the note and unfolded it directly.

It read:

hey asshole
guess who I got?
does this prezent look familar?
if u want to see ur clara again
cum to the mansion - u no the place.

if u don't cum by friday, I will send more gifts
she has such butiful purpel eyes, duzn't she?
would u like one?

hurry
u no who

Biggs balled the note in his fist and glanced at the day-planner on his desk. The postmark on the package wrapping read Saturday. Today was Wednesday. He had better get moving right away. He would leave a note telling Ellen that he had found Clara and was going to get her— nothing else. She would be hysterical if she knew the truth, and he did not need the additional stress and complication muddying the already murky waters.

He phoned the Impromptu Travel Agency and arranged for a red-eye flight from Columbus to Burlington. He had relied on them in the past and found their discretion worthy of his trust. The trip would have to appear kosher in order to allay suspicion. Fueling up his corporate jet and scheduling an emergency departure would attract unwanted attention from the Board of Directors and possibly the F.A.A. No, travelling via a scheduled airline flight would be the wiser course to follow.

Biggs was in Burlington by morning. The Ford Expedition he requested through his agent was waiting for him. From what he read about Vermont winters, he expected to be plowing through snowdrifts several feet high. The weather had ice in its veins, but normal mid-February snows were remarkably absent. The Expedition was hearty and reliable, a good choice, and it handled admirably as he sped northwest to his destination.

He considered bringing his Colt Detective Special along, but getting a revolver aboard a commercial airline would have been tricky and could possibly have caused precious delays. Besides, he needed no weapon to dispatch his puny adversary. When he found Roger Perry, he would tear him apart with his bare hands.

CHAPTER XXII

Twilight shades of blue-clay light swept the landscape free of some of the inherent dreariness outside Clara's window. The coming moon would entertain the land with another cosmic dance tonight, admirably bathing the trees and hillocks with the brash, silver edginess of a photographer's negative.

Clara was unrestrained and free to move about the room. However, the door remained securely bolted and locked. Roger spent the morning removing the wooden barrier to her room and replacing the haphazard security measure with an iron hasp and lock set. In addition to improved security, this measure facilitated speedier ingress and egress in keeping with Roger's accelerated schedule.

Roger had become more arrogant and self-possessed than ever. His mood had grown increasingly morose the past couple of days and his manner trite and abrupt. He was uppity and impatient, strolling about with an almost aristocratic swagger. His sulkiness seemed magnified tenfold, and he spat and cursed like a spoiled brat with needs far from being met.

Roger had discovered an ancient tome while salvaging construction materials from an attic crawlspace. The book was obtuse and oddly written. However, Roger believed he understood the gist of the messages therein. The book was in diary form with dates harkening back to the eighteenth century. Spells, incantations and assorted deviltries leapt from the pages and beguiled him with their promises of power.

Three generations of Lovingdales vied for equal measure of the young man's disturbed and impressionable mind. The force of Roger's personality might have dispelled an invasion by one, but an assault by all three was all but indefensible. Characteristics and mannerisms of the lordly lot manifested themselves insidiously. Roger adopted a lordly air as he paraded about, tome in hand, espousing the archaic rhetoric the past had bequeathed to him. The incarnate possession of his tortured soul (if he, indeed, had a soul to possess) coincided with the waxing gibbous moon, now past its three-quarter stage and entering the full glory of its lunar cycle.

A six-foot shaft of red cedar heartwood hewn with a drawknife and a burgundy cape sourced from tattered drapery were his new accoutrements of choice. He adorned the staff at the lesser end with a hollow brass doorknob. Roger eschewed battery driven light sources now (they never lasted) and lit his way with flaming torches through the near-night corridors he haunted.

Outside Clara's tiny prison, the wind rippled past the barren branches of the gnarled trees like phantom streams of water. From her discreet perch, Clara watched Roger pass back and forth below her with industry and fervor. She could only surmise as to what obsessed the poor man. She was perplexed by Roger's enigmatic peculiarities and frightened even more by their deepening shadows. As the world beyond her window grew more bleak and sere, she extinguished the stub of a candle near her chair. The energy from the vanquished light dashed from the room and spread inversely outside.

Clara pressed her forehead tightly against the windowpane and cupped her hands to either side of her face to better see. From the void, a dull-white thing emerged and fled on all fours from tree to tree. The sudden emergence of the glowing apparition startled her and she fell back. Was that Roger? Did she actually see what she thought she saw? She moved quickly back to the window again and peered into the night for answers.

Nothing seemed unusual now. Strange, she thought, to differentiate between the "usual" under such circumstance—as if her incredible situation was anything but singular. The inevitable normalization to perversity, thankfully, was still being offset by drawing upon her better angels. She must not surrender to this horror—this obscenity—this wicked betrayal of all she knew of humaneness and decency. Holding on to sanity was her one salvation. Thoughts of her mother materialized, and she prayed she inherited her mother's lucidity and fortitude. Clara retreated to the shadows when scratching at the door alerted her to Roger's presence. A glaring torch blinded her momentarily as he entered.

Roger was wiry, but powerful. He threw the full force of his weight against Clara and knocked her to the floor. He fell atop the addled girl nearly crushing the breath from her body while seating the torch in an improvised stand. His features were visible now and creepily alternated from mean-spirited and blank to lovingly indulgent and kind. Bands of illumination leaking between door and jamb conjoined with the fluttering torch flame to eerily transform Roger's countenance when he shifted from the shadows.

His face reminded Clara of the creatures she had seen as a child in the Spook House carnival ride that haunted her hometown every October. She shuddered when she recalled their awesome makeup aglow in the unnatural ultraviolet light.

Roger used strips of duct tape adhered to his clothing to bind her wrists and ankles. Other strips silenced her screams and hid his demented expressions from her eyes. When he found the 'package' trussed to his satisfaction, he threw her across his shoulders, firefighter style, retrieved his torch and hurried towards the door.

What was he doing? Clara arched her back and stiffened her legs in an effort to impede the assault. She wriggled like a worm on a hook. She would not go easy into that not so good night. She would make her captor work for every inch of ground he gained. Roger spun in circles until Clara's head smacked the wall. Her undulations flat-lined and she became much more manageable after that.

When her senses returned, Clara found herself strung by hefty rope lanyards between two trees on either side of the platform she had observed Roger building earlier in the week. Her eyes were free of duct tape now, but her mouth was not. The hemp ropes abrading her wrists and ankles and the balls of her feet were all that supported her. To her front, the heat from a pair of blazing torches seeped through the lightweight chemise that replaced her customary clothing. The invading breeze informed her of missing undergarments, and the thought made her blush and contract her limbs in embarrassment. Gooseflesh pimpled her skin from toe to topknot.

The moon, bloated and full of itself, spilled satin finish across the late winter land. The forest held a thousand terrors ready and waiting to spring upon her without warning. A hoot owl bellowed from a distant tree and its cousin, the screech owl, responded with the shrillness of a police whistle that reverberated from hill to hill.

Clara was terrified but acutely alert. Her ears tuned to each sound and magnified them a thousand fold. Her eyes, wide as a frightened foal's, wrung the air of every micro-watt of light. Rustling from behind filled her with dread. She could readily discern and prepare herself mentally for any frontal or peripheral attack, but the area to her rear was disarmingly exposed. Footfalls sounding ever closer behind her teased her breath away. She stretched her neck left and right until she thought it would break in a vain effort to see past her shoulder. As quickly as the footfalls began, they ceased. Whatever stalked her now stood directly to her rear. She swooned nearly fainting from the exhilaration of the imminent danger.

The ropes held her fast and ate into her wrists when she burdened them with the support of her trembling body. The pain kept her conscious, and she welcomed it. It reminded her that she was still alive and awake. If awake, she at least had a fighting chance.

Clara sensed the unknown inching closer. She could feel hot sticky breath warm her neck and shoulders. She felt what she believed to be saliva stream from the monster's mouth and run in rivulets between her shoulder blades and down her spine. She prayed she would die quickly and not be toyed with in cat and mouse fashion. Her agony was immeasurable.

Eerily, the hem of her garment began creeping slowly over her knees and up her thighs as if pulled by an invisible thread. She was powerless to prevent it. The duct tape holding fast to her mouth muffled her cries of indignation and protest. The chemise slipped from her tormentor's lusting hands, fell back, and then resumed a gradual rise upward to hover about her waist. She now knew her antagonist was no beast of the forest.

Clara was mortified, but completely helpless. Like an insect entangled in a spider's web, she endured the callous caresses. She feared the inevitable conclusion of the morbidly bestial behavior, but wished to hasten the act that it might be finished. No sooner had the thought passed, she perceived the thing's touch turn decidedly sexual.

Roger's compassionless arms encircled Clara's slender waist, gently pushing and pulling her body in a circular motion that caused her hips to gyrate seductively. He ran one hand over her buttocks, between her legs and up her belly to her navel while the other passed under her right arm and found her breast. Breathing near her ear grew irregular and heavy. Rough hands sought her secret places and lingered there. Vulgar, guttural grunts offended her ears. Human fingers, curled into claws, scraped her delicate skin and left harsh red trails wherever they passed, tearing the epidermis away to expose the more sensitive underlying layers.

Clara's stomach sickened in preparation for the insult that would shortly commence. She tried to move away but could not. Dangling like a marionette on a string, she could only respond to the whim of her deranged master. She knew nothing could curtail her violator's carnal delirium. Clara hid her face on her shoulder. In a minute or two, it was over.

The consummation turned Roger obsessively cold. A violent yank at Clara's hair snapped her head backwards and cut short the brief welcome relief. She responded with a throaty testament to pain. From the corner of her eye, she saw Roger's mouth agape and his teeth glistening with spittle.

Blood flowed down Clara's chest when Roger plunged his teeth into her neck. She had strength left for resignation only. Abduction and murder by a sadistic maniac was the worst that could befall her. She welcomed death, silently thanking God for closing her eyes and allowing her consciousness to faint away.

Roger stood behind the girl for several minutes more, holding her in his mouth and gorging on her blood. His fixed stare reflected the wan light of the moon while he relished the undead spoils of his devilish act. With the deed completed, he removed the harsh strands of hemp from Clara's wrists and allowed her to crumple to the deck of his sacrificial stage.

Looming over her body, he shattered the night with an unearthly howl. He shrank to a crouched position, listening for any response from fellow creatures of darkness. Hearing nothing save his own vociferous breathing, he lumbered off beyond the forest edge and disappeared. Night surged on.

Clara awoke for the second time that night seated in the rocking chair in her little room. Again, she was unrestrained. She sat facing the looking glass. She felt inexplicably drawn to the ancient thing and the urge to examine it more closely gnawed at her.

The mirror was tall as a man and twice as wide. Thick beveled glass held firmly in an elaborately carved frame bore signs of wear and age near its crazed corners. The frame, impaled between two gaudy pillars of mahogany, lent the entire contrivance a substantial and solid presence. The word '*vixen*' scrawled in red paint or blood shouted at her from the upper left corner of the glass.

The worn, haggard echo from the glass caused her to pity her own image. She turned her head slightly to one side to survey the marks on her neck. The distinct circular pattern of teeth marks sickened her. The wound was not as deep as she had feared, but the stained front of her clothing testified to profuse bleeding. She searched the fathomless depths of the darkened glass for clues to the meaning behind her unmerited entrapment.

Her mother's reflection soon supplanted her own. Sorrow in her mother's soft eyes spoke volumes. The realization of her failure to protect her only daughter from the ravages of a wicked world seemed to impose its bitter weight upon her carriage. Clara drew closer and reached out to embrace the only caring soul she had ever known and to bask in the nurturing circle of her mother's arms.

Her approach seemed to scare off the illusion and, in its place, an amorphous mass of entities mixed and mingled like steam from a boiling cauldron. Low dreadful moans and high-pitched pleading wails, scarcely audible at first, emanated from a force within the glass. An onslaught of ethereal and alien demons burst out upon her. Her sanity, no longer a given, paled before the implausible and failed to bolster her perceptions of reality.

As she fell back, her arms shot forward. A formidable energy seized her and pulled her relentlessly toward the mirror. The evil spirit-cloud coalesced into the witchy hag of her childhood dreams. Cackling insanely, the thing fought determinedly to draw her back into the nightmares of her past.

Utter terror doubled Clara's resolve to escape, but the force within the glass was too strong to resist. Her body inclined away from the source a full thirty degrees, yet, the magnetic phenomena reeled her in as easily as if she were drawn across a frozen pond. Her screams pierced the bolted door and travelled down the stair railing to Roger's ears.

Roger responded in seconds. As soon as he entered Clara's room, the poltergeists within the mirror released her. Clara collapsed to the floor in exhaustion. It was not Roger's intent to save her from the apparition. He could care less about her life, but her usefulness had not yet elapsed. Biggs would come as long as he knew Clara was alive. How much longer Clara remained so depended entirely upon the girl's will to survive.

Roger did not know the Lovingdales from jackshit, but he respected their blasphemous strength. But to allow the possession to grow beyond prediction and control was out of the question. Submission to any power outside his own might derail his plans. The intervention of the 'ghosts in the glass' apparently exorcised the Lovingdale demons from his body. Roger was determined to master his Id and not let his subconscious dictate terms. Ironically, he was both in tune and at odds with the evil nature of the decaying estate. But he rejected its sizable contribution, convinced his own damned soul and innate corruption were powers enough. He would neither need nor tolerate interference from the forces of darkness—be they fate, luck, deity or devil.

CHAPTER XXIII

I awoke in a disjointed state. It took several minutes to orient myself to my surroundings. The darkness around me was practically impenetrable except for a narrow shaft of light. A rectangular aperture six inches by eighteen inches in dimension and nearly ten feet from the damp concrete slab on which I lay sliced through the inky space like a laser knife.

My adversary had placed me on my side in a corner with my knees pulled to my chest. My wrists were bound tightly behind my back and to my ankles. I did not know how long I had been unconscious. It may have been over night; it might have been days. My last remembrance was of near strangulation as I bumped along in the bed of the old truck that brought me here.

Having no point of reference, it was impossible to triangulate my position relative to the house proper. I could be in a heretofore-undiscovered outbuilding or catacomb beneath the main structure. It was clear the being I battled on the second level and the cretin who coldcocked me in the Hotel Ambloy were one and the same. The man's ignoble countenance grimaced at me from every cobwebbed corner and dank recess into which I peered.

I felt relieved the threat I was facing was human—more or less. With considerable effort, I loosened my bonds sufficiently to slip my hands over my rump and feet to the front of my body. My wrists were still constrained by the rope around my ankles, but the new configuration allowed me to face my problem head-on.

Using my elbows, I patted the waistband of my trousers for the

Walther and found it missing. "Damn," I said, disgusted with my ineptness. "A lot of good a pistol does you, if you're always losing it." But in light of my situation, a lost firearm was the least of my worries. My immediate concern was to find a way to free myself from my restraints and escape.

By splaying my knees as widely as possible and bending my body double, I was able to reach my restraints with my teeth. The rope was bailing twine—tough, but fibrous. The loosely braided strands were easier to gnaw through than hemp or nylon, and I did so with rat-like efficiency, spitting the shredded matter in a little pile between my legs.

Unfortunately, before I completed my work, a low grating noise alerted me to the rear wall opposite the tiny window. I stared steadfastly in the sound's direction. A red line of light, like an acetylene torch, opened at the bottom of the wall and burned upward like an explosive fuse. It was followed by another line perpendicular to the first. The back wall grunted open.

In the space where the door had been, a silhouetted figure, statuesque and threatening, stood akimbo. As the shadow advanced towards me, the glare from a torch's dancing flame outshone my eyes. I could no longer determine my captor's proximity, for the intense light contracted my dilated pupils to pinpricks.

A sharp whack to the base of my skull rendered me senseless, and a vague sensation of someone dragging me towards the open door was all my fading consciousness could discern. The familiar state of blackness overcame me and time vanished, yet again.

Sometime later, a breeze as cold as a witch's tit tickled me awake. I found myself tethered to a post centered upright in another bleak and lightless space. The peculiar feeling of not being alone unnerved me, though no sound or movement in or from the shadows confirmed my suspicions. Pain in my head and neck was excruciating. Someone was always hitting me on the head, and I was getting damn tired of it.

Ropes separately binding my hands and feet and another encircling my neck effectively secured my body to the post at three points. My captor evidently noticed the abrasions on my restraints and deduced from their worried state that I was chewing my way to freedom. Repositioning me thusly insured I made no further progress towards extrication.

I could only see the area of the room ninety degrees to either side of a line normal to my nose. The corners of the room were dark. Dim luminescence between them was enough to define the extents of the dungeon. Scanning the enclosure from floor to ceiling revealed no obvious light source. The origin of the ambient light had to be either overhead or immediately behind me.

I returned my eyes front and was struck by the hint of a being crouching near the wall facing me. Even in the nearly impenetrable shadows, the creature's skin seemed pale as bleached bones. Two violet spots that could have been eyes fluoresced like uranium coals. I stared incredulously at the entity until it bounded away and vanished within the dank recesses of my prison. "Clara!" I called. "Clara, is that you? I'm here to help you." I received no response.

The tinkling of clanking metal and the creaking of another door announced a return visitation. Relative to the darkness to which I had grown accustomed, the light from the doorway was bright as sunshine. Indeed, it turned out to be just so for the door opened up to the outside. I could hear songbirds beyond my prison walls chirping merrily. I was convinced that my place of incarceration was inside the house proper. Still, I could not pinpoint my coordinates with any degree of accuracy.

For the first time, my captor seemed unconcerned with concealing his identity. He stepped before me and stared down like a sadist contemplating harm to a helpless victim. The black plastic grip of my stainless steel Walther PPK peaked from the top of his waistband. Noticing my attentions, he rested his fingertips on the pistol's anodized backstrap and patted it lightly with his fingertips.

"Looking for this?" he asked playfully. "I'll keep it for now, but I promise to send it to any surviving relatives you may have as a memento."

"What do you mean by that?" I asked, knowing full well the import behind his sardonic remark.

"It doesn't matter," he added. "On second thought, I think I'll keep it. Did you know Hitler killed himself with one of these?"

"No, I didn't," I answered, trying to keep him talking, "but that sounds like the kind of morbid detail you'd pick up on."

The boy grinned hideously. "Don't it, though?"

"Why don't you follow suite?" I suggested.

He kneeled before me, grabbed a handful of my hair and

rhythmically pulled my head forward and back against the post as if practicing dashing my brains out. "Why did you have to come here? Why didn't you just leave me and mine alone?" He asked, apparently lost in the recesses of his own mind.

When his efforts increased, I gritted my teeth and prayed a psychotic episode would not spirit the man away beyond reason. My brains were beginning to scramble like eggs. I could not make him stop but, by God, if I ever got my hands around his scrawny neck I could sure make him wish he had.

Suddenly, his eyes cleared and he returned to the here and now. He released my hair and brushed the dust from my shirt while stating matter-of-factly: "Now, you have to die. But first, I want to show you something. I'll be back for you when I'm ready." Then, he turned to leave without looking back or offering explanation.

"Don't come back on my account," I spat sarcastically, thinking a dose of humor might alleviate my own misery. "If I want your attention again, I'll send you a valentine."

The man acknowledged I had spoken, but it was doubtful my insult had registered. True to his twisted word, he returned after sunset and escorted me to an exterior location about twenty meters from a corner of the house. He strapped me to a thick wooden post centered in a ten-foot by ten-foot squared notch cut from a dense hedgerow.

My position afforded a view of the back of the house and an incongruous deck or stage queerly placed between two trees—the utility of which I could not fathom. Once the maniac secured me to his satisfaction, he left without speaking. His intentions were vague as bird tracks upon a boulder. My thoughts returned to the spectral female entity seen in the cellar-like space. Could it have been Clara? If so, how did she enter and depart the room so secretively, and where was she now?

My ruminations ended when the girl I presumed to be Clara appeared robed in sheer white linen and accompanied by our mutual tormentor. I could distinguish her form clearly through the material as she walked before the torch in her captor's hand. The man followed her holding a rope leash fastened around her neck. Had I the mobility to move, I would have felled the villain with a fatal blow for this blatant cruelty alone.

They stopped near the platform briefly before ascending the step.

The altar, as it now appeared to me to be, lent the scene a peculiar theatricality and I admit to being briefly and selfishly lost in the moment in a state of suspended belief. The inhumanity of the presentation snatched me back. This was no rehearsal for a Broadway performance; this was a life and death event of enormous and dire consequence. I felt ashamed at my voyeuristic lapse of reason, but I had no recourse but to watch the unsettling events unfold. The devil strung the girl between the two trees by her wrists and quickly departed.

Two wide strips of duct tape sealed my mouth. My hearing, however, was unimpaired and I distinguished the girl refer to the man by the name...'Roger'. How did she know him, and why would he mistreat her so? If she were indeed the girl I sought, why had Biggs not mentioned anyone named Roger in the background briefing he gave me? Nothing made any sense.

As the twilight dimmed to darkness and the moonlight had its say, a stiff northerly breeze swept the night air clean. The gale whipped the girl's tunic wildly about her torso and ripped tears from my eyes. Squinting into the blow, I angled my head slightly left and right to lessen the wind's influence upon my vision.

The primal sacrifice before me, if that was indeed what I was observing, compelled me to watch and held me spellbound. Strong emotions of disgust, rage, fatigue and, yes, even lust emerged from the vestiges of my reptile brain, buried though they were by thousands of years of civilized repression and social taboo. The moonlight spread in intermittent waves as the tempest-tossed clouds overhead passed between it and the midnight Earth. The air was icy. Tears froze on my cheeks before their time. An unearthly howl sent a gauntlet of goose bumps up my back and raised my hair and inch from my scalp.

An amorphous form beyond the girl's location suddenly materialized and appeared to change position. I questioned my perception, at first, thinking the movement to be a trick of light refracted from my frozen tears. However, further scrutiny convinced me the mass was, in fact, moving. I could not yet identify its shape or material composition. When the mound glided to within ten paces of the girl, the moonlight confirmed my fears. Roger had returned.

He stripped off his clothing and baby stepped towards the helpless girl. How he withstood the wintry forces was beyond me, yet he appeared completely indifferent to the raw wind and biting cold. Arching his back while supporting his posture with hands on his rump, he let loose the same ungodly howl I heard earlier. He turned to face me, intent that I be watching. His mischievous eyes sparkled like diamonds as the moonlight washed over them.

Sharpened awareness and a heightened perception of danger snapped every fiber of my being to attention, but there was no way I could conceive the turmoil in the poor lass' brain. I closed my eyes, foolishly thinking my inability to witness the event would preclude its occurrence. I castigated myself for such selfish denial in the face of the unconscionable acts unfolding in front of me. So, I opened my eyes and resumed my impotent vigil.

Roger wrapped his arms around the girl's waist and pulled her forcefully back against himself—timing his reflexive movements with the repetitive carnal lunging of his loins. The pitiful woman could do nothing. I winced when I considered the number of occasions she may have endured similar atrocities, and prayed her suffering would soon end. My heart bled for her, my soul cried for her and my utter incapacity to rescue her buried my self-esteem and confidence beneath layers of shame and indignation.

After Roger concluded his vulgar antics, I noticed a disturbing peculiarity of a different nature all together. He now seemed to be resting his head despondently on her shoulder with his face lost within the folds of her hair. I had no idea what he was doing. The girl's boneless posture slumped after this final assault. Her arms, stressed by her dead weight, stretched into sinewy strands no thicker than the ropes that held her suspended. The two bodies merged into one beneath the brooding tree branches, and I felt myself swoon into a semi-conscious state as blackness, my old ally, revisited.

It was still dark when I recovered from my delirium. My skin had turned blue from cold. Roger and Clara had both vanished. No evidence of the spectacle I witnessed remained save the dangling strands swaying slightly in the wind and the odious platform that played a no-less wicked part in the debauchery.

A disturbance within the hedgerow to my rear thrilled me with anticipation. Time would reveal what pernicious beast was about to pounce upon me, rend my body to pieces or devour me alive. Perhaps

Roger, with his perverted desires, had returned to perform similar obscenities upon my person. The rustling to my rear grew louder, followed by the distinct, gruff and exaggerated whisper of my name. Again, someone spoke my name, and I responded with guttural exclamations.

I cannot overstate my elation and surprise when I recognized the voice over my shoulder as that of Bernard Biggs. He quickly stripped away the duct tape sealing my mouth and untied the offensive cords from around my neck and hands. I crumpled to my knees upon my release, the strength in my legs inadequate to support my weight. Seconds elapsed before the flow of blood restored normal functionality and resilience to my cold-sapped extremities.

"Biggs!" I exclaimed. "How did you get here? How, on Earth, did you find us?"

"Us?" Biggs asked, blending hope and disbelief. "Is Clara here? Have you seen her?" He grabbed me by my biceps and spun me around to face him.

"Yes, she is here," I confirmed. "Some maniac she calls 'Roger' is holding her prisoner. She seems to know him from somewhere. Any idea who he is?"

"I know the bastard," Biggs disclosed ruefully. "It's my fault Clara is here."

I stared incredulously at my employer. "What else haven't you told me?" I spat, forgetting the place and time.

"Quiet, do you want him to hear us? He'll be back for you shortly. He might be on his way now. We have to get Clara out of there. Any suggestions?"

"Yeah, a few. But first, I want some answers."

"There is no time for explanations now. Here he comes!"

Biggs and I used our backs as battering rams to push a path through the dense shrubbery until we cleared the hedgerow's opposite exterior face. Once free of the hedge, Biggs went his way and I went mine. Biggs was right. This was no time for explanations. I focused on saving Clara and my sensitivity to perceived effrontery vanished with the moment.

Maneuvering through the mass of trees took considerable time and energy. Each step in the darkness could mean a serious tumble, impalement on broken branches or both. Ultimately, I arrived at a tall pine with a sturdy limb some twenty feet from the forest floor. The perch should provide an unobstructed view shed from which I could conduct surveillance of the old house and the hedge-rimmed alcove from which I had just escaped.

I shimmied to the vantage point. The full moon and light from the windows and open door illuminated the space I formerly occupied to twilight levels. I could see Roger prancing menacingly about in half-circles, stamping his feet and flapping his arms like a decapitated chicken. He was obviously incensed at my escape, and from his animations I deduced he had yet to formulate the method by which I slipped my bonds. I watched him study the uncut rope for a moment then toss it aside and hurry back into the house.

In a disturbingly long minute, Roger appeared at the second-story window and leaned out using his extended arms to support his weight. The streams of impurity coursing through his demented mind were his alone. His body language suggested that he was anxiously straining to see something. Perhaps, he had spotted Biggs? Subsequently, he straightened upright, withdrew back into the shadows and disappeared from view.

CHAPTER XXIV

I eased myself down the trunk of the yellow pine, but a small, jagged spur snagged my pants as I descended. My grip upon the coarse-barked trunk gave way and I slipped below the protruding stub. My left foot was now higher than my head. Bending in the middle, I struggled to inch my way skyward. I held fast to one side of the trunk with my left hand while I groped around the tree's considerable girth with my right. The awkwardness of my circumstance caused me to tip sideways. I again lost hold and fell backwards. After bashing about for a moment or two, I came to rest suspended upside-down by my trouser leg.

I, again, bent my body double and attempted to right myself, but the weakened stub let go and I crashed headfirst to the ground. Luckily, a dense growth of Rhododendron bushes near the base of the tree cushioned my fall. Unluckily, the mature formidable branches therein introduced themselves to my still smarting skull. Apparently, concussion favored my company, but I would be remiss to fail to acknowledge that a hard head is, in my line of work, a decided advantage

I awoke in the pre-dawn chill and smacked the brittle, fuzzy frost from off my clothing with the endearing, dry crackle a coroner might associate with refrigerated body bags. Speaking of refrigeration, I was cold and getting colder. I had to find shelter inside or I would soon die of exposure.

The roofline of the old house was visible where I stood and reminded me immediately of where I was and why I was here. My head was bleeding and I felt like whipped shit. I scarcely had the strength to stand let alone save someone. Still, I had to try.

Roger had my Walther. I kicked myself in the ass for that repeatedly, but it did not change a thing. He still had it. That was my greatest concern. Were it not for the 'equalizer' being in my enemy's hands, I would have stormed the front door. Outmaneuvering a bullet is not easily done. I would have to move extremely stealthily to gain entry into the house and avoid murder by my own artillery.

In my mind's eye, I reconstructed the house's blueprint by drawing on what I learned from my initial visit. I knew there was a basement entrance on the south side of the structure. I noted it before, but, in my haste on that occasion, I chose to inspect the main floors of the house first. Logically, the lower entrance would provide access to an upper level, but I could not be certain. The house was peculiar in many respects and could harbor a host of hidden passageways and crawlspaces.

I considered going for help, but from whom would I seek it? My experience with the locals left the impression they were all imbeciles. They had no real idea what was going on outside their own mini-spheres, nor did they seem to care. Everyone seemed to buy into the same local superstitious fear, and that fear was emptying the town faster than water down a drain. Anyway, civilization was some distance away and I had no expeditious way of getting from here to there. By the time I returned, Clara could be dead.

I hoped Biggs was having better luck than I was having. I had not heard from him since he untied me. The stubborn bull insisted on going his own way. What could I do? I could not stop him, nor did I want to try. He was an asshole, and he would do whatever he wanted regardless. I was willing to bet my last dollar he was solely responsible for the mess we were all now mired in.

The sky blazed with the first streaks of dawn, and the old adage 'red sky at morning, sailor take warning' sprang to mind. I dismissed it quickly. Pontificating on the *Farmer's Almanac* was the last thing I needed to do right now. Still, the sky was brilliant and portentous. Stranger things than thunderstorms in February had already happened. My mind raced.

The morning birds vocalized their customary raucous melodies and the distant hollow strains of a "rain crow" harmonized with the chorus. The birds were making quite merry—completely unaware of anything apart from their own existence. How lucky they were, I thought. I was a lot like that too, but lately, less so. There was barking off in the distance. Dogs or coyotes, I thought. Their calls were too yippy to be wolves. I remembered man exterminated wolves in this and nearly every other part of the country a century ago.

I decided to try to enter the house through the storm cellar. The inclined doors were heavy and hinged on their outer edges, but I believed I could lift one enough to slide my slender body through. I raised one door to thirty degrees and propped it open with a short timber that lay beneath it. The lack of light in the space beyond would be a problem. Roger had absconded with my flashlight, but, remarkably, I still had a book of matches I procured earlier from the lobby of the Ambloy Hotel. They came in handy as I descended the moss-covered steps.

Stale air at once introduced the acrid smell of mold and decay to my nostrils. The place was a jumble—filled with broken furniture, storage drums, candelabras, crates and discarded construction materials. On the far end of the space, an orphaned rail free stairway hugged the wall. Stealthily, I made my way, match by match, through the field of debris to the steps. I ascended them cautiously but stopped to grit my teeth with every creak of the shrunken treads. I placed my feet near the stringers to attenuate the sound.

At the top of the steps, a closed door halted my progress and presented its own puzzle for my consideration. The knob was missing, but the door would not open. After a brief analysis, I retraced my path down the creaking steps and searched the area until I found a strip of galvanized tin. The metal, possibly remnants of surplus roof edging, would serve my purpose well. A quick effort fashioned it into a shape sized to penetrate the void the knob once occupied. Several jiggles and twists later, I engaged the mechanism.

I pushed the door open in minute increments until I could evaluate the interior. The kitchen-like room was empty, though recent occupation was evident. A stout, glass container filled with orange liquid sat near the edge of a loathsome countertop and a cracker box lay belly-up near the blackened sink. The box's contents lay scattered about, presumably, by persnickety animals foraging for food.

Cautiously, I crossed the stone tiled floor to what looked to be a formal dining area. The house was silent except for the soft scuffling of my own footfalls. I tiptoed from room to room. Clara was nowhere to be seen—nor was Biggs or Roger. Biggs could be anywhere, but I knew Roger and Clara were inside somewhere. A spiral staircase with ornate balustrades dominated the next great room I explored and proclaimed the baroque mansion once comparable to any in Europe for entertaining royalty. Beneath years of layered grime, their ostentatious majesty and grace shown still.

Upstairs, I rediscovered the little room where the light had glowed. It was the space occupied by Clara, all right. Articles of women's clothing accessorized a mattress in the corner of the room and the red white-sleeved jacket, dirty but unmistakable, hung from the back of the small rocking chair that faced the window. I lifted the sleeve of the singular garment to my nose and inhaled the girl's essence woven among its threads.

"Where are you?" I asked.

A hazed mirror caught my eye and I found myself peering into the depths of its glass. A feeling of uneasiness swept over me and compelled me to leave the room at once. I turned to depart and was immediately aware of a tugging sensation at my sleeve. Thinking my garment snared by the mirrors decorative frame, I turned to free myself and saw the image of a haggard apparition smiling at me from the mirror's murky depths. The hair on my neck reared again.

Snakes of ectoplasm writhed from the mirrored surface and swirled about my extremities like Marley's chains. I was stifled for breath and panicked. I felt the muscles in my chest contract and my throat constrict. My body stiffened and glided inexorably toward the glass as the cackling spectre drew me nearer. As my face touched the surface of the glass, the stench of evil oppressed me. Whatever demons lurked in that macabre dimension on the far side reeked of malice and malevolence.

I was half in the glass and half out. My hot, heavy breathing condensed thickly on the dark pane. With the thumb of my left hand, I scribed a cross into the steamy film of condensation on the glass and the power within the portal ebbed as if my enemy fell back to reform its defensive line.

With a desperate lunge, I broke free of the influence and fled the room. I did not stop until I reached the lower level of the house. I paused at a base of the stairs to catch my breath and still my thumping heart with rationalizations. I was in shock and utter disbelief by what had just occurred. A tinny, barely audible whine emanated from somewhere deep within the belly of the mansion. The sound's volume increased to tinnitus levels and overpowered my senses. The room swirled as I swooned.

The repeated cranial abuse I had lately suffered was taking its toll and now held sway over my conscious mind. My weighted eyelids drooped and a searing pain between my ears dropped me to the floor. I needed rest and sleep like never before. I continued my vertical decline to a semi-horizontal slump at the foot of the stairs. Sleep came.

#

Biggs' knowledge of Lovingdale Manor was minimal despite being the proprietor and sole proponent of its grandiose renovation. He had perused the floor plans for the monolith on several occasions, but his cursory examinations and perfunctory comments were rudimentary in their understanding of architectural matters. Their purpose was designed more to impress the uninformed and would convince no consulting engineer of their supervisory merit. He did recall seeing a long-abandoned side entrance on the plans.

At one time, the access served as a connecting corridor to an adjacent building that housed the kitchen and pantry—a common practice during the pre- and post- Civil War eras before the advent of modern technologies. The introduction of natural gas and electricity eliminated the danger of fire spreading to the main house from open-hearth cooking practices, rendering the crude, if quaint, methods employed by generations obsolete.

With the necessity of separate facilities removed, Reynolds III integrated the kitchen into the main floor of the big house and ordered the corridor abandoned. However, being a man of incurably romantic and nostalgic nature, the Squire insisted the entrance remain open. He refused to allow workers then veneering the western exposure with brick to seal it.

Subsequent owners of the estate squandered any maintenance resources allocated for the upkeep and abandoned all but a handful of privileged rooms. The entrance remained, but the invasion of inquisitive forest creatures demanded the erection of a temporary barrier to inhibit their frequent intrusions. Being that the most feared and troublesome of forest denizens were quite large, those in charge of renovations placed the boards comprising the partition sparingly with gaps between as wide as a man's palm. As a result, insects, arachnids, reptiles, birds and small mammals had little difficulty trespassing and squatting where they pleased.

Large, ornately carved, wooden doors of German design framed with multi-paned windows created the interior wall of the space and effectively negated further penetration by unwelcome guests. This relative security satisfied the human inhabitants and they coexisted with their forest friends for decades in mutual, if not equiponderate, harmony.

Hordes of invasive plants and scraggly shrubs secured a foothold near the building's crumbling foundation and the shells of chest-high weeds that sprang up thick as thieves in summer hovered near the entrance. Despite these impediments, Biggs found the opening helped in part by the defining pyramidal cornice that projected over the entry. He tore away the rotting boards—their fasteners long ago rusted to dust. Some of the lumber held stubbornly to the jam by sheer determination and a cement-like, symbiotic mixture of algae and dissolved mortar. Despite these difficulties, Biggs exposed the entrance in minutes.

He paused in the archway and listened. He heard the naked nails of rats scarring trails beneath the piles of debris. Small saplings took root nearby at random intervals like neglected houseplants. Without warning, an army of bats exploded from their roost swooping and fluttering their wings with aggressive defiance. Biggs nearly left his skin. He swatted at the flying beasts with mocking, comical gestures. After he calmed himself, he ventured forward. Thick spider webs adorned with the shrouded caskets of unfortunate insects hung in gooey masses throughout the foyer. Biggs retrieved a length of splintered windowsill nearby and brushed the disgusting webs from his path. He advanced down the corridor, swiping the web destroyer before him like a Samurai's katana until he reached the far end.

Two large multi-paned windows installed to either side of massive double doors greeted him. The window to his left had numerous missing panes. The contrast between the dark interior and the reflections on their outer surfaces gave the unit the whimsical appearance of a great crossword puzzle or an enormous toothless grin.

Biggs stepped to the right of the double doors. This window was intact and the sudden appearance of the reflection of his body in the glass charged him like a cattle prod. The atmospheric dreariness and dangerous potential inherent in his mission heightened the intensity of the smallest of alarms. Upon realizing the distorted reflection's true identity, he paused again for a deep cleansing breath. He did not feel like laughing at his foolishness. He put his shoulder to the double doors and brought his weight to bear against them. One door groaned miserably in its old age. He stepped beyond the threshold where darkness enveloped him again. Thankfully, his eyes quickly adjusted to the diminished light and allowed him to continue cautiously ahead.

Noises emanating from another room caught his ear. He inched toward the sounds with Loris-like movements. He stopped near an archway that led to a hall beyond. He flattened his body to the edge of the opening and extended his neck and head through the archway.

The hallway was clear. Sounds deep within the mansion called him closer. He feathered the wall with his fingertips as he advanced toward the sound. A fiery glow from a room at the hall's terminus cast shadows on the grimy walls mimicking the dancing gyrations of maniacal moths. As Biggs moved closer, he recognized Roger's raving alto. When he reached a corner, he craned his head to one side to afford one eye a view of the interior of the room. Roger was nowhere in sight, but Clara sat bound securely to a chair in the center of the room. He stepped closer.

Clara, became aware of Bernard's presence and responded with urgent unintelligible grunts and powerful contractions of her body that caused the chair in which she sat to hop an inch or more from the floor and drop with a sharp clatter. Several loops of rope encircled her from chest to ankles and her mouth was muzzled by wrappings of some kind. Her terrified gaze shot across the room and met his own. Her eyes held the stuff of madness.

CHAPTER XXV

Forgetting about Roger and the present danger, Biggs sprinted to the young woman's aid. "Clara, oh, my darling, what has he done to you?" He pushed and pulled at the offensive bindings to loosen their hold. "I'll kill the son-of-a-bitch!"

The ropes, double-knotted and swollen from the damp environment, would not be easily undone. One length encircled the girl's head at mouth level. Biggs tore at the stubborn strands until his fingers bled. He swore aloud as his movements grew frantic with exasperation. "I'll have you free in a minute," he promised in a strained whisper.

Clara's tensed muscles relaxed as she felt the ropes slacken. The promise Biggs made had scarcely consoled her before her body tensed again. Her agitation signaled Biggs that something was about to happen. He caught a glimmer of motion in the irises of Clara's eyes.

Before Biggs could rise to confront the threat, Roger swung a three-foot length of galvanized pipe over Biggs' head and withdrew it violently against his throat. Biggs lurched instinctively backwards to repel the attack. He clawed at the cold metal in an effort to force his hands between the crushing steel and his fragile larynx. His legs kicked forward and he lost balance when he tried to straighten vertically.

Roger seized the initiative. He moved backwards and sideways strategically anticipating his opponent's manic attempts to find his center. In less than two minutes, oxygen quit flowing from lungs to brain. Biggs stiffened into dead weight and slid to the floor. Roger threw the pipe aside and puffed his chest victoriously. His cadmium yellow eyes rolled back into his skull as he released his valedictorian cry. Twin streams of condensed breath burst forth from his nostrils. His eyes, cold as dry ice, burned through Clara's fading hopes. A smile got the best of him and settled on his thin lips until an autonomic torrent of drool swept it away to the stone floor.

Clara slumped into her chair and closed her eyes. She could hear Roger struggling with Bernard's body, but she dared not look. To see another tormented by this insane subhuman would add immeasurably to her miseries and she could not bear it. Five minutes later, the scuffling was over. She cautiously opened one eye, then the other, and found herself alone and forsaken once more.

Roger ensconced Biggs in the east wing of the estate. His next move was to locate Biggs's vehicle and move it out of sight. The car should have been visible from the upstairs window, but it was not. Ample opportunities for parking and avoiding detection from the main house dotted the driveway's winding length. He discovered the keys to Biggs' vehicle while rummaging through the fool's pockets. All he had to do was stroll down the driveway. The car would be there. He left through the building's front entrance. Near the end of the driveway, about two hundred feet from where it intersected with the road to town, he found the car. He drove it back without incident and stashed it behind the stable doors.

Roger scanned the visible extents of the property for signs of the intruder. He had no idea where the meddler had gone, and the uncertainty troubled him. Maybe, he went for help...maybe. But he could be lurking in the thick undergrowth or peering in any of the unguarded windows. Maybe, he waited around the next bend...maybe. But he did so at his own risk. Roger brushed his paranoia aside with reassurances that he really did not care. He had the investigator's gun nestled snuggly in the waistband of his jeans to mitigate interference. There were only six rounds in the magazine; adequate for his needs, he reasoned. If resolving a situation required more than six rounds, he had one hell of a problem. Six would do. He had all the wherewithal he needed. He would destroy the two-bit private dick as easily as swatting a fly.

He revisited the Great Room to check on Clara and found her bound securely to the chair just as he had left her. The investigator was still lurking about, and he wanted to insure the bait was still ripe and waiting. The sight of the poor girl's fragile beaten condition comforted him. Her tear-stained cheeks and imploring gaze reached his Teflon heart but sloughed away.

Roger's thoughts returned to Biggs. Biggs was no fool, but he was fool enough to come here. Roger cackled insanely as another piece of his plan fell into place. He could afford to laugh now. Victory was his. As he strode to the east wing, the combined Lovingdale energy his psyche fought to stave off for so long returned as formidable as ever. It impregnated his being and spiked through his veins with devilish purpose.

The change in Roger was remarkable. He forgot his duties and charged about the interior of Lovingdale Manor like a cock-of-the walk—his head craned jauntily back. He donned his cape and swirled it about his shoulders like a matador's brega. He conversed with himself and answered with an accent that reflected nineteenth-century sensitivities previously foreign to him. He exhorted each room of the mansion to awaken and recapitulate its scarlet history. He marveled at the illustrative old tapestries remaining on the walls and pretended to divine their secrets. The wall coverings, luxurious in their time, were now stained, moth-eaten and rotting—like the inner lining of Roger's soul. He revisited the ancient tome he previously discarded and kept it ever near. He exhibited no awareness of the change in his intonation and speech patterns though, and he still retained a portion of himself despite the alien presence. Roger felt right at home now. His transformation was complete.

The dispossessions of his past seemed a lifetime away. He existed entirely in the present now, immersed in the moment. He was ready, willing and able to do anything and everything. The world would cringe before his power. The toll for meddling in his plans would exact the ultimate price, and those responsible would suffer for their insolence for the rest of their short lives.

In a few hours, Roger was himself again, although he was exhausted. He felt too wired inside, too engorged, too engrossed for anything as habitual and simplistic as sleep. He had transcended the rudimentary physical limitations of mortals, but his indisposed guests were still human and required attention. So, like any gracious host, he busied himself in the kitchen preparing food for breakfast.

Roger performed as concierge in as courteous a manner as any schizophrenic could. He freed Clara from the bulk of her restraints to allow her to feed herself. Clara consumed her meal with the conviction that maintaining her strength was vital to insure her survival. Roger sat enthralled at her feet, as usual, watching her bird-like motions as she swallowed the meager meal he had prepared.

It would be the last time he would watch. His charming passion play had to end at some point. Roger knew it was only a matter of time before the authorities caught up with him. He was sane enough to understand that much, and insane enough not to let it stop him. His plan would accelerate, now, that was all. The only hitch was the meddler. He could ruin everything if not brought under control.

Roger stood erect after Clara finished her breakfast and rebound her hands to the back of the chair. He patted her head in a rough, inconsiderate manner leaving her tousled mane more so for the effort. The upper portion of her ivory breasts shone like lighted globes. He cupped them one more time in his hands and teased the nipples with his thumbs through her sheer chemise until they firmed up beneath his touch.

Clara turned her head to one side in shame to avoid looking at the monster, but she could not ignore the stimulation nor control her body's response. Her nipples grew proud and stood out in bas-relief despite her desire they remain desensitized and lifeless. The icy breath of the devil himself could not have hastened their contraction more effectively.

When Roger was satisfied with his achievement, he ceased his manipulations and left the room with a haughty air. He remembered Biggs. He did not give a good damn if Biggs ate or not, but years of nutritional deprivation as a child left him with lingering convictions about the sins of wastefulness. He had plenty of cider and crackers left. "I must extend every effort to sustain my guest for one more day or so," he spoke to know one in particular.

Roger's ardently anticipated desire was to force Biggs to watch the death of his beloved. He would show Biggs what a real man could do. It did not matter that Clara was Clara. She could be anyone. What mattered was that it would hurt Biggs. He had nothing personal against the girl. In another life, they could have been friends…lovers…hell, even betrothed. But under the circumstances, she was nothing more than a means to an end—a pound of flesh to be exacted to deprive the treacherous Biggs the cherished core of his existence. The scenario must play out to its inevitable conclusion. Death would be the final act. His thoughts began to chafe, so he shooed them away with a hand before his eyes as if dispelling thirsty gnats. He gathered more breakfast morsels and headed to the east wing.

Lightning struck the area of the mansion where Biggs lay years ago, and the immense power of the strike blew the entire corner of the room away. It was the perfect place to view the clouds passing; see the stars overhead at night and the full moon when it chose to reveal itself, or to hear the howls and moans of the night creatures and fear their loathsome proximity. Roger wanted Biggs to see, hear and feel it all and to know his time was fast coming.

#

Back in town, the residents scurried around like rodents. They believed whole-heartedly in the myths and superstitions surrounding Lovingdale Manor. For decades, villagers awaited the vengeance of Squire Lovingdale, who swore to return from the grave and punish those who dared impede his work or disturb the sanctity of his home. Curse upon curse for the Viscount's enemies filled the pages of the journals he left behind and promised no less.

It was true the Squire had murdered his family and aired their lifeless corpses upon blasphemous crosses, but to him the act was the ultimate expression of love. His hunger for power had rotted away his humanity. All that remained was the sickness that drove him to sacrifice his own blood relations in exchange for passage to his infernal eternity. What Lovingdale did not learn, for all his decades of devotion to wickedness, was that Satan was a qualifier and would have his way. The Devil collects on outstanding debts in his own good time and has little to fear from humans who disprove of his methods.

When dealing with two separate planes of existence, who can say that eternity, measured by the Devil's clock, is no more or no less an instant in human terms. The lightning bolt that splintered the Squire's world filled him with more power than any mortal had ever known before, yet that same power destroyed him just as quickly. He made a pact with Satan and Satan honored the agreement. It bears remembering that though time is man's conception, the concept of evil is timeless. And although evil can always be trusted to manifest itself, Evil, being evil, can never be trusted.

Continued isolation from modern concepts and beliefs lent credence to Lovingdale's vow to return and conditioned the simple townsfolk to swallow his malarkey without question. The unusual synergy in town, the abominable night howling and the resumption of slaughtered livestock confirmed their suspicions that Satan had reanimated the Squire to do his bidding. They could not risk having their sons and daughters destroyed in similar fashion or trapped in hellish enslavement. No, superstition or not, it was a risk too great to take.

When news of the reincarnation of Squire Lovingdale surfaced, it spread like prairie fire from mouth to ear. Families abandoned their homes. Store keepers closed their businesses and usurped trucks, trailers, buses, wagons, sedans and every conceivable form of transportation in their mad haste to evacuate. The chaos was amazing and contagious. Everyone feared what they feared most—the guilt of their collective conscience for allowing evil to thrive within their midst. That they would pay for the apathy of their ancestors left them little choice but to run, and run they did. It seemed only the clerk at the Ambloy Hotel, Roger, Biggs, Clara, and Harry were naive enough to remain.

#

Fragmented images and gross phantasms plagued Biggs' unconscious mind. He saw himself spiraling through blackness—his body illuminated by flashing lights. Strangely, his form did not diminish in size, as one would expect when observing one's self plummeting from a superior elevation to a lesser one. Instead, his tumbling and spinning body gyrated on a constant plane of action as if suspended by invisible wires. As the void beneath his spastic body rushed upwards, the claustrophobic walls that contained him growled and pressed ever closer to one another, intent on snuffing out his existence with glacial certainty.

The space was tight as a well-digger's ass. His chest heaved taut and full as if bearing a great weight. His diaphragm, absent the dictates of autonomy, responded only to deliberate commands to rise and fall. The dusky smell of moldy wood was so strong he could taste it. His open eyes might well have been unhatched eggs and his skull a basket. He inferred interment underground unlikely. His puzzled mind worked feverishly to resolve his predicament.

Answers came with his next breath. Unseen forces ripped the blackness away and exposed a field of dirty white. The relative brightness shut his eyes like the throw of a switch. After the orange-red afterimage dispelled, he opened his eyes again. He now clearly discerned the rhythmic, swirling ridges of a plasterer's trowel on what remained of the textured ceiling above. He understood immediately that he was conscious and above ground. He attempted to rise from where he lay but his legs and arms were useless, his head immobilized. His mind was a muddle.

Roger's insipid cooing—the high-pitched, strangely feminine music he employed on occasions of great pleasure or satisfaction—began again. Then, his manic countenance sprang immediately into Biggs' field of vision. Roger clapped his hands in child-like merriment and bent over his old friend like a concerned saint tending a leper. "How we doing, Love?" He asked in a peculiar English accent. "Did you miss me? How do you like your new wardrobe, eh? Oh, I forgot, you can't see it, can you?" Roger giggled.

Biggs lay within a pine casket atop a large oak table. He swore incomprehensible oaths only to swallow them again, trapped as they were beneath the woven fabric tightly drawn over his lower face. He prayed for intervention from the gods, any god, to destroy his deviant tormentor without mercy and neutralize whatever evil fueled his neurosis.

"I'll have you out of that box in a jiffy," Roger chimed. With several astounding crashes of a 'single jack', he smashed the sides of the makeshift burial box to the floor. "There we go." I'll let you admire yourself in a minute, mate. But I have to finish dressing you first, don't I?"

Biggs found that by bending his torso at midpoint and sustaining a contraction of his abdominal muscles, he could raise his upper body three or four inches. He was horrified to discover Roger expeditiously wrapping large torn strips of linen fabric around his lower extremities in the fashion of an Egyptian mummy. This situation explained his 'dream' and his immobilization.

When Roger finished, he returned to gloat over his prize. He held up a large, jagged shard of broken mirror and rested it on his victim's shoulder—angled to reflect his masterpiece with maximum efficacy. "What do you think, Biggsie? Nice wrapping, huh? If it was Christmas, I'd 'ave you under the tree, I would."

Biggs strained his gaze to the lower corners of his eye sockets and discerned his shrouded image reflected in the broken mirror. He could hardly move a muscle. He pumped his physique to the degree possible while Roger wrapped him, but attempts to exaggerate his musculature created too little slack in the bindings to be advantageous. The lunatic had performed his task well. Disbelief confounded his ego for allowing capture and mummification by so meager an adversary as Roger Perry. Admittedly, Roger was not so meager an adversary as Biggs had led himself to believe. Now, his underestimation may cost him his life and quite possibly the life of his darling Clara.

Roger mused at his former partner's pitiable wiggling and tossed the mirror against the wall where it shattered into smaller fragments. He bent over the poor man's face and scrutinized his features with deftness and precision, as an archeologist would inspect an historic artifact or Paleozoic fossil. Abruptly, he placed his thumbs on his makeshift mummy's eyelids and stretched them open until the eyes bulged to an extraordinary size. He glared menacingly into the man's straining orbs, then spat in his face and laughed.

Biggs writhed on the table as much as his confining wardrobe allowed. Cotton gauze wicked the moisture from his mouth and salivary glands like desert sand. Duct tape, Roger's miracle accessory of choice (employed to stifle his victim's insufferable blathering and not from fear that his cries would be heard) sealed the gauze in place.

Roger placed a tray of cider and crackers on Biggs' chest. He wisely left a portion of the man's midsection unwrapped. This clever forethought facilitated bending him in a semi-upright position as need arose. He wanted to keep Biggs alive as long as possible, but not indefinitely.

"I brought you some breakfast, Biggsie. I hope you are fond of crackers. We've got crackers, crackers, and more crackers." Roger laughed.

Biggs' rolled his head from side to side to scan the makeshift mortuary for a way out. The bare walls were blotched with grey-green mildew and signs of black mold. Small saplings sprang up like the skeletal arms of zealous volunteers from beneath the dead leaves that carpeted the floor. The remains of what appeared to be small animal carcasses lay rotting in the corners. The sinking realization that there was no apparent escape caused his eyes to roll back into his head and his head to fall back against the table.

"We're going to have a play tonight," Roger explained, chatting like an old friend catching up after a lengthy absence. "Well, more like opera, really, and you are the guest of honor. Looks like you'll be the only one there, I'm afraid, unless your bungling friend decides to join us. I'll have to find him first, but that shouldn't prove too difficult." As Roger rambled on, he orbited the table on which Biggs lay, never releasing the helpless man from his penetrating gaze for an instant.

"You know what they say: 'If you build it, they will come'. I thought of inviting the whole town. But the last time I was in town, everyone was packing up and leaving. They were running, they were. And do you know who they were running from? They were running from me, Biggs…and good riddance." He emphasized his last statement with quick, self-identifying jabs of his thumb to his chest.

"They were right to run, and you were stupid for coming here. Did you think I couldn't hurt you? There was no way a bug like me could bite the almighty Biggs, eh? Well, consider yourself bitten, Mr. Bernard Biggs." Roger stopped circling the table and paused just behind Biggs' head. "Nobody could touch *you*, eh, Biggs?" He teased. "Nobody, but yours truly."

CHAPTER XXVI

Roger's malice oddly melted to magnanimity. He picked up a rotting cushion from a refuse pile near the table. He folded Biggs' body, fluffed the pillow with two back-hand punches from his free hand and positioned the item between the man's shoulder blades. "There you go, Love", he whispered mockingly. "Is that better?"

Biggs glared at the maniac until the strain of his stare forced tears from his eyes. "Son-of-a-bitch! I'll kill you!" His muffled, angry threats grunted through his rag-covered mouth lost their meaning but little intensity.

Roger heard nothing but the rattling pratfall of a delirious patient. "What? What's that?" He feigned interest, leaning closer and turning his ear towards him. "Here, let me help you." He carefully unwrapped the linen from around Biggs's head, tossed the fabric onto the floor and then ripped the duct tape away from the man's mouth with one fluid motion.

Biggs let out a guttural shriek of pain as Roger tore the tape away. A sizeable portion of a two-day old stubble went with it. Biggs coughed out the soggy gauze and cursed wildly. "You bastard! I'll kill you! I'll murder you! I'll pull you're fucking toenails out, you..."

Before the threat was complete, Roger dipped a cracker into a cup of warm stringent liquid and shoved it into Biggs' foaming mouth. He cupped one hand over the helpless man's mouth and used his other hand to encourage swallowing with forceful vibrations of the man's throat. Roger repeated his offering between murderous oaths. When Biggs closed his mouth tightly and turned his head, Roger grabbed a handful of his hair, jerked his head back and secured it in the crook of his left elbow. He wanted his old friend to see who was in control. He squeezed Biggs' nose smartly between thumb and forefinger until a desperate gasp for air provided Roger a ready passage through which to propel the gruel into the man's gullet.

Roger now pressed the full weight of his body upon Biggs' sizable stomach to counter the anticipated objections. He crammed two more crackers into his mouth, cupped his palm to prevent a spiteful spit and again warbled Biggs' throat to induce swallowing. This unhealthy pattern continued for several more cycles. The revolting mixture bubbled up and over Roger's hand and oozed like yellow lava from between his fingers. Roger used a fresh cracker to scoop up the jaundiced mush and promptly reintroduced it to the obdurate cavity from whence it came.

There were several crackers left on the tray, and Roger was growing increasingly frantic and impatient. Dipping the crackers in the cider was proving too tedious. He decided it was time to accelerate the exercise. Clamping Biggs' nose shut caused his mouth to again open reflexively. Roger promptly filled it with the remaining liquid. The open mouth would not hold the jar's entire volume and nearly half spilled out and flowed down both sides of the wretched man's neck, staining the linen bandages a putrid ochre.

Biggs repeatedly lifted his shoulders and hips from the table in the spasmodic undulations. His air supply exhausted quickly. He arched his back and seizured about like a fish on land until he was forced to swallow.

Roger was obsessed, now. No connection to the dregs of his humanity remained. Like an automaton, he smashed the remaining crackers into a thousand pieces in his fist and force-fed the gagging handful to his mummified captive.

Biggs convulsed like a rabid dog as he choked on his own vomit. His eyes rolled madly and widened to saucers. In less than a minute, his protestations ceased. His pupils turned fixed and dilated. A dusky, waxen film clouded his eyes as his life ebbed away.

Roger had witnessed that phenomena before. He remembered how eyes glazed over whenever the spirit left its earthly shell. Strangely, the passing of life seemed to awaken Roger's innate self-awareness. Roger was pissed that Biggs had passed prematurely, then the piss quickly turned to full-blown panic. Conflicting thoughts collided in his brain. What to do?

What was to become of his planned performance—his *grande finale*? Was the guest of honor to miss the show? He could never allow that to happen. Roger forced his fingers into the man's iron trap of a mouth and scraped the occluded airway free. A drip or two of debris-laden water from the exposed timbers above polluted the hollows of Biggs' eyes. Roger swabbed the sockets dry.

In his mindful state, Roger discerned that everything around him was soaking wet. He was normally more observant and sharp, but today he had seen only Biggs, the elephant in the room. He had been blinded by revenge and he chastised himself for his weakness.

Roger glanced furtively around the room and then upwards through the ragged breach in the building's ceiling and roof. The skies were thick and blue-grey as the winter coats of Nebelung cats. Rolls of thunder, distant at first, soon resounded through the empty halls preceded by lightning bright enough to sear retinas. The cacophony grew maddening. Swirls of mist and rain vented into the room from the opening above.

His only recourse was to resuscitate Biggs, but what could he do? Think! Suddenly, as if spawned by the thunderous applause and theatrical lighting, a splendid idea lit his face. Of course! If his consummate power destroyed Biggs, perhaps Nature's own awesome energy could restore his life! But he needed to acquire the items necessary before resurrection could commence. Time was a crucial element, as his success hinged on the storm's longevity and intensity. The unyielding forces of Nature were notoriously unpredictable. One could tap the energy but never harness it for long.

"Wire, rope, steel pipe" ...he counted off the essentials on his fingers as he hurried to the basement level. The lines between fiction and reality blurred. He remembered Baron Frankenstein performing similar experiments years ago. Images flooded back in refreshing detail. He had seen with his own eyes the experiments work for his heroes. Why should comparable efforts fail here?

He returned to the east wing forthwith with an armload of equipment. The basement was a treasure trove of usable materials. He imagined converting the lower-level rooms into a laboratory when this was all over. A Barlow knife pulled from his back pocket aided in removing the strips that bound Biggs' body to the table. Quickly, he tore the mummy rags away from the lifeless torso.

He threaded the galvanized pipe used earlier as a weapon through Biggs' shirt sleeves and behind the man's neck to support his outstretched arms. He then fitted a larger steel pipe, two inches in diameter, perpendicular to the first and parallel to the body's spine. He lashed the two together to form a makeshift cross and wired the body to the cross with triple strands of oxidized copper wire. With some difficulty, he inserted ten-penny nails through the fleshy portions of the dead man's arms and legs and connected them to each other with lines of similar wire. The loose ends of the wires he then twined around the galvanized pipe.

Roger admired his artistry then utilized a crude block and tackle long abandoned by bricklayers from a distant time. He flung the pull rope across an exposed rafter and encircled the stiffening corpse with the hook end before configuring the ropes to facilitate lifting. He raised the body enough to maneuver it to the floor and piled the wooden table high with bricks, marble and every item of respectable weight in the room.

Biggs weighed a ton. It took every ounce of Roger's strength to pull the man skyward. After achieving sufficient height, he secured the loose end of the rope to the wooden table. Now, he must wait until a well-aimed electrical strike infused the mass of corpuscles with the energy necessary to rekindle life.

#

After awakening, I, somehow, found my way to the room where Clara sat strapped to a straight-backed chair. I ran to the girl's side, freed her from her restraints and assisted her to her feet. She was faint, weak and barely able to stand under her own power. I ushered her halfway to the doorway before her rubbery legs returned to flesh and bone.

"Who are you?" Clara cried.

"Clara, my name is Harry. Bernard Biggs hired me to help you. I'll explain everything later. Right now, we have to get you out of here!"

"Roger took him" Clara explained. "Do you know where he is?"

"No, I don't," I admitted. "But I promise I'll find him."

"He's hurt. He needs your help, now!" She pleaded.

"I'll find him later." I reiterated. "Right now, you are the one most important to me."

We advanced through the doorway and moved toward the kitchen where I had entered the evening before. Clara leaned on me the entire way. I quickly removed my jacket and draped it around her trembling shoulders. I had not noticed her feet were bare.

"Clara, listen to me." I began in earnest. "If we get separated, you have to make your way to the nearest stream and follow it down to the Rundle River. Stay off the road. That way is easier, but too obvious. Roger will catch you quickly. Do you understand"?

She nodded in the affirmative.

"Once you get to the river, turn to the left and follow it downstream until you find a small settlement. I passed it on my first trip here. You can find shelter there until I can join you, ok?"

She nodded again.

We hurried back the way I had come, but detoured to the abandoned corridor near the kitchen after finding the knobless door shut fast by a draft. We made it through the double doors, but then we zigged where we should have zagged.

The roof suddenly gave way under the tremendous weight of its sodden timbers. Terracotta roofing tiles, six-by-eight rafters, ceiling lathe and two-by-six trusses crashed down around us. Luckily, a cripple-studded windowsill, a third of the distance from floor to ceiling, arrested the fall of the main truss before it completed its journey. Ironically, this fortunate happenstance offered a measure of protection. The unit that knocked us both unconscious served as a wedge that divided the major portion of the debris into two large piles to either side of the beam. The bulk of the near fatal masses lay harmlessly distant from our prostrate bodies.

Sometime later, I awoke with a start, re-animated by the steady drip-drip-dripping of water on my forehead. I rose on wobbly stems. My immediate thoughts were of Clara. I tore wildly at the piles of wreckage while I called her name. After several desperate minutes, I saw the jacket I had given her partially buried by debris. I concluded she must have escaped serious injury and left without me. I shook the foreign matter from the garment and put it on. I was the one shivering now. Moving quickly outside, I shouted her name loudly enough to rise above the din of distant thunder and howling wind.

A denizen of the forest, apparently disturbed from its slumbers by the savageness of the passing tempest, responded in kind. There was something uncanny about the howling, though. It was mysterious, dark and disquieting like no other sound I had ever heard. I decided to follow the frequent cry and use it as a point of reference. When I arrived at the stream bank and the sound grew louder, I knew I was on the right track.

#

At the point where Clara stood, the stream was about fifteen feet across and deeply incised into the rocky soil. The banks were steep and strewn with boulders, some as large as automobiles. The water level was at least twenty feet below her. Various deciduous and evergreen trees thrived in abundance on both sides of the torrent.

The stream served as the main hydrological departure for the watershed that began innocuously enough in the higher elevations behind the Lovingdale house. It emptied after a mile or so into the Rundle River. Explosive rapids cascaded in sharp steps for as far up and down the channel as she could see.

Her knowledge of geology and hydrology was rudimentary, but she understood simple gravitational theory. Ephemeral rivulets flow into creeks, creeks add their volumes to streams and streams feed rivers. Most settlements sprang up near bodies of water, and the northeastern United States was no exception. She remembered Harry's advice and found it solid. Following a watercourse to its confluence with another would lead ultimately to civilization and assistance. It was her only hope of finding her way free of this remote, desolate section of Vermont.

Her naked feet and legs were exposed and vulnerable. Roger hid her shoes, thinking that bare feet alone would prevent her from escaping. After emerging from beneath the collapsed ceiling, her impulse was to run, but she could not leave without her beloved jacket. Better instincts aside, she retrieved it from the little upstairs room. While there, she searched briefly for her shoes but could not find them. Delaying escape further would have been unwise. The gloom of the corridor and layered debris prevented her from seeing Harry. She had no idea he remained next to where she once lay.

As Clara descended the creek bank to the edge of the water, she transported into an unfamiliar world—a primeval place far removed from the society and comforts of the small hometown she knew as a child. The wilderness was raw, visceral and dangerous. She loved it and hated it. Only the most primitive of creatures could find comfort within such a harsh labyrinth rife with torment and brutality. Beasts like the one that kidnapped her—the very same she feared was now howling at her heels.

Clara began working her way down the treacherous embankment. Grasping shrubby stems and saplings helped to counter the tendency to plunge face forward. The menacing nests of brambles and greenbriers rested their wickedness while she passed, and for that she was thankful. A narrow, relatively flat terrace about five feet from the water's edge offered a respite from the exertions of her descent. The area was a remnant of the stream's historic floodplain into which the channel had more deeply incised. She immediately turned downstream.

She passed by the stumps of fallen trees, now serving as tombstones in deference to their former majesty. Nearby, in the throes of decay, the remains of their giant trunks lay dead but unburied on the earth that once nourished them. Though no longer numbered among the living, their presence still defiantly commanded huge linear territories. Rhododendron and mountain laurel, thick and luxurious, covered the cobbled ground at the water's edge. Her struggle was monumental, but she gradually realized progress through the ungainly boulders, gnarly vines and impenetrable shrubbery that confronted her at every turn.

Smilax, less forgiving than its kinder cousins, tore large fragments of her clothing away, leaving tiny, blood speckled battle flags to mark her path. Corkscrew vines, thick and fibrous, dangled like ropes from the tops of trees. Some assisted Clara as she negotiated the terrain. Others drove their tendrils from the earth, wrapped them about her ankles and caused her to blunder beyond control.

Normally, the far reaches of North-central Vermont exceeded the native range of *gleditsia triacanthos*, or Honey Locust, but it thrived here after introduction by Squire Lovingdale. He planted hundreds of them as a windbreak and natural security perimeter that aided in confining the large herds of Devon cattle he raised. He also indulged an unhealthy fascination with this singular species of tree and found their off-putting appearance strangely compatible with his own dark leanings. After more than a century of profligation and evolution in the harsher northern clime, their evil-looking thorns mutated to greater girth and length than their southern counterparts.

Her present torment inspired great feats of daring—achievements totally alien to her and unthinkable under less duress. Her course was preordained. She could not go back, she could not cross the torrential channel, nor could she stay where she was. Her place was forward—to the Rundle River—to a homestead or farm where she hoped to find people humane enough to lend succor to one so sorely in need.

Moving beneath the expansive canopy she was scarcely aware of the sky, but bits and pieces of bright blue and welcome shafts of sunlight offered reminders of a dimension outside the one from which she sought escape. She paused for as long as she dared in the precious golden rooms until the infernal wailing, sounding ever nearer, compelled her to struggle on.

Her blessed adrenal glands provided her with full benefit of their intended function. The miracle substance plagued her heart with palpitations, quickened her breathing and generally made her feel as if she were experiencing slow death from asphyxiation, but its protective effects shielded her from the bitter cold and sharp bites of pain. It also gave her the clarity of vision she needed to navigate through the unfamiliar maze of wilderness.

Around one bend, the sight of a tawny black bear on the opposite bank froze her in her tracks. The animal stopped and stared at her with equal alarm. They eyed each other for several minutes, both wondering what the other was about to do. The bear sniffed the air and reared on its hind legs to magnify its presence and aid it visually. Clara remained deathly still.

Remarkably, woman and bruin simultaneously arrived at the same conclusion. The bear spun to its right and scrambled dexterously up the bank, while Clara pirouetted left; both seeking the marginal difference in elevation that gave the perception of relative dominance and security.

When Clara was certain the threat from the omnivore had lessened, she retuned her attention to recapturing forward momentum. The ungodly howling of her pursuer grew nearer. She knew it was Roger bellowing, and there was no doubt he was as much a beast as the bruin and several times more dangerous. The instinct for self-preservation and desire to see her mother again drove her on.

Suddenly, she became aware of a low murmur, constant in level and sustain—an ambient sound she could not quite distinguish, like the continuous shush of a theater usher. The rustle of leaves, the breath of wind and the stirrings of forest creatures fell silent as her ears tuned to the sound's unique frequency. It apparently originated from the direction she was travelling. She hurried her pace and soon the provocative music increased in volume to a roar.

The water at this point, though at high stage, calmed to placidity and gave no indication of the stream's schizoid nature. The banks, however, grew increasingly steep. The floodplain vanished, segueing into a forty-five-degree incline that forced her to walk with her right leg stiffened and straight and her left leg bent at the knee. When she could no longer advance vertically, she adopted the 'four-legged' posture of her friend the bruin and scrambled up the bank to a passable contour. One could hardly call the new elevation level but, all things being relative in the wilderness, she accepted it gladly.

A clear and present danger alerted her now. She turned to scope the area behind her expecting to see Roger jump from tree to nearer tree. She tried to discern movement in the early morning gloom but could not see past the dense undergrowth for more than fifty feet or so. Seeing nothing, she moved forward only to freeze again.

A beast of a different sort confronted her now. Her abrupt halt caused her feet nearly to slip from beneath her and convinced her at once of the area's deadly potential. She stood spellbound on the brink of an awesome, moss-covered cliff nearly hidden by mist and dripping with slimy wetness. From the lip of the precipice, a ninety-foot waterfall spun dizzily into the depths below awash in a wealth of glory.

CHAPTER XXVII

Clara could not determine Roger's proximity with any measure of confidence. The applause of falling water drowned out every other sound. She surveyed the surrounding land for signs of his approach but saw nothing. The intimidating force before her stood in stark contrast to the placid quality she observed a hundred yards upstream. The sight inspired deep meditations of a religious nature, but this was no time for theological musings. Still, the wonder of the spectacle held her in its grip and her thoughts deepened.

How many times had she questioned the existence of a Supreme Being? An argument could certainly be made that a true and just god, if he were indeed omnipotent and worthy of our devotion and respect, would never allow the myriad atrocities that defile a world of his own creation. 'God is everywhere' fundamentalists spout, but the horrors abounding in this world were also universal. The deductive conclusion based on this fallible premise alone might induce one to believe that ubiquitous inhumanity and the god of religion were one and the same.

Ironically, challenging her beliefs frightened her now that she knew the depths to which the human soul could sink. She thought of praying for a sign to convince her of God's existence but preferred hope to prayer, given that the latter implied the wonderment of miracles and the former reassurances of more tangible merit.

She also entertained thoughts of her own existence and place in the universe. Who or what had selectively placed her being, her soul, within this singular shell of a body? What was the energy that made her unique? When she stared in a mirror, did her soul not stare back? She realized her essence in the glass, but what preternatural phenomena made her aware? She knew no more now than she did on those reflective occasions, but the thoughts she entertained then and now were unequivocally her own. All that is undeniable and paramount is the innate instinct to survive, the will to preserve that extinguishable light in one's eyes.

The waterfall's incessant hissing beckoned her back from her ruminations as quickly as it stole her away. She stared at the wide insurmountable chasm fearful of its aggressive and turbulent cascades. The frothy water, jetting out ten feet under incredible force where the rock fell away to open air, culminated in a swirling mist upon rejoining the stream ninety feet below. The eroding torrent scoured a great pool of undeterminable depth at the cataract's base. The river widened below the falls. Enormous tree trunks stripped of bark and limb and worn smooth by tumbling submersion in the fierce currents lay helter-skelter at irregular intervals along the stream banks.

Impressive granite cliffs rose to great heights on both sides of the gorge. Huge hemlock trees, hundreds of years old, clung magically at the foot of the rock faces, their low-lying limbs nearest the water's edge caressing the churning urgency in vain attempts to calm it. A shy sun, peeking meekly over the treetops, offered weak yellow rays but no accompanying warmth. Her body shivered in the mist. She reminded herself of her precarious situation and terror, again, trumped her weakening constitution.

Strangely, the continued absence of Roger Perry worried her. She had not heard nor seen any sign of him, but sensed his clammy breath on her neck with every hypothermic breeze that whistled by. Roger could be so close that howls were no longer necessary. Perhaps, he was waiting just ahead to spring upon her. Vigilance was paramount. Roger would never give up, so neither could she. The consequences of inaction would speak for themselves.

The canopy opened marvelously near the pool. Dark clouds boiled overhead in time lapse. The winds aloft must have been incredible to stir the black, ominous mass into such fury. Evidently, she passed the last few hours 'in the eye' of the morning storm and now the back end was primed to unleash.

The finality of a fall from so great a height frightened her into turning away. She stopped in mid-turn, more afraid of what may be behind her. Gooseflesh erupted in early warning and soon had goose pimples of its own. Hairs snapped to attention on her arms and back of neck. A tingling sensation swept across her scalp and a super acuteness of the senses took control. She turned fully just as Roger emerged from behind a large conifer at a two o'clock position.

Roger's face was demonic and pale as the froth from the waterfall. He moved towards her with staccato, zombie-like steps. The plopping of his feet upon the ground caused his body to shutter with each stride. His undead appearance, dark with depravity, made him all the more repugnant and scary. The same sickening grin he always wore adorned his face. He seemed unfazed by serious gashes in his flesh—signatures left, no doubt, by the merciless locust thorns and smilax as he tore after his prey.

Clara locked eyes with her nemeses, but knew better than to lock horns. She matched his movements, step for step, countering his manipulations at positioning her to disadvantage. Nevertheless, his movements forced her backwards toward the stream. Her back was soon dangerously near the precipice she faced frontally minutes before. She turned her head to scan for routes of escape. The unknown depths of the cold water seemed to call to her, but she shut out its siren duplicity from her mind lest she answer in the affirmative. Remarkably, down seemed to be the only way out.

The clouds warned with a low throaty rumble that sharp outbursts would follow. Rain began spattering like diamonds dropped in great numbers from a great height, albeit shattering upon the rocks and forest floor like true diamonds never would. The generous shower soaked them to the skin immediately. Wind whirled down upon them through the break in the canopy and stirred the wet leaves into sticky globs that clung to their feet.

Roger crouched within springing distance. She could feel his mouth upon her throat. It was only a matter of time, she thought, until his icy fingers and venal bite snuffed out her life. The conclusion made her retch violently. She forestalled collapse with the realization that such a contracted position curtailed her chances.

The morning grew incredibly dark, as if a vacuum had sucked the light from the air. The sky erupted. Roger's position changed with every lightning flash. For a moment, Clara stood transfixed as if watching an old movie flicker on the sheets of rain.

Realizing it was fight or flight, she turned to run along a course paralleling the channel and cliff. Immediately, lightning split a towering evergreen in half and hurled splinters of wood in all directions. The enormity of the flash and accompanying explosion dropped Clara and Roger to their knees. The top two-thirds of the forest giant fell perpendicular to the stream, spanning three-fourths of the distance to the far cliff. Circumventing the colossal obstacle was out of the question.

With timely decision, Clara grabbed a branch nearest her and pounced with feline poise upon the arc of the mighty stem. All grew eerily silent except for a distant ringing in her head. The thunderous lightning crack had stunned her eardrums and left her feeling more alone and isolated than ever. She made her way down the tree's tapering trunk aided greatly, but also impeded, by the exponentially increasing quantity of branches. When she reached halfway, she turned to evaluate Roger's progress. He had stopped near the broken shaft and appeared to be monitoring her exertions with interest and bemusement. Maybe he was waiting for her to fall or to realize her folly and return. He seemed oddly disinterested in pursuing her farther.

The rain upon the tree's moss-covered trunk turned it into a treacherous icicle. Clara directed her steps along the tree's centerline as nearly as possible but grew frustrated sidestepping the great number of limbs sprouting vertically in her path. She gave no forethought as to her actions upon reaching the tree's terminus, where options were clear. She would either rise into the heavens above, or plunge into the hell below. It made no difference which fate prevailed. She would be just as dead.

Everything is relative in the wilderness, she remembered. The continued wrestling of the warring protagonists in the sky produced crashing thunder that reduced the roar of the waterfall to a kind of white noise—a baby's cry in a maelstrom. To her left, the stream resumed its descent into the canyon by way of numerous cascades and smaller falls until vanishing around a bend. The dissonance of thunder and the swirling water beneath her confused her terribly. Her disorientation caused her to close her eyes and cling to the supportive limbs. Another ear-spitting clap of thunder bent Clara into a crouch.

Roger appeared unfazed, although he did look up. However, his casual dismissal of the superiority of Nature did not last. He moved several feet away for reasons of his own, but his eyes still bored into his quarry like heated irons. Again, he glanced skyward with increasingly frantic awareness. He paced a minute or two along the perimeter of his limited space, then scrambled up the bank to the protection of a stand of locust trees. Upon reaching the copse of trees, he stood with his back to the rank of spiny trunks. He still had his eye firmly fixed on Clara's position several yards away. He pulled the pistol from the waistband of his trousers and resolved his scampering prey in the notch of the gun's Patridge sights.

Just as Harry entered the scene, an icy blue shaft of lightning struck the earth with incredible energy, fusing the rocky soil to conglomerate and fouling the space between them with the acrid smell of ozone. Soggy leaves served as efficient conductors and transmitted the destructive power undiminished up the hillside and focused it like a prism. The explosive energy channeled fulgurites to the tree's massive root network and surged up the branching fibers of increasing girth to where they culminated at the tree's base where Roger waited.

Simultaneously, the bolt surged from the foot of the tree, up Roger's wet pant legs and out the top of his head. His face lit up like a backlit mask. Roger's body uplifted three feet and flew backwards, into the arms of the foot-long thorns erupting in black and deadly profusion from the locust trees' trunks.

The needle-sharp tips easily penetrated Roger's torso and buttocks. One in particular tore through his heart like a dagger and erupted proudly from the center of his chest. Spasmodic contractions jerked his legs and arms about in a jittery dance. Luminance emanated from the hollows of his eyes. Drool and blood ran like molasses from his gaping mouth and covered the front of his shirt. Roger hung crucified with a final surprised look of utter disbelief frozen on his face. His movements stilled, the thorns broke away and he dropped to his feet.

Somehow, he stayed erect, denying his death while still facing Clara. Roger's left arm slowly uplifted and reached for the girl in an epileptic salute, unaware that the bolt had fried his brain and reduced his internal organs to pudding. He stumbled forward dragging his feet like a plow through the sodden earth. Roger advanced until he reached the cliff's edge. He teetered there until a final step reeled him into the depths below.

Clara screamed. She watched horrified as the merciless hydraulic forces at the base of the falls sucked Roger's body into its cauldron. Ultimately, the churning water vomited him out as if his presence left a bitter taste upon its tongue. Roger's corpse, buoyed by his hollowed-out interior, surfaced again with his left arm still outstretched. He floated beneath the tree where Clara clung trembling. He submerged beneath the water with his trademark grin plastered on his face and his eyes dead as snuffed embers. His twisted fingers were the last to go under.

Clara turned away to a new patch of blue visible above her and uttered a silent prayer of thanks. She opened her eyes at the sound of her name. Someone was calling to her. At first, she had difficulty discerning the direction from whence it came. Her searching gaze pierced the clouds above her. Could it be the voice of God?

When her hearing regained its normal acuity, she pinpointed the source. At the spot where the tree cantilevered over the abyss, stood Harry beckoning to her with an outstretched hand. He moved toward her with great caution lest his presence startle her into falling. When Clara recognized who he was, and where she was, she moved to meet him halfway. They embraced briefly then, with hand welded to hand, stepped carefully back to terra firma.

Harry turned and stared at the spot where Roger disappeared. "Good riddance," he said, suppressing the urge to spit in Roger's direction. He would inform the authorities of what happened, and they could retrieve Roger's body if they felt it was worth their time. It was difficult to believe their trial was over.

When Clara composed herself, her thoughts turned back to her benefactor. "You've got to help Bernard, Harry," she cried.

"Clara", I began, choosing my words carefully. "I don't think..."

She interrupted me in desperate tones and a hushing touch to my lips, "You don't know that! We have to go back. We have to be sure. Roger can't hurt us, now."

"You're right. Let's go." I agreed. I covered her poor tortured feet with my heavy socks. My shoes were much too large and I possessed no strength to carry her. I put my arm around her waist and helped her get started. "Clara," I began when the moment presented itself. "I can't even imagine what you have been through. If only I had come sooner. If only I knew where to look. If only I read the clues differently, I could have saved you so much pain at the hands of that monster. I'm sorry."

"You have nothing to be sorry for. You saved my life. I will never forget it. I know Bernard paid you to find me, but I believe there is something more to you. You're a good man, Harry."

"I don't know about that, but I'm glad you think so." I paused again, allowing the compliment to sink in. I needed it desperately. "That gives me a lot to live up to. I'll try not to disappoint you."

While departing, I nearly stepped on 'Old Betsy'. Her stainless steel slide glistened from beneath a clump of wet leaves. I picked her up and marveled at her distorted shape. The lightning had melted her stock plastic grips and welded the slide to the frame. "What good is a gun, if you're always losing it?" I asked with rhetorical finality. I tossed the worthless article into the turgid torrent. "I won't need you anymore."

#

In about an hour, we arrived back at the house. The day was improving considerably and the interior of the house was brighter, if not cheerful. We wandered the length of the old house searching room by room for Bernard. The windows and exposed rafters provided sufficient light that eventually guided us to the east wing. Despite the atrocious violence we had just survived, we were still unprepared for the sight that awaited us.

The body of Bernard Biggs, hoisted the full distance from the floor, hung suspended on the cruel device of his ill-fated resurrection. Upon reaching the ceiling rafters, his head bent sideways under the force of Roger's exertions. Denuded of the linen rags, his upper torso glowed like foxfire. His arms and chest bore blue-black marks from repeated lightning strikes to the attached copper wires. His face, with its toothy leer, was an exercise in horror. His tongue dangled two inches from behind blackened lips boiled away by the intense heat. His hair singed to bare scalp along one side of his head and his eyes, what were left of them, smoldered gruesomely in burnt sockets from which wisps of unsavory incense emanated.

Clara turned away with a frightful 'Ugh!' She fell against the wall, covered her face with her hands and sank beneath the weight of her repulsion to the leaf-littered floor.

I hurried to the configuration of pulleys and three-quarter inch hemp rope, unfastened it and quickly lowered Biggs' body to the table. I picked up the pile of mummy wrappings from the floor and covered his dreadful remains. I then rushed back to Clara, placed my hands upon her sobbing shoulders and whispered, "Come on, let's go. There's nothing we can do for him now. We'll send an ambulance back for the body when we get to town. We have to get you home."

Clara fought bravely to control her sobbing. She knew Harry was right. They left the room and the house without looking back. It was nearly dusk when they reached the road to Milford. An hour passed, but no cars did. "What we need is a guardian angel." Clara observed, breaking the silence.

"Fat chance of that happening," I replied wearily.

As if on cue, the sound of rattling cylinders swept around the far curve to their rear and resounded in their ears. To my surprise, the farmer in the '58 International Scout slowed to a stop. "My word," the farmer exclaimed upon seeing our disheveled condition. "You two look like you've been through hell!"

Clara had no response. She merely climbed into the front seat of the pickup truck with me a close second. "We have been," I answered, after a pause. "We've been to hell and back. If you don't mind, we'd rather not tell you about it."

"That's ok," the farmer answered sympathetically. "I've been there a time or two myself."

No one spoke for the remainder of the fifteen miles back to town. On the way, Clara bathed her legs and feet in the welcome warmth from the trucks generous heater. Our guardian angel let us off at the bus station where we thanked him for his kindness.

Despite rumors to the contrary, not everyone in town was devoid of courage. There were signs of activity suggesting those that fled had regained their senses and were returning home. I located a pay phone inside the bus station and called the police. The nearest cruiser positioned to respond was a good twenty minutes away.

We collapsed on a nearby bench and stared at the floor. I put my arm around Clara and she leaned into me to rest her beleaguered frame on my shoulder. We sat in silence until the authorities arrived. The sheriff approached, hat in hand, and stood before us while we related our incredible tale.

"Well, that's about as far-fetched a thing as I ever heard," the sheriff proclaimed, shaking his head in disbelief after digesting their story. "I know you won't mind if I confirm your facts. I'm going back to that old house. Meanwhile, we'll have some divers and rescue people search the river. If he fell in, it's my guess he's in the Rundle by now. With all the rain this winter, the streams are flowing pretty high. Strange weather...we have never had this much rain and thunder in February before. Can't explain it, we usually get snow, and tons of it. Oh well, the ambulance will be here shortly to attend to your needs and take you on to Montpelier. I'll call the authorities there directly and relate the particulars, just to keep us on the same page. Good luck to you, folks." The sheriff turned and left.

The ambulance arrived shortly, just as promised. After a careful physical examination and adroit attention to Clara's numerous cuts and abrasions, the medical technicians kindly provided Clara with suitable winter attire at no charge. An hour later, we were enjoying a well-earned meal at a diner in Montpelier. Clara called her mother. I watched tears of joy spring from Clara's eyes when her mother answered the phone. The girl's mood brightened measurably after the phone call. "She's on her way!" Clara declared joyously.

I had no idea what I would do once Clara's mother arrived. I imagined I would drive back to Ohio. I still had substantial remuneration coming from Biggs, but I would have a hell of a time collecting it considering the circumstances. At any rate, I was not sure I wanted the money now. It had a dirty stink about it.

CHAPTER XXVIII

Clara was safe. That was the important thing. Who knew finding someone could be so complicated...or rewarding? All I needed was someone to believe in me and a chance to prove it. They say good can come from tragedy, and I felt good about myself for the first time in a long while. I would not squander this chance to do the right thing as I had so many others. It was high time for a change, and this experience had definitely changed me for the better.

Ellen booked a flight scheduled to arrive at eight a.m. the next morning, so Clara and I had ample time to acquaint and reveal. I felt I knew Clara better than I had ever known anyone, despite knowing nothing about her. Except for the exhausting experience we recently shared and the information Biggs provided in the manila envelope on the day I accepted the case, I actually knew very little.

I wanted to find the key to Clara's heart and hoped we would talk of many things. As it was, I did most of the talking. The frivolities of my past, in excruciating and embarrassing detail, the numerous poor decisions and the blundered episodes in which I was participant over the years poured out of me like beer from a wide-mouthed bottle. It was not that I was prone to self-absorption as much as it was a release of potential nervous energy.

Clara's mind was elsewhere. She feigned attentiveness at first, even smiled on occasion and made a remark or two. A distant yearning colored her thoughts and she seldom blinked. She could have been a million miles away. If there was any true justice for the deserving, she was on some peaceful exotic island in the South Pacific. That is where a beauty and innocence such as hers belonged. When it was Clara's turn, she spoke of her mother; she spoke of her industrious father and his premature passing; she spoke of Bernard Biggs, however briefly. She did not elaborate on their relationship.

I accepted her brevity, and let it go at that. I had no right to pry into this poor girl's life, especially after what she had just endured. I kept the subsequent conversation as light as possible and steered away from whatever lurked in the dark recesses of her past. Better to let the dead remain so and learn from history, not relive it.

Clara seemed to have a hollow leg. She could not get enough of Vermont's signature maple syrup. At nine o'clock that night, she ordered another helping of French toast smothered with fresh New England butter and half a cup of the sweet viscous condiment. She took her coffee black.

I was still full from our earlier meal, but I choked down a hamburger and fries for the sake of projecting sociability and of mitigating my recent caloric deprivation. I insisted this wonderful young woman have the best of everything, and pledged to do my upmost to provide it as long as I was able.

Clara chatted more over her second helping of French toast. The information now verily bubbled out of the girl as if long contained under high pressure. After anecdotes about her horse, her culinary debacles in school and the heir to the throne in Iran she met after her first weeks at the institute, the conversation waxed philosophical.

"What makes people the way that they are, Harry?" She asked, toying with her last corner of toast before shoving it into her mouth and washing it down with the last gulp of lukewarm java.

I must have looked puzzled. "I don't know. I imagine it has to do with a lot of things, where we grow up, who we're born to, what happens to us while we are young...a whole host of things."

"Yeah, I know all that, but what turns some people into monsters or devils and others into angels or saints? What dark force or bright light coerces someone into doing evil or doing good?"

I glanced down at the crumbs on my plate and pretended to arrange them in a meaningful way, but I failed to use my fork to profound effect on the fugitive scraps. In my own case, the driving forces controlling my actions were those of greed and lust. I was a typical human male, nothing more.

I had a good heart, for the most part, but when a beautiful woman bared her bosom or the prospect of a quick fortune dangled beguilingly in front of me, I felt my heart shrink and my ego take over. With all that money, I could win a harem of beautiful women. Gold-diggers, as a rule, were hardly worth a shit except in bed, and some even failed in that regard. But that was all I was concerned with anyway, in my earlier life. No apologies—that was just the way I had been.

I felt ashamed now and regretful for many things I had done. My time with Clara made me want to do and be better. In the years to come, if there were to be any years, I would clean up my act. I hoped I would have time to reconcile my past and direct my future along a truer line.

"Harry?" Clara said, touching my arm to awaken me from my reverie. "You didn't answer my question."

"Oh, I was just thinking."

"Yeah, I know. You have been quiet for a couple of minutes. I thought you were formulating an answer, but by the look on your face you were deeply involved somewhere else."

"I'm sorry," was all I could say.

The waitress appeared just then with a fresh pot of piping hot 'joe' and filled our waiting cups to the brim. We both grabbed the handles of our respective vessels in anticipation and raised them to our lips scarcely before the server finished pouring.

"You know," I began refreshed, "some people are born lucky. They have rich parents, a good home, nice things...a privileged existence, you know, and turn out to be the biggest buggers on the planet. Others are born to poverty and deprivation. They grow up starving, yearning for the things they can never have, but instead of coveting their neighbor's property and their neighbor's life, they mature into the finest people the world has ever seen. There is no explanation for it, Clara. It's just the way things are."

I stared at the clouds in my coffee as I spun the cup absentmindedly on the turquoise Formica table top. "Some things you have to accept as truth. Hell, what do you think prompted the development of psychiatry and psychology in the first place? It was the perplexities of human behavior and the desire to understand it. Even the experts don't have an answer. They are all just as befuddled as you and me. There is an angelic side to everyone's nature and a devilish side, too. They are in constant conflict throughout our lives. Every now and then, depending on which one we feed the most, one side will take over and control our actions. We just have to be careful of feeding the right one."

Clara nodded, surprised at the breadth and depth of Harry's insight. "Yeah, I know what you mean. It seems that every person on Earth is an amalgam of good and bad, just as any society in any country is an amalgam of its people."

"And our planet is an amalgam of countries and continents," I added, "and our galaxy an amalgam of planets."

"Yeah, exactly…and the universe an amalgam of galaxies, and on and on," Clara continued, totally absorbed and excited by the conversation, "and in the end, I guess, society gets the people it deserves. I think, in a way, we create them...by the way we live, by the laws we choose to have and enforce, and by the priorities and values we place on ourselves and expect of others."

I smiled. "That is pretty deep thinking for someone your age," I said admiringly, "But I guess you've earned the right to say it."

Clara smiled too, and lowered her head. We finished the remainder of our coffee in silence and reflection.

I wired my brother in Atlanta for some cash. My brother, lame as he was, would send money when asked but he was not overly enthusiastic about bailing out his less fortunate kinfolk for the umpteenth time. He had come through a number of times over the years and was growing weary of the incessant drain on his bank account. Still, whatever he could spare would be welcome. I figured if I spent the money wisely and sparingly, it should tie me over until I secured additional funds.

The bus station had a Western Union office near the ticket window. I sprang for the best room in the best hotel in town for Clara. I slept in a lobby chair. I woke early the next morning to an impatient Clara's jostling.

The hotel had a shuttle service on stand-by for Gold Card customers, but after some cajoling and a twenty-dollar bill we induced the shuttle driver to convey us to the nearest car rental agency where I leased the finest sedan on the lot. Clara deserved first class, if anyone ever did. In less than an hour, we arrived at the airport terminal.

Ellen's plane touched down on schedule. I remained in the

shadows for a lengthy fifteen minutes watching the two women hug and cry on each other's shoulder. When they had sobbed themselves out, Clara told her mother she wanted to introduce her to someone. They strolled, arm in arm, to where I stood leaning against a pillar in the airport lobby.

"Mom, I'd like you to meet my good friend, Harry. Harry, this is my mom, Ellen Connor."

"Harry Case," I said, extending my hand.

Ellen smiled at the name.

I recognized the reason behind the smile and smiled along with her. "I know," I admitted. "It's a funny name, especially for a private investigator."

All three of us shared a long and much-needed laugh.

"Mr. Case, I..."

"Call, me Harry" I insisted, cradling her elbow in my hand. "Please?"

"Harry," Ellen began again, "I can't tell you how much I appreciate what you have done for me and my daughter. There is no way we could ever repay you. You risked your life and almost lost it to save my precious girl, and we will always be in your debt." She turned to her daughter and stroked the back of her head with loving hands only a mother could possess.

I absorbed the complement with grace and humility but insisted that having Clara back where she belonged was enough. "Any reward or reciprocation is out of the question." I explained. "I did what I had to do and would do it again in a heartbeat." Most of my remaining wired money went to pay for a nourishing lunch and a nice hotel room for Clara and Ellen. I left them alone for the rest of the day, and I spent the night in the back seat of the rental sedan.

The next morning, after another hearty helping of French toast courtesy of Alice's Waffle Barn, we all drove back to the airport. I escorted the women safely to the gate and sat there with them until they boarded. I watched their jet taxi down the runway and never considered abandoning my post until the plane disappeared over the blue horizon. I slung my grungy, crumpled jacket over my shoulder and strolled outside to where my rental vehicle waited.

Without further ado, I was off. I had heard it said that there was nothing like a hundred miles to soothe a worried mind, but the great state of Vermont was two hundred and fifty miles behind me before the weariness of my adventure began to fade away. A semblance of my former self slowly emerged as I drove through the quilted terrain. Overhead, a V-formation of Canada geese carved the skies on their way north. "Looks like we'll have an early spring," I said.

Hoar frost covered the fields on both sides of the ribbon of highway and glittered like gold as the glancing rays of morning sun softened its crystalline edges. I rolled the window down to let the crisp, invigorating air stream into my lungs. I have been known to be flat as a pancake at times but, by God, I felt like singing.

I belted out a few bars of the Meredith Wilson tune *"Till There Was You"*. The meadows I zoomed past lay speckled with great numbers of wintering birds. A clever smile shaped my vowels when I fancied the cringing expressions on the faces of the snow buntings and horned larks as the discordant strains of my vocal stylings assaulted their discerning avian ears.

Dissonant or not, I liked the song and I liked singing. As I crooned the blues away, every verse and chorus chimed with new and profound meaning. Despite my monstrous pitch and performance or, perhaps because of it, the awakening landscape echoed a refrain long after my fifteen minutes of fame dissolved into fairy dust.

I did not intend to stop. I would drive straight through until I reached Columbus. With so much caffeine and adrenaline still thinning my veins, sleep was out of the question anyway. I glanced at my eyes in the rear view mirror and imagined Clara in the back seat. I thought about Clara most of time while driving the long road home. I wanted to see her again in the worst way. I longed to see laughter replace the despair on her face. Maybe I would tease her fair hair and chuck her chin, as I wanted to do in the diner. It was not appropriate then and may not be appropriate a year from now, but I wanted to do it just the same.

I was much older than the alluring beauty and shared little common ground except for our recent extraordinary time together. "Maybe if I took up cooking...," I laughed. Hell, I had trouble boiling water without burning it. However, I did confess to a fondness for 'stirring the pot' at times. I whimsically juggled romantic scenarios in my mind as the miles along the lost highway melted away.

#

After the legalities and complexities swirling around Clara's kidnapping settled down, things went well. Biggs had an unshakable confidence in the benefits of insurance and knew the dangers of neglecting to establish a living will. In a remarkable display of unprecedented munificence, Biggs bequeathed Ellen and Clara Connor to be joint beneficiaries to substantial cash and an esteemed portfolio of valuable holdings.

Credit life cancelled all outstanding debts, and a term life policy alone netted the Connors nearly three quarters of a million dollars. In addition, there were three separate bank accounts with combined assets of over five hundred thousand dollars. Talk about poetic justice.

Under Ohio law, executorial duties would fall to the parent or guardian of an underage beneficiary. Ellen accepted the role and hired a real estate management broker to negotiate liquidation of the extensive and varied properties to which she and Clara now held title. She had no interest in any of Biggs' holdings with the exception of *The Village Clarion*. Her husband worked for the newspaper many years and often entertained notions of playing a larger role in the day-to-day operations. With Clara's blessing, she renamed the concern the *Carl Connor Crier* in his honor. She also contacted Harry while settling Bernard's legion of outstanding invoices.

Harry explained the details of their arrangement to her and was willing to forgo any monies due, but Ellen insisted. She also offered him the position of general manager of the paper, which he accepted with deep gratitude. His promise to better himself took root this time and did not diminish with time like so many previous resolutions.

He still talked to his reflection in the mirror, but resolved his self-image issues by concluding that "unattractive" people, like himself, had no reason to fret over their relative attractiveness. There were advantages. For one, handsome people were plagued with worry over losing their looks with age—the 'ugly' are 'ugly' forever. Accepting that fact saves a lot of stress, when one thinks about it. Besides, his 'bare-chested Brando' days were far behind him.

Clara obtained a position in Dayton hosting her own midday cooking show at WHIO TV 7. She called it simply: *Cooking with Clara.*

She infused each episode with profound joy and attention to detail unprecedented in the station's broadcast history. There was talk of national syndication but, for the present, she was content to don her flowered apron and muss her modern kitchen with the best of them. Flour on her forehead became the hallmark of her craft. It marked a culmination of a life-long dream, and she was happy as a clam.

Her recipe for French toast stuffed with blackberries won national accolades in *Cuisine Magazine* and quickly became a local institution. The marvelous confection garnered quite a lot of publicity for Dayton from gourmet critics around the globe.

The trio reunited on holidays and special occasions, growing close as extended families ever get, and they enjoyed a depth of trust and love for each other that few people ever share. In time, the terror and despair of the years preceding the 'big event' paled in comparison to the happiness of their new lives. The notorious video tape never resurfaced, and concern that it might one day show up dampened Ellen's triumphant spirit only a bit. The sick, sordid nightmare world in which they never again would visit became as surreal as a distant dream.

Golden Path Cemetery won the honor of being the final resting place of Bernard Biggs. He was interred with all the fanfare and outpourings of sympathy befitting a citizen of his enviable stature. Ellen and Clara attended—more to allay suspicions and discourage inquiries had their absence been noticed than from admiration or devotion.

Harry passed on attending the affair and mourned (read celebrated) the passing of his former employer with a handful of bourbons at Talley's tavern on Ninth Street. He had known enough disillusionment for a lifetime and had no stomach for more. The hypocrisy of the scene would have made him retch and, true to form, he would have soiled the minister's robes.

Roger Perry's body was never recovered. Some said he did not drown that day as reported. Some said his profile blotted the pale light from the mansion's single upper story window. Others swore a young man fitting Roger's description, complete with his signature flaming red Mohawk, hitchhiked the road between Milford and Lovingdale Manor when the moon was full. Townsfolk in Milford accustomed to the comfort of their superstitious natures continue to avoid the stretch of road at night, full moon or not.

CHAPTER XXVIX

In the End

Shadows of the psyche and the depths of depravity attractive to the human soul have eluded probing, inquisitive minds for eons. The keys to the mysteries of humankind's malevolence are ironically locked away within the inaccessible vaults of our collective subconscious. No one can ever truly understand the motivations and causations for aberrant behavior. We can only coalesce facts, formulate theories, and sanctify treatment for those conditions most abhorrent and intolerable in 'civilized' societies.

How, you may ask, could a place like Lovingdale Manor, devoid of life's essence and relieved of the afflictions of human intrusion, inspire such a tale such as this? A fair question, to be sure. Suffice it to say, there are fantastic forces at work in the universe, good and evil, with influences far beyond the threshold of death. Only spirits adrift in the ether of eternity have the insight to inculcate the vestiges of the living. It is equally so that the power held in the hands of these nameless spirits is theirs to wield but for the brief time they are adrift.

In the end, it is the policies society initiates to control the deranged among us that define us as who we truly are. Adhering to the archaic doctrine of 'an eye for an eye, and a tooth for a tooth' only cheapens the noble precepts of right and wrong and undermines the potential of the enlightened human animal. The practice denigrates our species to the order of lower forms of life. Reciprocating with equal vigor and violence, though the target of our hatred be those most deserving for crimes heinous and repugnant, reduces mankind to a commonality with evil; whereby we, as judge, jury and executioner have no more right to hold the reins of those judicious responsibilities than the cowardly accused.

We have within us the aspirations of righteousness, the mental acuities to conceive idyllic social orders and the means and wherewithal to destroy our planet sanctuary. We have not yet achieved the wisdom to focus our collective faculties nor tune our creative energies toward achieving the one goal common to people everywhere—a life of peace and well-being—an existence free from want and fear. We must strive to be more than human...we must be humane. That we are capable is without doubt but the nature of humankind, as it is with all life forms, has been one of survival of the fittest.

Survival, by its very definition, implies sacrifice—sacrifice not of one's self, but of another life. The universal instinct for self-preservation far outweighs any treatise or manifesto conceived and codified by the higher noble mind. Equanimity and peaceful coexistence, goals undeniably worthy of pursuing will, perhaps, through due diligence and adherence to a kinder more empathic creed, mark our evolution into a species worthy of inheriting our planet and ruling our universal destiny.

The amalgam of atoms, animals, people, personalities, countries, planets and galaxies comprising the universe are as varied and mysterious as they are innumerable. No 'right way' has risen above all others, no beauty exists that may not be surpassed by the perceptions of the beholder, no action or attitude is ever thoroughly understood or absolutely analyzed. Societies are but a conglomeration of accepted beliefs, practiced philosophies and theoretical proofs. We are who we believe we are, and should dare not expect others to see us as we see ourselves. Myopia is the curse of prejudice, for a voyeur who refuses to see is far less perceptive and informed than those born without eyes.

And so, dear reader, at the risk of boring you with the oppressive diatribe of my ranting mind I am extending to you, to tempters of fate, subscribers and proponents of wickedness and, yes, for my own salvation, a warning:

Evil can never be truly destroyed, but only cast out from one repose to the next.

For thine unfettered soul, once dissolute,
To wealth and power must forever bow.
That vile and vicious mouth awaits.
Be not attuned to yon horrific howl!

#

Lovingdale Manor, stood unopposed on its lofty bluff until catching fire during a great storm shortly after the conclusion of the last tragic episode in its dark history. Only the elemental brick, stone and mortar remains to this day—a sad, hollow symbol of a formerly grand and eloquent age.

It was the only holding in Ellen's bequeathed portfolio she failed to liquidate. She finally donated the property to the Vermont Historical Preservation Society on the condition they protect it in perpetuity, but with the stipulation they allow the land to revert to its natural state. As of yet, no one but the uninformed has had the gumption or ignorance to set foot on the grounds. By all accounts, spirits of the unfortunate who perished there haunt still the infernal landscape and cremated remains.

On occasion, out-of-town squatters unfamiliar with local legend seek temporary shelter in the immolated shell only to be found shortly thereafter wandering the road to Milford, crazed and incoherent. On storm-tossed evenings, passers-by regularly report seeing a faint, bluish illumination where the singular window opening on the upper floor once glowed. No one, yet, has had nerve enough to confirm the veracity of the sightings. Believers write off the repeated episodes as another chapter in the continuing legacy of Squire Lovingdale and proof his curse still lives.

Blustering billows continue to rake the blasted ruins, scattering the ashes of the manor's unfortunate victims to the extent of their formidable influence. Yes, and rumors of satanic conjurations still spread like wildfire through the forgotten town of Milford when evil weather brews wantonly to the west.

The gnarled trees clinging to the eroded slopes near the House of Lovingdale still arch their remorseful branches heavenward, begging absolution for their inaction to the brutalities they have witnessed. Yes, and the Rundle River, sullen and fetid, flows timelessly on...silent and still as a pauper's grave.